NATIVE LAND

Other books in this series from Lumen Editions:

Too Late for Man
Essays by William Ospina

The Joy of Being Awake
by Hector Abad

Diary of a Humiliated Man
by Félix de Azúa

Silk
Stories by Grace Dane Mazur

Urban Oracles
Stories by Mayra Santos-Febres

Dialogue for the Left and Right Hand
Poems by Steven Cramer

S
by Harry Mathews, Mark Polizzotti, Jean Echenoz, et al.

Pursuit of a Woman on the Hinge of History
by Hans Koning

NATIVE LAND

by

Nadja Tesich

Lumen Editions
a division of Brookline Books

ISBN 1-57129-042-7

Library of Congress Cataloging-in-Publication Information
Tesich, Nadja.
    Native land / by Nadja Tesich.
        p.   cm.
    ISBN 1-57129-042-7
    1. Yugoslav Americans--Travel--Yugoslavia--Fiction. I. Title.
PS3570.E78N38   1997
813'.54--dc21   97-17844
                                               CIP

Book design and typography by Erica Schultz.

Printed in the USA by Data Reproductions, Auburn Hills, MI.

10 9 8 7 6 5 4 3 2 1

Published by:
Lumen Editions
Brookline Books
P.O. Box 1047
Cambridge, Massachusetts 02238-1047

For Stefan and Dean

in memory of my brother

The author would like to thank the Djerassi Artists Program, the MacDowell Colony, and Yaddo, where she wrote this book.

Part One

Chapter One

The arrival was smooth, a barely noticeable landing in the midst of a very luminous sky. The customs officials seemed sleepy, languorous somehow; nobody checked the suitcases for explosives or forbidden fruit. I couldn't detect the signs of unrest and internal difficulties that *The New York Times* had mentioned in passing a few months ago. You couldn't tell if the vagueness of that one paragraph was due to an absence of real information, or because the country was too small to merit full attention. Still, common sense told me there was nothing to worry about—the customs officials don't look so relaxed during a civil war. Around me, the chatter of pilgrims coming from as far away as New Orleans and San Francisco to see the Virgin appear somewhere in the mountains off the coast. I didn't pay attention to miracles, or to them, and on the plane these travellers didn't look any different from tourists in polyester suits, squat, tired, middle-aged. I noticed them now because they were herded together under a sign that said MIRACLE TOURS and then a handsome young man led them toward the bus.

Two women on my left were probably going to the same conference as me but I wasn't sure of anything except their looks. Both had that air of university professors, something austere about skirts and blouses, a neatness in the face I had also seen on social workers and nuns. When I asked them about the conference, both shouted—how could you tell? Just a long habit of casting, looking at people, I told them, noticing as if for the first time that American women, when surprised or overjoyed, jump up and down, exclaim dramatically, squeal, do all sorts of little rituals, including a few that Marilyn Monroe had perfected. It occurred to me that nineteenth century American women, before the movies, had very different poses, other gestures for surprise. Of course their clothes were different too, corsets and such, I was right to insist on costumes in my classes, Juliet would act one way in a long dress and another wearing blue jeans.

Two husbands appeared in a rented car; they were professors too but not connected to the conference. In the absence of any dramatic gestures, or facial expressions, they seemed almost invisible next to their wives even though they were much taller. They said they would only drive and lay low since it was too dangerous to show their faces at a feminist conference. They were joking of course but still I knew they had to be from a small town; in New York nobody talked about feminism as dangerous any longer. Betty and John had been in Bloomington, Indiana for ten years, Teresa and Paul had just moved there from South Bend.

It was nice of them to take me along; the town built by Venetians was five miles away, along the narrow curvy road with the sea on one side. I was tempted to say I had been there before but changed my mind and watched the sea instead, something like anticipation in my chest, a feeling I had forgotten. Almost fifteen years. I had never come to Ragusa this way, never directly from the States, on the plane. And this was the first time I almost used my red passport, had it ready but chickened out at the last moment, afraid for some reason. Of what?

Chapter Two

I stayed in an old merchant house on top of the street that was all steps. The room was perfect—sunny, large, a garden below, the view of the sea directly in front. Everything hidden behind a wall, invisible from the street. A girl at the tourist office in New York had arranged it all, for proximity to the conference and my rest; she had laughed when I asked about internal problems, just rumors, she said, forget it.

I fell asleep right away and didn't know I had slept for a long time. It was the smell of coffee and the sound of children playing that woke me up. My watch said 3 a.m., but it was ten o'clock here, the sun already strong. The smell of coffee was still there but the kids were gone, maybe it was a dream about kids, an old game I remembered, round and round you go in a circle then you fall.

Below, in the garden, the old man was watering the roses; he said, "You should have closed the shutters last night."

"Did it rain? I thought the month of May was dry."

"Of course it's dry," he laughed at my ignorance, "but

there are the cats. Didn't you hear them?"

No, I heard nothing at all last night, was only aware of an immense hunger right now. I devoured everything his wife brought in with a pot of very strong coffee, made Italian style.

The woman laughed, "You eat like my grandson. I'll get you some more."

She spoke with a melodious accent that made me think of guitars, mandolins, the seashore. A pretty dialect, gentle somehow. I wondered how I sounded to them, it was hard to tell; I had not spoken the language in years. Not at all really, if you excluded the same old words to my mother on the phone. It wasn't natural any more. Even yesterday at the airport I had stuck to English and my American passport, although I didn't have to—I had the other one.

The last roll gone, I stretched by window and watched the two shades of blue merge on the horizon. The smell of roses and shrubs filled the room; sleepy again, I didn't want to do anything now, not even the smallest gesture, the conference was the last thing on my mind but it was the official reason I had come. An invitation to participate and then write about it came from an old classmate in Boston and the university paid for the trip in the name of faculty advancement, or whatever they called it. Others did this constantly, a conference in Italy, France, Mexico, Spain but I was never tempted before. It was a last minute invitation, a bit confusing, I was not a scholar or journalist but Marsha insisted I'd be perfect and so I said sure, why not, thinking about the sea and this town I had known as a child. Here we had stopped for a day to rest from a long train ride, then a boat took us to an island, two hours away. I must have been eight, mother looked young in that picture of the two of us dressed in white, in Ragusa, an old name that stuck in my mind. Grandma used it more than the other one. "Ages ago, when I was girl, father took me to Ragusa," she said.

The town of Ragusa was protected, all the booklets said so, you couldn't alter, build or demolish, it's the only one that remained the same thanks to the thick walls and the gates and the narrow streets which were like corridors. Cars drove up to the town but couldn't enter.

I got up. Time to go.

The conference building was only minutes away, in an old mansion which was like this merchant's house, built in the nineteenth century outside the old city by people who wanted gardens, space, privacy, impossible in the medieval world. I vaguely remembered sleeping there—it had been a youth hostel at one time.

Nobody inside the mansion was very young except two local girls in charge of programs which announced in large letters LANGUAGE AND LITERATURE, Feminist Theory and Practice. They were printed on very expensive beige-pink paper and you were supposed to save one for the university—when they saw your name, they paid for the trip. Looking at the names and topics I was surprised—they were not writers, but professors of literature and feminism, scholars who had spent years getting their Ph.D.s, which was not the case with me. I had written some plays and was teaching theater, but scholarly papers were foreign to me. Somebody made a mistake. I shouldn't be here. I wasn't sure what that crazy Marsha from Boston wanted me to write, something funny? Why did she insist that I, Anna, was right for it. Right how? She was supposed to be here instead of me, but changed her mind. Didn't want token anything, she said, still touchy about it all.

My name, together with a poet from Minnesota and a novelist from India, was on the last page; we were scheduled to talk about "I, Me, Us—Women's Voices." Again I didn't know what they wanted me to do, either read from a play or talk about how I wrote it. Why did they call it 'I, me, us'? Nobody in the crowd looked like Indira from Bombay but far away I saw Teresa and Betty both wearing crisp cotton dresses that fell to their ankles. I wondered what the poet from Minnesota looked like and if she knew more about 'I, me, us,' when Betty ran up to say that their hotel was just great and their husbands had left sightseeing, then another woman interrupted to ask Betty about her tenure. She said 'tenure' in a standard way, low, respectful, not smiling, mouth slightly pinched, the same way you might ask about a sick old mother, 'is she OK?' I noticed these things, saved them for my students who are touchingly ignorant about everything, yet every one of them wants to direct.

I didn't hear what Betty said next. The place was buzzing in French, German, and English, with Americans clearly a majority. Here and there snatches of conversations about jobs, promotions, names of so and so and such and such. Some important feminist critic was coming soon or was already there, but the name they repeated I didn't recognize or her book on Djuna Barnes. It's true, I didn't care for criticism or critics nor did I understand their passion to examine then tear apart. If all the theater critics died suddenly, theater would still go on, I had told a well-known man some years back at a party; the way he looked at me was pure murder. Next door, in a large room converted into a canteen with tables and stools, a woman in an old skirt was making coffee for the participants who in large numbers came through the door. She had a white kerchief around her head and some special look around the eyes. They were eyes you don't see in New York even though they were ordinary enough—large, brown, round but with a gaze that had some familiar weariness which stretched, went far. I had seen her eyes before on someone else but I didn't remember who.

"Eh," the woman moaned. Her skirt looked homemade, shiny around the seat. She was making standard Turkish coffee in a blue pot that was too small for such a large number of women, all crisp and efficient and in a hurry. They wanted a fast cup of coffee without having to wait so damn long. If only she had an electric coffee maker or two everything would go faster, could have been ready in advance but that was not the kind of coffee they drank here; the scholars weren't prepared for this, the water wouldn't boil fast out of spite and you can't do anything until the water bubbles up. Then you add coffee and sugar in equal amounts, the way my mother did, every single time.

The blue pot gave only five cups each time; the line of women extended then withdrew. The first session started.

I asked for a cup of coffee in English then watched the woman straighten up, rub her back along the spine; her legs were swollen around the ankles. She sponged the sink area, washed the cups and then another woman came over, obviously a friend, and the two of them started talking about the kids, and how one is sick and she is worried to death. Her friend just nodded and soon they switched to the kids' shoes, school bags, how expensive it all is and kids wear everything out in six months, "but then everything gets worn out," said the other woman, "including us." This set them laughing temporarily, establishing some clear perspective on things. "Fuck this life," the woman in the white kerchief said.

"Yes," said the other, "but it's the only one you've got."

They were younger than they appeared, I realized, and felt guilty. They are much younger than me. Kids' shoes, kids' bags, I've never worried about that, my mother did. They had her movements, her mix of gloom and laughter, but their speech had elongated vowels, slight nasal tones.

I picked up her cup of coffee and was going to drink it fast and leave when suddenly I heard them talk about the participants; certain that I couldn't understand them, they used farm words to describe them—this one became a chicken, that one a cow, a duck. I waited, dying to know what they would say about me, what animal would I become, and if I would recognize it as me.

I longed for it, one word that would define me, fix me from the outside for good, a simple one I couldn't push away. In New York, they took me for this or that, depending on my mood or my dress, and then they said, "Ann is an actress, she prefers actors to us, Ann is not a team player, Ann is fun." Not as good as being called a cow, or a duck.

The women said nothing about me. Having exhausted the subject of animals and participants, they settled down to drink their coffee slowly, with a cigarette, tiny sips and long pauses—the way you are supposed to drink coffee here. Sighing occasionally about life, our sad destiny and youth that passes in a blink. I thought about Bosnia for some reason, or towns away from the coast.

Their talk looked intimate, warm, intensely loving, from where I stood and just watched. I wanted to say something, maybe join them but that would change things and it was better to remain as simple as possible for everyone—a playwright, American (no accent at all), a woman with an ordinary name, not Anna, which could be questioned, but Ann.

I forced myself to leave the kitchen, then tiptoed inside a large lecture hall and sat in the last row by the window. In front, an energetic woman in a summer suit was reading a paper about Virginia Woolf with conviction, waving her arms, her voice strong, but her speech was full of technical words, the names Derrida, Barthes, and so forth; *subject position, deconstruct, signify, signifier* became like a drone, a steady hum and soon I gave up trying to comprehend and drifted out of the window, the smell of shrubs strong. This was an old habit since childhood, to take off, disappear, and nobody ever noticed, not even me, except for certain gaps in time. At some point I left the women with Virginia Woolf, and entered another conference room, a smaller one where they spoke French. I gathered it had something to do with Marguerite Duras whose work I knew and I spoke French but again the words the speaker used to describe Duras were uninteresting, with harsh sounds, and they bounced off me without penetrating. Instead, I remembered the real Duras and how funny she was about everything, her drinking, her love of young men, and how she flipped TV channels without getting any satisfaction because it was all the same, one big car chase on

TV through the night. That must have been three years ago.

I drifted off again, hypnotized by the sailboat on the horizon. The light shimmered on the surface of the water, the boat moved to the right, then to the left, then it stopped. Somewhere near the water my fingers taste of salt. I am nineteen years old, maybe twenty.

Chapter Three

A sound of cats like baby cries woke me up. I was sure they were sick kids until I heard somebody shout, then pour water on them. The painful lament stopped in one short yowl. The owner was watering the roses, he now looked up, "You didn't close the shutters again," he said. "Did you sleep at all?"

"Yes," I said, "I slept well. What happened?"

"The cats were unbearable last night." He used an old-fashioned term for what they did, 'adventures,' he called it. "They are in love," he said, "this is their month." He spoke then about insects, lizards, the passionate lovemaking of the scorpions and snakes and how he always found snake skin in the garden around this time because the month of May was their time for love. I didn't know much about the snakes, how they made love, but the idea of just leaving your old skin on the ground seemed amazing, even if it happened regularly and without any effort on their part.

In the garden, he showed me a snake skin, grayish, dry, with an interesting pattern on it. I was tempted but didn't dare ask him for it, he might think I was weird and what would I do with the skin except show off in New York in front of my sons. He wanted to tell me in detail about his attempts to grow a certain type of yellow rose which was very large, perfect except for its smell. He laughed that maybe he couldn't smell as keenly as when he was young. "I lose something new everyday. You smell it," he said.

The yellow rose was more beautiful than the others, with a deeper yellow inside it and a bit of purple. Its petals glistened, it was lovely but had no smell. None. It wasn't his age. Maybe in perfecting it something was lost, a bit like those large tomatoes in New York, other supermarket fruit. I realized I was now thinking of Teresa, tall, blond, perfect too.

"What is that called," I asked him about the shrub which grew everywhere in the garden, all over the city. The white flowers had a very strong sweet aroma that made me sleep too much.

"Oh, that's myrtle," he said. "You don't have to water it. It's wild. You know the Greeks wrote about it."

"Yes," I remembered, "myrtle and honey is what the gods liked."

"They knew how to live," he said, "didn't they?" He was tall, thin with a very straight back, seventy or so, I thought. When he smiled and winked at me, I saw him as young, he had lived fully once, adventures included. Something like a memory of desire still lingered around them, him and his wife, a handsome dark woman who brought me breakfast on an embroidered cloth that had small roses and leaves.

The breakfast tray was made of old silver, just like my

mother's, and the doilies were the same, even the furniture
was of similar color and shape as hers, except this room didn't
have a large mirror with two small drawers on each side. It
was called *psiha* and mother said it was dangerous to stare in
it for a long time. You could see things, she said without
explaining. Scary stuff. Didn't one woman see her own death
one day and another the man she would marry? I had stared
often in all sorts of mirrors and never saw anything special
but now I saw that the old man and his wife thought I was
from Dalmatia and I did nothing to correct them. It would
mean going into details about my life, when, how, why we
left, what year, explain all sorts of things about my parents;
with all the problems in the country, it was better to play
safe, not get involved. As a precaution, I told them my mother
came from the coast which was true in a way, but I said
nothing about religion at all. Being old, they might not understand that I had no religion of any sort, nothing I was
aware of. Somewhere I remembered it wasn't good to be a
Jew or a non-Catholic around here.

They knew I lived in New York, my room was reserved
from there. They didn't ask any questions about my life or
New York, which was nice. They didn't seem to notice my
accent which most likely I had; after all I had not spoken the
language in years. I had no problem understanding or reading, but my physical expressions were different, my R's muted;
years ago in the capital somebody said I sounded like John
Wayne. If at least they had said James Dean or somebody I
liked. When was that, maybe in the seventies, I wondered,
but wasn't sure.

It bothered me that I couldn't remember who said it, or

the exact time I had been in this town, although it had to be in the seventies after a trip to the capital. I stopped coming after that, disgusted by the invasion. My private word for it, the one I don't use. Around 1975 or so, all the big hotels went up, the fishing villages died, even the most hidden coves had bodies in them. Meanwhile in the papers they bragged about the rich harvest, this new crop better than any other which brought dollars, francs, marks. It's their fault, not mine. Why didn't they say no, I think as I dress.

The trolley went in the same direction as before, clamoring, clanking, rusty. I followed it on foot. In front of the tourist office, it made a half circle, picked up two people, then started a slow climb up the hill toward the train station, two hills away. I was outside the old city walls, in front of the gate. The tourists were not to be seen, maybe because it was still too cold for them. Any day now, they'd descend, and in July or August every room would be occupied. I was lucky to be here now. Absolutely. Maybe Marsha remembered what I told her about Ragusa once, maybe it was meant as a gift.

I ran across the bridge. After a moment, the city opened up and once again I saw the white polished stones of the main street which extended all the way to the small harbor. Always a surprise, this part of it, every single time. I took my sandals off. The stones were smooth, already warm. And once again my heart jumped and there was that longing for something I couldn't name. From here, the island seemed near, only a couple of strokes away, but it wasn't true—it took a half-hour by boat to get there, a natural preserve great for swimming in hidden coves, nude.

It was there I had seen a man who looked like me but was taller. The sudden smell of the sea and salt brings him back to the point of pain, I had forgotten him and his name; he was from the North, we communicated in French, he had a fever blister on his lower lip.

I can't remember the details, the day or the month time when he came to my room here, in one of those stone houses. The room had a view of the sea, the owner must have been absent, this wasn't done and I hadn't done it before, no way. This was an exception, maybe because I didn't have a room of my own. Not then, not at that time. Maybe I never had a room of my own, I think now. Other people's places.

Would I recognize the house, probably not. They were built in the same style, of the same white stone and the day I met him was almost thirty years ago. Thirty? Is it possible? Did I meet him here or on the island first, does it matter? Yes, it does for some reason, but nothing definite comes up. It's silly, it's not important. I'll never know.

We must have met here, in town after the play and the next day we went to the beach and then he came to my room or maybe that's not how it went but the salt is what I remember better than anything else now. Maybe I had met him there after all. Then we took the boat back and he walked me home, up and up those steps and I must have said, could have said, "Come on in, I have the most beautiful view." And then what?

No, I couldn't have written such a bad dialogue, *the most beautiful view*, how corny, I probably said nothing at all, just opened the door, the owners were absent and then we made love and that's all.

I could never find that house or the street, nor can I see myself, but wish I could. Something small, a haircut, a dress, anything would do. I remember his mouth, not mine; he was beautiful and had beautiful arms but something else was needed for a real passion. Something. After all he was from the North and spoke a language I didn't know and he didn't know mine. Maybe that was the problem. Still I must have liked something about him, maybe that we looked so much alike, what others said often. But I don't remember either one of us well, only this city is clear, the heat, the salt, the special smell of the harbor. Much stronger than now, much much more. On the horizon small boats came and went but in my memory there are no cars anywhere to be seen.

Is it possible?

To the left, outside the city walls, where once a single hotel stood, surrounded by pines, the entire hill was now covered with villas, restaurants and further up above all this, a steady line of trucks and cars. Of course! The highway along the coast didn't exist! That's why there were no cars in my memory, I didn't invent anything. The narrow dirt road was there, further inland, but only the bravest English and French travelers took it, in Deux Chevaux, or Minis, equipped with tents, and people marvelled at their strangeness, how fast their skin freckled or turned bright red. These people from the outside world were like kids and had to be told everything, about staying indoors at noon, what and where to eat; the town didn't have many restaurants, and there were no menus in English or French.

No, there were no tourists then or they were so rare that in some places away from the coast they attracted attention;

when an English family suddenly showed up in my home town, there were many arguments about where they would stay, whose house would be the most comfortable for them. Money? Of course not. It was an honor to receive, part of tradition, even the poor gave the best food and the most comfortable bed to a guest. There was a benefit—they loved watching them, these funny-looking strangers, carefully examining their features, their dress; it was better than the movies in the summer months. They watched them constantly.

When did the invasion start? What year?

Maybe that very summer, the summer I had met the blond boy who looked like me but was taller. Didn't I meet French students in a youth hostel near the border around the same time and they took me along, happy to have a native girl as a guide. I shared their tent and food but there were no other involvements, nothing romantic. We descended slowly, the coast empty, nobody on the beaches, nobody on the road except an occasional truck. Children minding the sheep watched us and the car, not comprehending fully, without asking for anything yet, not even candy or chewing gum. But how could they, they didn't even know what gum was.

The French couldn't get over it, the beauty of the landscape and the people, how could they grow so tall, the French marvelled, in the midst of such barren landscapes of sea and rocks. How could the sheep survive on that bit of grass that grew around the stones?

The French students were too charming to look like an occupying force, but I didn't feel right sitting with them. Guilt and that café I remember now. A waitress, a young

girl, was serving us. She wore a cotton dress that was homemade, the kind of dress you saw in *The Bicycle Thief* and
other films by DeSica. Even in their beat-up Simca and plain
blue jeans, the Parisian students contrasted sharply with the
native boys whose pants were either too short, too baggy, or
too long, depending who wore them before. For the first
time, there was envy, maybe hatred, when the local men
looked at us and the car, and whenever local girls glanced at
the bathing suits French women wore—their own were made
out of scarves or a bit of leftover fabric. This envy was not
openly expressed, they might not have been aware of it, as
they would be later on. Local men, tall, muscled, strong,
would just glance at the strangers, then dive into the sea
with more daring; coming out they would adjust their minimal trunks, and casually in passing caress their balls. But
their eyes at me, sitting with the French, spelled contempt—
you slut, you whore.

That word doesn't bother me now, it even helps me consider that there were no prostitutes anywhere, none, or maybe
they were invisible to me. Or did they come along with the
tourism and cars, the big hotels, and all those shiny trinkets
from abroad, from the West, where nobody believed me when
I said, "No, we have no whores."

"Of course you do," they said. "Everybody has them."

You slut, you whore, their eyes said. No, not a whore.
My betrayal was of a different sort, in my faultless French
that amazed the French, in the way I resembled them, mim-
icking perfectly their speech and gestures, you must really be
French, the Parisian students said. Flattered in something, I
did nothing to correct them. And didn't I tell him, the blond

boy whom I would meet soon after, that I was half-French? Why? A costume? A role? A mask?

And why was I thinking about all this now, why not before? Now when everything had been settled, my life smooth, without friction, the pain appeared too, bursting, pulling me along. Something old. Along with the waves of confusion, came disorientation—who am I? What else have I erased, what other people?

The sudden noise of the tower made me stop. The church clock struck ten slowly, then more thunder came from the other ones. I was sitting on the stone you tie boats to, staring at the water. The white city and the tower looked like a painting out of Di Chirico, a landscape dreamt.

Jet lag can make you weird, I'd better go back, I thought.

At the mansion, they were between two sessions. Judging from the facial expressions and raised voices, an important event took place moments before. In the courtyard, I moved to the edge of a small group, attempting to decipher without being seen.

"I don't think her paper added anything new to the scholarship on Virginia Woolf," said a woman with a slight Midwestern twang, maybe from Chicago, maybe Indiana.

"It doesn't matter," said an angry looking one, "everyone is courting her since her new book on Djuna Barnes."

"Wasn't she offered tenure at Cornell?"

"Cornell! That's not all. She was offered ..."

They lowered their voices abruptly. I couldn't hear what the woman was offered, but I followed their glances, the reason why they grew quiet—the woman who was in demand and was courted by everyone appeared. She had a tiny head with close-cropped hair and an immense body that made me think of whales. I chuckled, then was aware that it was not nice to think this way; lately too many things had become forbidden in the States.

A circle formed around the woman, all sorts of smaller and bigger fish nibbled at her, then enveloped her; only their backs could be seen.

I walked over to a different group by the fountain when a woman with a ponytail said to me, "I only heard the last part. Is it true that Djuna Barnes was seduced by her grandmother?"

"I wasn't there," I said.

"She was not seduced," a blond woman said. "It all depends on your subject position."

"But I just heard the part about the letters," the ponytail started.

"Oh, that," another woman said. "I suppose it could be called seduction if you include the letters."

"What letters?" I asked.

"The letters her grandmother wrote—she called her sweet names and she said she missed her terribly," the woman explained. "And there were pictures."

"Pictures?" I asked.

"Yeah. She'd send her paintings, you know postcards of paintings with two women hugging each other and would write underneath them how much she missed her. She seduced her head, I think it's clear."

"Oh, really! Too bad I missed all this," said the young woman with the ponytail, looking disappointed. Turning to-

ward me, she said, "What do you think their sexual politics
are here?"

"Whose?" I asked, confused. In New York I knew what
those words meant. Not any more.

"The men," the woman almost giggled. "They are gorgeous, aren't they, but you never knew about their sexual
politics."

"I don't know either. I've never known anyone here," I
said.

In the conference room I heard nothing as interesting as
Djuna Barnes' grandmother. They have switched on, talking
in jargon which included 'subject position' over and over
again, this position, that one. For some reason, I assumed it
was something sexual in nature, maybe some positions were
forbidden, or were NOT to be done, bad for your health.
Wasn't the so-called missionary position condemned by the
feminists in the seventies as too passive, not good enough? I
was not too involved with them and if I can't remember
exactly, it's not important; it happened on the periphery of
my awareness. But having revived the blond boy with the
blister on his lower lip in this town empty of cars, I think,
almost out loud, "Wait, how is it possible? Didn't I spend the
summer with the other, the dark one with gold eyes?" He
was not a gypsy but looked like one. Not a clue.

No, I'm not happy that maybe I'll turn out to be a superficial person, maybe worse. To stay with the blond one right
after the dark one seems cynical for a young girl at that time.
And what's more I didn't love either one really. That's the
horrible part. Why is it horrible?

Why did I say that I knew nobody here, why lie?

I didn't love anyone here, would be more accurate, but that would mean explaining, getting involved. *Better not.*

Chairs moved, hands clapped. I was sitting in program number five. They were discussing Colette's ambiguity in French. *Ambiguité.* Of course, he used the same word when he wrote to me in French, care of a university in Boston, which means I didn't know them at the same time but a year apart. I knew the dark one from before, from a ways back then, and we were never here in this town or anywhere on the seashore although he talked about it, didn't he? The place for our honeymoon.

I am glad I didn't know them at the same time. There is something reassuring about all this knowledge, and it's easier to look at them, the blond and the dark boy, now that they are separated for good.

Chapter Four

The cats went at it every night. I heard them now in between two dreams. Their lovemaking had terror, pain, and
passion all at once; half-asleep I was sure they were dying.

In the morning the old man was watering the roses as
usual; near him in the sun, a bloody cat barely moved. You
couldn't tell if the cat's horrible state had to do with love or
if someone just beat her up, but I didn't ask, out of embar-
rassment. Looking at the cat sprawled, haggard, eyes shut,
made me ill. It resembled someone I knew, a woman from
my childhood who had many lovers and even more my Aunt
Yanna after she went to seed. Mother disapproved of both
Yanna and the other slut for their absence of dignity, their
lack of control.

Throughout the morning I saw more and more cats,
bloody, thin, starved, all over town. One was even lying near
the myrtle bush in front of the mansion, in total abandon,
oblivious to the conference and us.

Inside the mansion, I looked for an Indian woman in a

sari but couldn't spot her. I was going to inquire about her and the poet from Minnesota but was distracted by Betty on the coffee line.

"I wonder why they don't have an electric pot," she said. "It would simplify everything."

"They don't drink American coffee here," I said.

"Why not?" she said, surprised.

The cook in the white kerchief was bent over the same blue pot; her friend was making more coffee in a chipped white pan. Still not enough, just a drop in the bucket, these two pans.

"The French are starting to act snotty, did you notice?" Betty said.

"Really?" The French didn't arouse any violent emotions in me. They were a small group of women, less loud, shorter in size, and dressed in muted shades of beige and gray. Americans and French irritate each other wherever they meet.

"Just an impression," Betty said. "I know Mrs. Trintignant speaks fluent English, I heard her once in New Orleans at the conference on Foucault but she watched me suffer yesterday with my ten French words ... Oh well, I'm not going to let it upset me. We found a great place last night, really interesting food. Where were you? We looked for you, you can't get up there without a car."

"I had some sardines last night," I said. "Fresh sardines," I added, noticing her grimace. Did she think I just opened a can?

"I love sardines too, that's the first thing I asked for last night but they said, no sardines, no fish."

"There are less of them now. Almost all gone."

"Where is this place you went to?"

"It's not a restaurant," I said, afraid that the entire mob would suddenly find the little old man who cooked the sardines whenever he caught them. "It's this fisherman's place."

"Oh, one of those," Betty raised her eyebrows, moved her shoulders, mouth opened slightly then twisted to one side—gestures American women make to indicate romance, adventure, occasionally rich food.

The old fisherman hadn't recognized me; I was surprised he was still alive and that I found his place by the small harbor. And as before, his restaurant consisted of an old table with a few chairs and his two buddies drank white wine that was very strong. I had come here with the blond boy the first time; it's here we always had the best sardines, just caught. In my memory, as the night fell the men sang, harmonizing, and when they stopped, there was no other sound except the sea gently hitting the shore, moving the pebbles. I am not going to tell her about that place, call me nasty if you wish.

"What's with the cats?" Betty said, "did you see them?"

"Sure."

"I can't stand the way they treat them, most of them are half-wild and they could be rabid. Poor things, nobody feeds them."

"It's a poor country," I said, "that's why they are not fed."

"Still," Betty said, "still … "

Betty irritated me, a sign that my own difference was greater than I imagined. I should have expected it, but then I had never been with Americans in this landscape. Too bad we have to be together, without them I'd feel better.

"If they can't feed them, they should fix them. That can

be done," Betty continued, "It's the humane thing to do."
What does she know about human or humane, a silly twit!

"They used to cook them and eat them during the war,"
I said, having forgotten this detail.

"You're kidding me!" Betty made a horrible face, as if
hit.

"It's true. The Italians ate them. They loved roast cats,"
I said. Why did I say that? It wasn't necessary. Still it *was*
true.

Luckily, the crowd moved—the French, dark and small,
to one side, and the Germans, Swedes, and Americans, united
by the English, to another. New sessions started.

Inside Program Seven, I tried to concentrate, thinking
about that essay I had promised to write, but it wasn't easy.
Nothing resembling an essay entered my head. Through the
window the young woman with the ponytail who had asked
me about sexual politics and Djuna Barnes was talking to a
young man in blue jeans, obviously in English, but the way
he gestured and how he laughed made it clear he was a native. He stood too close to her, and I expected her to take a
step or two backwards, to establish a more comfortable distance when talking to a perfect stranger; instead, she laughed
at something he had said and their shoulders touched. Bravo!
Wonderful to see that first moment, so rare.

It was like beginning of an old film, too bad they had to
run off screen and only the myrtle bushes were left splattered
with sun.

I got it, I almost shout, Stanko, that's who! He was an
actor, a dancer, he looked like me. And that's not all! I had
run into him again, in another summer, a year later. No,

wrong. I saw him on the ship leaving Ragusa, going north and he couldn't believe it, this second meeting in the same place which only proved it was meant to happen. It was awkward soon after, I had forgotten him and his love letters in French (why did I forget him, who else was there, another man?); he reprimanded me that I never wrote and so I changed my itinerary (what was it, where was I planning to go instead?), because he persuaded me to come home with him to a small village in the Alps. Why did I do it? Guilt maybe. It wasn't love.

He was sterner looking, the second time, he did classical plays, big parts, but his cold sore disgusted me; it bled on my mouth when we kissed. No! It's not possible he would have a fever blister both times, it just isn't, I have forgotten, then merged the two summers, no point in trying to separate them, I can't worry too much about a cold sore.

His people were silent and efficient, very different from me, almost another country, but they found it natural that the two of us should have a large bedroom full of cherries, apricots in glass jars, and the smell of quince ripening on the window sills. In the North, Mother said, they were different about many things; there pregnant girls married without shame or problems, even before the war, but they were known for their calculating side. The German influence, what else.

In that large silent bedroom with fruit jars, we didn't make love that night because I was suddenly seized by panic of pregnancy and my life ending abruptly. I had wild notions about my life at that time, something linked freedom and roads but I didn't have the common sense to think about contraception, either because it wasn't romantic, or it was too premeditated, or maybe making love wasn't on my mind. Love was. I was not different from other girls of that generation, whose lives ended abruptly with a pregnancy. Where are they now? I wonder about Judy and Sandra and Lois, married at twenty. And Tina who died from a botched abortion.

He was bitter, he said I was not afraid to risk everything the summer before. True. I can't think of a single reason why I slept with him one year and not another, maybe it had to do with the sea and the sun; in the North it was colder.

In the morning I rushed to leave him, get into any car on the road going toward the capital. He waited with me without saying a word, looking like something out of Bergman.

I don't remember what I wore, what my hair looked like, but I must have had a pair of blue jeans, I always wore that for hitchhiking, and an old army parka. I can't even see him as he was then by the road but his last words come out just as I am about to get into the car. He shouts, "coward! coward!"

"Absolutely not. He is wrong," I said out loud.

"I agree with you 100 percent," a woman next to me smiled, "Barthes has nothing to do with her thesis."

My arm burned; the sun fell on it and on the floor. Almost noon. An hour has passed. Outside the window everything was luminous, still, as if in anticipation. Sun, I think, sun is the reason I am digging this up, nothing ever happened to me in the fall. Sun must be the reason. It will destroy me, it passes through my head and I just know that's how I used to think at twenty.

Chapter Five

There was no doubt about it, I couldn't write anything, my mind was empty. In a restaurant near the mansion, I had attempted a few lines about this or that but nothing happened; my thoughts vanished; without a focus, nothing held them together.

The sea from the terrace was deep blue, almost indigo with white caps. It looked like the beginning of a storm, I wasn't sure what the wind was called, was it sirocco or mistral, the one that brought the rain. The waiter could tell me if it's one or the other, except it made no difference, he couldn't stop anything. If it's supposed to rain, it will rain.

At the next table, two women couldn't decide what to order. I had seen both of them at the conference, wasn't the tall one an important feminist from Cornell, or did I confuse her with a woman from Yale? She was clean-cut, handsome like a young football player around the shoulders and jaw. "I miss my cereals," she said. "I'm getting bored with rolls and butter and jam." Her voice was surprisingly squeaky, a young girl's.

The other one said, "I know exactly how you feel. You can't imagine what's it like for vegetarians here. The conference should've been better organized."

"You can say that again. It's a mess," the tall one said. "I hear they left it all to the locals, just like the coffee break."

"Fortunately I don't drink coffee. I carry my teas with me wherever I go."

"Smart girl! Why didn't I think of that?" the tall one exclaimed.

"I wonder what to order," the vegetarian said.

"Don't you think we should have a party? I still haven't said a word to any of the French. Not a word. We have too many papers and no time for serious discussion. A party might be good," said the other.

"That would be nice. I still don't know what to order," the vegetarian said, looking hungry and sad staring at the menu she couldn't read. She was thin and dark, with that special look in the eyes that I associate with vegetarians and my friend Sally, who always talks about purifying her body with plants.

It was an old state restaurant that didn't have translated menus out of season, but I was sure that the waiter was bound to speak English or German or French. If he wanted to. The young one who took my order was gone; he had addressed me in English and I kept to it, not letting on. It was better. But the vegetarian looked so pained and the new waiter so surly, I broke the rule, "I can help you, I speak the language," I said.

"Great," they shouted and invited me to stay with them. My calamari in butter and garlic appeared at the same time. The tall woman gestured to the waiter to bring her the same, only the vegetarian wasn't sure. "What I really need is a plate of raw vegetables, I haven't had any for days. My whole system is out of whack."

"You won't get it here," I said. "Cooked vegetables maybe."

"I know that, but they overcook them and kill the benefits, so what's the point," she said with despair.

"Try one," I said, giving her a bit of calamari from my plate. This gesture, or my fork, frightened her. She recoiled as if I would stab her, giggled, then said, "Oh hell, I'll risk it."

She loved it immediately, her love for it was as big as her fear had been, and finally her problems were over. We gestured to the waiter to bring another plate of the same.

"Are you from this town?" the tall one asked.

"No, inland. But ... I've spent most of my life in the States."

"You don't have any accent ... but what's it like where you are from, is it like here?"

"No, it's quite different."

"Really? What's different about it?"

"The coast was built by Venetians, inland it's a different climate, different history, religion, everything." I began lecturing like a tourist guide and was annoyed. They didn't even look at the map or it would've been obvious that everything would not be the same behind those high mountains. The sun, the mild climate didn't penetrate very far; inland you had snows, dark skies, mosques.

"Really? God, I wish I had another week," said the short one.

"How did you escape?" the tall one said earnestly, prob-

ably out of a need to say something. This was an old question, the one I remember from New York, from the days
when I used to talk about my native land, in detail. And this
too I know—their expectations, visible in the eyes, in the
tone of voice—dogs, snow, danger, guns—as I run across the
border with my mother, or maybe my mother carries me
wounded in her arms. Blood drips on the snow, my shoes are
gone, but we make it. We talk about freedom next, in a
close-up. In all these years nothing had changed—they ask
the same questions. They'll expect the same Hollywood answer too.

"It was easy," I said slowly. "We took the train to England, then left on the Queen Elizabeth. That was a beautiful ship." Here too nothing has changed, in spite of my new
self, the one I had managed to acquire finally. My answer
was same as then, and with it a feeling of rage I had sup-
pressed. I refused to invent for them.

My answer, or my voice, must have produced an effect;
they didn't ask any more questions about the country but
drifted off into promotions, articles, papers for the next conference, in Greece. They didn't see me any more; not being
a part of their professional interests, I was not what they
looked at.

The waiter and the waitress looked at the clock. It was
late, past their usual lunch shift. I heard the waitress say,
"My kids are waiting at home, hungry. Fuck these cows."

"Fuck this life," the waiter harmonized, "Fuck it one hundred times. They'll probably want some coffee next."

A part of me wanted to remain camouflaged so I can
hear the rest, all the curses that'll fall on their heads, it

might be funny, they might say all sorts of things about me too, but there was another more violent need not to be in the same pack with these two, a need to reveal myself. "Bring us the check," I said to the waiter, imitating his speech from the central parts.

"She is ours," he exclaimed with that smile that had love in it, a bit of my childhood, memory of warmth. It was a usual smile for him but I could've cried now, had I been alone.

"I told you," he said to the waitress, "didn't I?"

"Why, how did you know?" I asked.

"Like that," he said, "you look and you know. I can tell you a thing or two about them," he said winking toward the women next to me, and I knew what he knew, what he meant. He didn't want them in his bed, his wink said. A part of me laughed with him, native-to-native appraisal, the other portion became confused, it's not fair to talk about women this way, a piggish thing to do, yet, at that instant I was closer to him, no doubt about it, bound by something old, our country, overrun, misunderstood, unknown, forgotten, invaded. I couldn't find the right word for my feeling, 'cultural imperialism' seemed heavy, old fashioned, but it enabled me to see it all in a larger perspective and then it was my feeling but not mine alone. Marsha would forgive this switch. Her allegiance shifted often.

"What did he say?" the vegetarian asked.

"He said the storm is coming," I said. On the horizon a small ship moved with difficulty in the midst of the white caps.

Chapter Six

It was easy to spot her at the reception even though Indira didn't wear a sari but a white travel suit Indian style, loose fitting with baggy pants, and a white transparent scarf. She had travelled for a few days, further up the coast, had seen the Roman ruins and everything was wonderful until now. Indira had imagined that writers and scholars would talk about writing, together. She said all her books are about women—mothers, grandmothers, mothers-in-law. Didn't they want to know about these women and herself in India. "Do you know what textual spaces are?" she said looking at the program.

"No," I said, laughing. Indira spoke fast and her accent was funny, with strong dramatic r's.

"Good. I understand 'genre' … but here is another one … look, 'Subject position on textual bisexuality.' Are you confused? I am confused. Very confused. It is all right. It doesn't matter. I saw a pretty city on the coast. Maybe I'll see another."

This was the first official reception, with dinner in the old city later on, an attempt, I heard from Teresa, to get everyone together. But the divisions were apparent, small groups whispered here and there, plotted, grew silent at intervals. Some looked angry, some hurt. I couldn't decide if the divisions were due to hidden nationalism along French/American lines or personal ambition, but I was glad to be neutral. I was sure Indira would do the same, a nice spot, a perfect position to be in, same as our countries in the UN. We were called 'nonaligned,' it used to be an important movement for the Third World.

There were no natives at the reception or I would have noticed them—they would laugh loudly and be overdressed. Two English women stood to one side talking to each other. Only their mouths moved, a peculiar cultural style that passes as well-brought up. You couldn't tell Germans or Scandinavians from Americans until you came closer. New Yorkers, recognizable by their fiercer gestures, had their own group; they discussed real estate and where their kids went to school. A Dutch woman with flaming red hair complained about her movement sisters who dropped her after her book made a lot of money. The French continued to talk only in French and to each other but would welcome anyone who spoke French, I knew they would. I almost gravitated towards them but they didn't interest me enough; my love was gone, maybe the language was too precise, maybe the geometry of their minds too boring. I can't remember why I loved them so much. The woman with a ponytail and two other women talked about a fascinating secret topic, judging by the glances they threw around, their eyebrows raised. One said, "I've heard that lesbians hold all the power here, they schedule things the way they wish."

"I've heard that too," said another. "All of them are from New York."

"I doubt that," said the ponytail.

"I know they have their own parties," said a short woman with a southern drawl, "the best food, with champagne, all catered. I saw this boy bring them a case right to …"

"The lesbians?"

"Of course. They had picked the best hotel for themselves, the one on the beach. They can swim and party anytime they wish. The reason I know …"

"You mean everybody at that hotel is gay?"

"Most likely, judging by their papers."

"That's not fair," said the ponytail. "I could get real pissed. Why should only they get to use that hotel."

I got inspired for the first time, imagining lesbian committees judging everything either by looks or titles. What if I wrote something about this? It might be funny. The next moment, I censored it—the feminist scholars wouldn't go for it. I had tried to joke yesterday about my lack of inspiration and how humor is always a good way out when the whale woman stopped me like a cop, "If you have nothing constructive to say, don't bother!" Too bad. "Fuck this life," I thought, "fuck it one hundred times."

"Nobody, nobody will tell me my mother's life is the same as Margaret Thatcher's," the black man was shouting at Indira.

"I know," Indira said, calmly. "I have five children, my mother had eight."

Five kids, I though, and moved closer to her. I liked the way she looked. The man kept up his rage against England, then a young blonde woman with very large hips joined us and she too was enraged. Pointing to the program, she said her name was misspelled and she is not from Minnesota but Maine.

"You must be Jane," I said. "We are on the same program, the three of us."

"The very last day," she said, "did you notice?"

"We should get together and plan what to do. I still ..." I began.

"I'm only going to read my poems. They don't give a shit about us, living poets and writers, did you notice?"

"If they don't want to hear about Indian women, they lose, I think," Indira said, serene.

"The Third World is underrepresented here," the black man said, furious.

In the midst of all this, I saw a young couple I had not seen before. Both had blue jeans on, his hair was slightly longer than hers. They stood against the tree kissing, then he laughed at something the girl must have said, she stuck her tongue at him, then he grabbed her around the waist. I liked watching them and they were having a good time; too bad the bell interrupted us. Everybody rushed toward the door, then we were herded together for a communal dinner in the old city where a portion of a street was converted into a restaurant for us.

I couldn't find the young couple again. At the table there was no room next to Indira, who was sitting with the French and a man from Nigeria. I wished for something pleasant, a bit of warmth; it was chilly suddenly, the strong wind moved the paper place mats, rattled the forks.

I sat in a empty seat next to the women with a ponytail, across from the woman I privately referred to as a whale. There was nowhere else to sit. Eat fast and leave, I decided, but with only two waiters it looked like it would take forever just to order. To speed things up I recommended certain plates, explained the ingredients, had them order en masse. "Thank God you're here," the waiter said. "What are you, a guide?"

"Yes," I lied.

"I don't envy you the job," he said. "It's not easy, is it, for us."

He was in his late twenties with olive skin and very blue eyes, an ordinary guy from the islands.

"What a hunk!" one woman said. I had never used that word, was unclear about it, or the word couldn't describe anything I would ever say.

"Mmmm, he is gorgeous," the woman next to me said. "Look how he moves, look at those thighs. Are they good lovers?" This was directed at me.

"I don't know."

"Aren't you from here?"

"No, I'm not."

"They are so fit," the woman said, "but I'd better not get involved. I have a relationship already and ... I shouldn't self-destruct."

I knew this one better than some because I had seen her through the window with the native guy and because she had asked that question about sexual politics. She was younger than the rest with her ponytail, edgy, restless; her nails were well bitten off. With this new question it sounded as if she were both attracted and scared, yet it was stated in public, openly, something girls couldn't do here. Nor could I.

I tried translating 'self-destruct' but it was too new, too modern used this way; although you could destroy buildings, towns, culture. To 'destroy self and remain alive' couldn't be said in this country, while this girl didn't mean anything as drastic as suicide. Some other lesser state I didn't know, cooler, more metallic. I realized I didn't know what she meant, separated from her by so much.

Then I heard another tough one, "I've been working this whole past year on my life," a woman said to the one who didn't want to self-destruct.

It was peculiar. I had heard this sentence before in New York without paying attention. I must have heard it many times on the buses, subways, at parties too. Now, these words stood separate from the person, by themselves, as if suspended in air, for me to look at them. Zero again. It was hard because it didn't exist as an idea—to work on your life, not the way this woman worked, or maybe the main problem was with that word. Worked. Too practical. Here nobody liked to work and if you didn't like it on the job, why would you bother to work at home too. No, it wouldn't occur to them, life passed this way or that way, that's all. To work on it implied results too, some improvement after a year of working hard, you just wouldn't invest your time for nothing. There has to be a profit of some sort.

My heart jumped—a brand new thought—it meant the pragmatic approach to economy extended to everything before and after the job, how you felt, for how long, is it worth it—he wasn't worth it, she was a waste of time—and how you expressed yourself, what words you used. Will they start talking like this here, too? Now that socialism was ending. They might.

'Work on myself' was untranslatable, or it would sound like masturbating. I almost giggled, imagining it in print.

The whale turned suddenly toward me; she had been talking to a slight man with a goatee who looked like Trotsky.

"You're a native?" she asked.

"I guess so," I said.

"Why do you say you guess? Are you from this town?"

"No, another one."

"How come you don't have an accent?"

"I'm American too. We are supposed to have a gift for languages," I said.

"Really! How come you said 'we'? How do you think of yourself?"

"I don't think of myself as anything," I said. I said *we*, I thought. I haven't done that in years.

"I can't believe that," she said. "What do you teach?"

"Theater. I write plays," I said.

"Have I seen any?"

"*Che* is the best known, but that was a while back."

"Che Guevara?"

"Yes, him."

"It's not about women?"

"No, it's about Che."

"You don't like to write about women?"

"There are women in all my plays. Men too."

"Do they have any good writers here?"

"One won the Nobel Prize."

"Really! Does he live here?"

"He is dead."

"You can't keep up with everything," she said. "Some-body told me they eat cats here," she said looking at her plate. "Is it true?"

"Yes, once in a while, they do," I said, with great plea-sure. She'll eat and worry about every bite. I watched her push her plate away. I'm turning nasty, I thought. I should have kept my mouth shut.

I shouldn't have told them about me, it was better be-fore. No questions or answers, no irritation. I was getting distracted; just as I was on the point of remembering some-thing important, they had to intrude.

The whale had no more questions. After the last one, she turned toward the man who looked like he could be her husband, a quiet man half her size. But others began, now that they had an expert for free, to ask question after ques-tion about politics, life, death, history, all wanting nice pre-cise answers which I couldn't give fast, nor did I want to. They were exhausting me when I only wanted to eat. This I observed: nobody asked about the Germans. That hasn't changed. They never asked about them.

"Was it hard to live under a dictatorship?" A woman asked an old one, making that special gesture with a wrinkled forehead that stood for sorrow and earnest concern. Jane Fonda was good at such roles.

"No, it wasn't," I said as always. "At ten, I didn't know it was a dictatorship. I didn't know we were poor either."

"Your family was poor?"

"No, everybody was," I said, not wanting to explain how *Death of a Salesman* wouldn't be understood here. Dreams vary from nation to nation, don't they?

The woman wasn't happy with that answer, she would've preferred "yes, it was awful," or something like that. Communism was romantic to them, evil, sexy, what will they do from now on? It looked like Communism was fading away, not that it ever really existed in any country except as an idea.

I could have obliged them, it wouldn't have been hard. I could've said yes once in a while, or varied my performance for fun, and then it might be interesting to see what happened next, but it would all lead to one simple conclusion— life is horrible here and good in the States and I should be grateful to be a part of it. If they didn't push so hard, I might have given it to them.

I'm a fool, I thought. I should've stuck to my decision. They'll get me, I am bound to lose. My stomach turned yet I tried to be nice, but it wasn't easy. They didn't play fair, just kept on provoking me, pushing me to react, and then they would blame me for the outcome. What would I do? You never know, do you? A woman with a horse face complained she couldn't find a single English bookstore in town. Poor dear, imagine that!

Then another one who looked like a frazzled cat complained about men. They had chased her last night, pinched her too. I was grateful to her for changing the subject from 'life under socialism' to more contemporary themes. Warmed by the food and wine, they attacked relationships and men in general, and got right to the main problem—how can you have both a good relationship and good sex. I relaxed—this would be good. Actually the best dialogues in New York are on this subject—women talking to each other about the absence of men. Anywhere you go, that's what you hear, the major shortage of males, as if they were killed off in a war.

It's not just me. It was obvious, any actor would tell you this just by looking at them—they were madly attracted to local men, on the street, in restaurants, anywhere, but were unwilling to risk it. It had to be safe.

There was a problem—nothing was safe anymore, as the disease spread in every country, even to China where apparently the sick were quarantined. There was nothing about it in the local papers, not a peep, just their usual problems, the impending end of socialism and various nationalist bickerings. Which didn't mean they didn't have it. Of course they did. They had to.

"See," the frazzled woman said, lifting her skirt up. Her thigh was dimpled, white, with a large bruise in the middle.

At first, I thought it was a problem of mixed signals, the usual cultural misunderstandings, but then my view changed, shifted 180 degrees, and I who had complained in the past about native machismo, saw it differently, with our waiter's eyes. For one, it was not a pretty thigh. Cheesy, soft, local boys could find better. They pinched, attacked out of vengeance maybe.

Rage is what I knew, looking at them. Waiter, waiter, bring me another glass of water, another cup, more ice, it's not cold enough, no not that, bring me another dessert, I've changed my mind, are they good lovers, did you get everything out of it, out of it, they shrieked, go to hell, the waiter muttered, running back and forth, and I thought his thoughts—I would rape them. I hate them, I repeated, just as in the sixties, when anger, hatred, and love exploded but even then I didn't shout my own rage fully. I had hated with Americans; it was different.

I hate America, I thought, I've always hated it, I still do.

I hate them was a revelation, my identity, a disclosure, the way poor Allan must have felt when he went shouting to his parents he was gay. Something hidden. Something big, dying to erupt. I hate, I repeated. Deliriously happy, I could spit at them. Everything carefully constructed over the past years was crumbling now, all that had been my orderly life.

It had to be stopped or else. I approached my hateful self gently, the way I did with kids, let's talk this one over, OK, guys?

Do you hate all of them?

(No, not all.)

Of course not. You have American friends, right?

(Yes ... but ...)

And your sons and Marc?

(Well ... yes ...)

Not their fault. The U.S. has only two borders and one is with Canada.

(True.)

You don't hate them really, be serious? You don't want to hurt anyone.

(I guess not.)

The reasonable voice covered it all up, then gained control. Slowly, the rage left me. Nobody noticed a thing. It was just my own internal explosion, an invisible epileptic fit, yet my separateness stayed, even seemed bigger; the women's voices reached me as if from Mars.

"I like the pill the best. You take it and forget it," said one.

"Did you ever try the sponge?"

"Too messy."

"Not if you get used to it. The pill is not for me."

"Why not?"

"It gave me a discharge."

"I stick to a diaphragm. It can't hurt you."

"And it lubricates."

"True, but none of them are safe. I carry my own condoms wherever I go."

"It's true, you just don't know if they're any good outside the U.S."

"I am sure the German ones are OK. I was there last year. Everything they make is first-class."

"I've heard they don't have it here," I heard the ponytail say.

"I wouldn't be so sure," another woman said.

"Do they have it here?" the ponytail looked at me for an answer.

"AIDS? I'm sure they do," I said, regretting it. Maybe she had slept with that guy in a brief moment of madness and now she'll worry to death, poor thing. The blond boy had a fever blister on his lips. Would I sleep with him now if we were both twenty? Can you catch AIDS with a kiss?

"It must be minimal, or I would have heard about it," I added, wanting to console her. She looked young, ponytail and all; I could have a daughter her age, I thought.

They were leaving; I made sure they left a large tip, a pile of inflated dinars which looked like toy money. The waiter looked up and waved to me, then went back to his dirty plates. He didn't have to say anything. His eyes were enough. A feeling of betrayal entered me again—I was with THEM, they had money for things, for the disco where they were heading now. And I with them. I was in the mood for it, anything mindless.

I had asked the old man about the dancing place I used to go to. It had stayed with me like a memory of films I saw—rhumba, soft lights, sea in the background and me as a girl in the white dress. Waiting for the music to start. Something marvelous will happen on that dance floor. That must have been around the same time as the blond boy.

The old man had looked at me with suspicion. "How could you remember it? That place is gone ages ago. Nobody dances well anymore, they only jump up and down like kangaroos." He said they now dance in horrible dark dungeons where he would never go, very expensive places that only rich foreigners could afford. Not fit for mature people, either, the way the old ballroom used to be. And now I was going there, to a native disco for the first time, in the cellars of the old fort.

By the entrance, two young women with wigs, and leather suits pranced and pouted, their eyes dead. Of course I recognized them, now that they looked the same as in the West, but it wasn't always so. Maybe I was naive at twenty, or maybe they didn't look the same, but there must have been prostitutes before, always, maybe not many, but some, hidden, invisible on the small streets by the port. I was a child when I left, and didn't know how to observe well, that's why I said I never saw any. They were always there, they had to be. I lied about the other stuff or I chose not to tell that some ordinary girls, students on vacation, sold themselves casually for a dress, stockings, even a ride in a car, during that first wave of invasion. Every summer the tourists descended with suitcases of new clothes to party for a month, for pennies, the way they couldn't do it in the West, more and more of them every year, until the very shape of the coast was transformed to accommodate them. The Germans won this time.

"You scum, you whore," I hear the local boys shout at me. It must have been around sixty-seven or eight; I had forgotten it.

Why would they say that, my costume didn't fit, I had blue jeans and sneakers on, no make-up, none. What did I do wrong? At that time they still considered me theirs and just talking to an American ballet dancer was enough. They didn't believe, couldn't imagine I knew him from New York, had only stopped to say hi, and he was gay anyway. For them, there was only one reason why a native girl would talk to a Western man, stockings, dresses, you whore, you scum, they said. Here.

Nobody would shout scum, whore, any more. The fight was over. Nobody is shocked by anything any more or maybe it's not in the open, or maybe they had forgotten what used to shock them once. The beautiful dancer is dead too, from AIDS; I saw it in the papers, three months ago.

"Just a bunch of cunts inside," a whore who looked like a transvestite said to the guy selling tickets at the door. Her voice had a hoarse resonance of voices dreamt. "Why the hell are you staring at me?" she said to me, making an ugly grimace. "You don't like me, or what? Men fuck their own money, that's all."

"Excuse me," I said, "I didn't know I was staring."

"Excuse me, I didn't know, she didn't know," the woman mimicked me, kept stabbing me with words. It was OK to have whores in New York, here no. It hurt. It didn't seem right. My pain was big, but couldn't be named.

"Get out of here," the man yelled, "or I'll go and get the cops."

"Go ahead. I've screwed every one of them," she yelled back.

He made a gesture to hit her and she ran, looking crippled in her red shoes that were too high. Both of them looked familiar, his jacket, her wig, a replica of 42nd Street, a movie they saw. I ran inside.

After a brief darkness, a large space with strobe lights. Generic disco went *pam, pam,* pounding hard. The floor was jam-packed with conference women doing their thing, looking transformed. Even Martha, the whale, danced with energy, her flesh rippling in silk pants. Teresa shook all over as if tortured by electricity, Betty stayed in the same spot, her ass sticking out while her hands made all sorts of defensive movements, go away, go, don't come near. A tall blond galloped across the floor bumping into everyone, one kept on boxing with the ponytail who threw her head and hair back and forth in an agony of some sort.

The old man was wrong. There was more to it than up and down. They were briefly possessed but nothing of all this will

remain tomorrow morning. That's what Western meant, madness tucked away, selective loss of control, I pursued my own
thoughts, a form of entertainment. What else could I do,
there was no room on the dance floor. Around me a slew of
young men watched the floor too, but you couldn't tell what
they thought. *Pam pam* the music went for a long time and I
got bored. I was heading for the exit when a different music
came on, resembling a folk tune from the South. The women
went 'oh, no,' disappointed, and scrambled off the floor. Three
young men jumped in, obviously the leaders of the coup.
They danced like they have been rehearsing for this number,
arms raised, hips swaying, and it looked serious, tense, a prelude to some dramatic event. It's life or death, their faces
said. Fortunately, they smiled and waved toward us, come,
come, they said, in English, but nobody budged, intimidated
most likely. Disco is democratic. For this dance, you had to
know the steps. The boys looked disappointed, their coup
was not staged for them alone.

As the drums accelerated, the tension inside the disco
became unbearable and I found myself on the dance floor
without knowing what I was doing, what this dance was
called. It might have been an old courtship ritual, or a sword
fight, sometimes I was attacked, other times I charged and
they retreated, then fell dying on the floor. I had never danced
this before, but the rhythm was familiar and strong so I didn't
think about the steps. I knew I danced well, even though we
were dancing a prelude to the war.

They talked while they danced, they urged me and each
other with all sorts of words. I wasn't sure of their age, they
didn't seem to notice mine. We were just dancers on the

dance floor and I loved it, I had not danced like this in years and would have stayed on with them if Teresa and Betty didn't say something about leaving. And then, one of the boys reacted, "You can't leave. We won't let you," he said, his hand gripping my shoulder. I pulled away and left them. They didn't try to keep me by force.

Outside, we were a large group which split up into smaller ones. The town was silent, shut, only our feet echoed on the white stone. We crossed the bridge over into the street with trolleys. Right here, outside the city walls, I was left with the whale and her husband; they lived, it turned out, not far from me. I had just said goodbye to Teresa and Betty and promised them something or other when, turning toward the old city, I saw my three boys walking toward us. Were they following me?

"Do you mind walking me home?" I said. "I couldn't get rid of them," I added nodding toward the boys.

"Of course," her husband said, "we don't mind."

"At your age I wouldn't put up with any nonsense," the whale said. "Just tell the bastards to get lost."

I was sorry I had said anything, I couldn't easily explain that it was different for me, these boys were like relatives, sons, perhaps. I wasn't really afraid of them, I wasn't even sure if fear was the right word. I had betrayed them now, and the dance, with my stupid words, and with a woman I despised in addition. I had betrayed the blond boy too. He must have loved me to write nonstop for years, letters I didn't even open.

Chapter Seven

I had forgotten about the miracles in the morning. Half-asleep I was drifting toward the memory of us, without tourists or cars, was on the point of figuring out something important, something dreamt, when I remembered—I had promised Teresa last night I would come with them to the village where the Virgin appeared. Damn. I could have said no, was going to but hesitated, we'll be lost without you, Teresa said. It was too late to change things, by now everyone knew who I was, a mistake, Ann was easier to live with. That's the problem, I thought, getting ready, I am always in unclear situations, except when I say no, when I run away.

Instead, half-awake, tired, in a bad mood, I was in their car heading away from the coast. From the highway, high up, I saw Dubrovnik from the postcards—palms, white houses, red roofs, small harbors and blue water on all sides except one. It was beautiful but they exclaimed too much. I was sleepy, not a morning person. They took pictures, two sets, a peculiar habit, to duplicate what's done already. The road climbed, all curves. Betty complained about her ears. Teresa got ill. Half an hour inland, the vegetation changed completely, it got colder, the houses grew thicker, more squat without any elegance or charm; the light of the coast seemed far away, an illusion.

Betty said she felt guilty about playing hookey especially since they'd miss an important paper on Lacan but they had planned this trip to the village ages ago, had also promised their relatives and friends to make this trip. They had a bag full of rosaries to be blessed.

They didn't really need me if they had planned it all along; they knew what to do. And I could still be in my bed thinking my own thoughts. I couldn't stand the word 'hookey' for some reason, nor the way Betty said to her husband, "Will you get me a dessert if I'm a good girl?" She had an annoying habit of asking small favors, then bragging about it, "Look what he gave me yesterday, he said he'll buy me this." In her thirties, Betty had a girlishness that wouldn't go away.

It was too late to retreat, I was stuck with them now. If only they didn't carry on so much over everything, how unspoiled, how perfect, if only they said nothing about it. I kept silent, not wanting to spoil it for them, I could've said you don't know what you are talking about, this is a shit hole now, a raped country, a ruined coast. And then they had a strange tic about money, and kept dividing the bills evenly in three parts, coffee included, then discussions followed. They were thrilled by a bargain, they saved money with a joy that resembled passion. At the rent-a-car place, I helped them repair some minor accounting error, and they looked grateful, as if they had won an extension on life.

The man handed them the ten dollars with contempt, stingy worms, his eyes said, but then he didn't understand their world, I thought, he can't judge them like that, it's not fair, yet I too judged them, cringing every time they said, 'it's worth it, it's worth it.' Who was petty, me or them? I couldn't remember if I said, 'it's worth it' in the States. Maybe I did. So hard to be fair.

Still there was no point in denying it—something had happened. Too late to retreat now. After many years of calm, once again I was on the outside looking, judging them. It wasn't as if I ever became a part of anything, no, but I had reached a certain neutral state of functioning, a good place, a restful one. Somewhere during this week, for some reason a switch took place, didn't I say *we* for the first time in years. *We*. I had forgotten what that meant. Now in the car *we* took over. I could even hear my speech change, the accent I had lost was coming back slowly and I was powerless to stop it. I noticed the first symptoms—very precise English, almost British, an attempt at control. Soon, I'll start changing the entire sentence structure, then will even forget some words.

The conference was a mistake, I shouldn't have come. It'll cost me.

The miracles had to be recent. I had not heard about this village before. Teresa said the village was tiny and poor, so poor they starved. Then the Virgin appeared to some local kids and told them all sorts of things, she forgot what the Virgin said exactly. Betty specified that the church hadn't taken a stand; the miracles weren't proven yet; you have to

have seven proven miracles in order for the church to make
it official. I had all sorts of questions about this—how do you
prove it, do you have a selection committee, is it like a jury
system, what if they disagree and so on. "The Virgin appears
around three p.m.," Betty said ignoring my question, "then
speaks with the kids for a while, who later in the church
reveal what she said. That's why we'd better be there on
time," Betty concluded, lilting her voice, the way teachers
do.

They didn't ask any questions about my religion, maybe
because my ignorance about details said it all.

A mile away from the village, we got into a traffic jam,
then it took half an hour to find a parking spot, far away
from the church, behind the Miracle Tour buses. The village
didn't look small or poor any longer. The road to the church
was lined with brand new houses, some half-finished, some
getting built. Here and there couples painted window frames,
women shook their rugs, hung their wash to dry and everywhere in front of the houses from the windows the signs said
"Zimmer, Chambre, Eat, Room To Let." I couldn't imagine
what sort of church they had seven years ago, what the village looked like. Now, the church was visible no matter where
you stood because it was the tallest building in the area, built
on a rise so it seemed to dominate everything, a bit like
colonial cathedrals in Brazil. This one was brand new and
unusually ugly, graceless, done in the same exaggerated style
as night clubs in Las Vegas, the kind of building that makes
you wish an earthquake would occur.

On an unpaved clearing in front, thousands stood waiting, some in wheelchairs, some on crutches. Beggars sat on

the ground, hands extended, while the healthy workers hammered the tile pieces forming a mosaic pattern with a face that would eventually cover the red clay in front of the church. They hammered evenly without looking at anyone, with the indifference you see in domestic animals, cows, mules. Just another day, a job to do.

The church was full all the way up to the door. You could see nothing but backs, packed thick; to get to the altar seemed impossible but Betty said she had to see the kids, hear their message. Next, the bell sounded, people lifted their arms to make the sign of the cross; when I looked for Betty and the others I saw they had managed to get inside, were pushing their way toward the altar.

Outside, the sermon over the loud speakers was translated in English, then in German, and French in a husky monotonous announcer's voice. An actor's voice, sexy somehow. The hammering of the workers continued uninterrupted but was less noticeable, or it appeared to blend in with the sermon in the same steady rhythm. Quiet oppression settled in me. I should've brought a book along. In back of the church there was no one. Grass and cherry trees in bloom. Further out, behind a wooden gate, almost hidden on the back lawn, I saw some people and priests in white robes. They sat in chairs that were marked in black signs, a bit like directors' chairs—ENGLISH, FRANÇAIS, ITALIANO, PORTUGUÊS, DEUTSCH.

People who couldn't get inside the church waited in line to confess, kneeling on the grass as their turn came. Those waiting kept a respectful distance between themselves and the kneeling person, about the same five feet as in the bank.

The lines were uneven, with the German and English the longest, a surprise, if you think about it. But then maybe the Spaniards and other Latins had their own miracle places to go to.

Out of boredom, I imagined—what if I confessed some story to two different priests, would it come out differently in substance in different languages, would they disagree on my sins, for example? He might smile and say, oh it's nothing in French, while in English I would be condemned. I had never confessed anything to anyone, not that I remember, was unsure even of what my sin would be. Mama's religion, or what was left of it, didn't bother too much with sin and confessions, our Christianity was a veneer: from my childhood, I only retained the stories about witchcraft and ghosts and my grandma talking to God directly from her kitchen. In her demands for justice, she included me and our neighbors. "Listen, God, let me tell you the way things are," she began.

Looking at the Franciscan priests and kneeling people, I gave up on confession—it was only amusing as an idea. It would take too much work deciding what to say, and besides I didn't like the way the priests looked. There was a profound boredom in their faces, just like my colleagues—years and years lecturing from the same textbook, winter, spring, fall, the same boring verbs in French, and in English, freshman composition, Introduction to Western Civ. Some turned old overnight like Rob who still talked about the novel he intended to write.

It wouldn't be easy confessing so many, month after month. The priest who handled the Germans chain-smoked, he even had his own little silver ashtray on the grass; the

Portuguese one was chewing something pink, gum? He had nobody in front of him, his very beautiful eyes just stared ahead toward the hillside. He was the best-looking one, most likely gay. I followed his gaze over the rocks—I saw groups of people moving slowly in some sort of procession. They carried an immense wooden cross on their backs.

Away from the priests, to the right, the toilet line curled and extended, composed mostly of middle-aged women, then, next to it, they waited for something else. This other line in front of the makeshift store was longer than any other, and whoever was in it would miss that important drama inside the church when the kids reveal what the Virgin said. Just as I was going to inquire, a woman with a strong accent from Brooklyn turned to me in a gesture of friendliness, the way it happens in supermarkets in New York, and said, "I got ten, then I realize it's dumb. I should get more, I says to myself. Five medals for a buck! I figure why not get ten bucks worth. The nuisance is I had no money on me and by the time I got it, I lost my spot. Had to start all over. What can you do … I won't be able to do anything else today. See, my husband is inside the church so we got the place covered."

I liked her for some reason, or I liked her monologue, well said. Her voice brought a memory of a woman who had the same speech pattern, a way of talking about herself in monologues, less nasal maybe and it wasn't medals and money but different boyfriends she talked about. Where is Jackie now … maybe Hawaii. We had travelled together all over Europe, were considered good friends, where did she end up, with whom, wasn't the last one the snake charmer? No, that was in Phoenix, she had moved since, we lost touch, maybe in the eighties when she moved to L.A., then Alaska, and nothing since but a card.

In front of the church, the crowd seemed denser now, more nervous, waiting for something. A woman carried a deformed girl in her arms, her face turned upward, her arms extended in offering. God, take her, the mother's eyes said; she was not praying for a cure. The bell sounded. There was a low hum, a music of voices in different languages, a prayer, a lament, but each time the bell sounded everything grew hushed temporarily, then resumed with more force. Some fell on their knees, some stood still, some sobbed. Then I saw him, a young man with a face I had seen many times in New York recently, he had the same skin patches, recognizable. I remembered Bill and David and Dan, all gone, all young. Bill was in my last play, he was so happy, poor baby, when he got the part. He couldn't believe his luck; he had just moved to New York from Omaha.

The young man with AIDS had his eyes shut, a woman next to him looked toward the sky, near them a couple of Japanese held hands praying too. The bell kept going and going, urging without a break, then other bells joined in, one by one until there was nothing but this sound, magnified by the hills, everything else erased, and we stood united, just like ages ago on a peace march, and I was crying too. I don't want to hate, please help me love, I prayed upon my knees with all those sad people, an excess of feeling in my chest, a need for a miracle of my own.

The bells stopped. Next to me, the deformed girl screamed, her tongue was blood red. The arms of the young man with AIDS were covered with sores. Flies buzzed. It was hot. The

sun appeared huge and terrible. I had been taken in. Bells
and whatnot. I was ashamed of my stupidity. In rage, I wished
I could blow up something. Instead I moved away, looking
for a place else to eat.

The souvenir stands began immediately, right after the
church. It was the usual assortment of key chains, tee shirts,
sunglasses, but I didn't expect to see the kids in color on the
postcards. Some were regular size postcards, some much larger,
some life-size posters and the kids were not kids anymore—
seven years had passed since the original appearance of the
Virgin.

The pictures showed them as well-dressed adolescents
now, hair combed, girls all made up, eyes lifted upward, mouths
slightly open. Someone was directing them. They seemed
disturbed, especially one girl; seven years of miracles every
day at three p.m. showed on their faces. I knew that love or
miracles don't thrive on regularity; if anything, regularity
would kill it.

The beginning must have been easy—the original appearance was 'real,' in a country prone to tales and madness,
where the dead came back to visit at night. Then came the
second time and the third and things got out of hand—
obligation, duty to report, more and more tourists came, the
economy boomed and the kids couldn't retreat even if they
wanted to. I was sure they wanted to escape but didn't know
how. There were really just two ways to do their job; either
lie about it or go mad and do it for real. They probably didn't
even remember who they were before the Virgin.

I shuddered. Their disturbed faces disturbed me too. *Go
away, it's dangerous*, someone whispers in my ear, *they butch-*

ered us near here during the war. Run away! My head spun, the
postcards in my hands were not real, throat slashed I fell into
the pit silently, and others fell on top of me, and my words
were not there when I wanted to scream. I was brought to
life by the gypsies who lived in the shacks behind their souvenir stores; my unreality stopped with a real cry of someone
getting strangled. More shouts came next, then a gypsy woman
flew out of her shack spitting and cursing at another swarthy
woman, pulling her hair too. They kicked, hit, bit each other
unsparingly. Nobody separated them until they knocked a
table over, a plate broke and then a man ran out and splashed
a pitcher of water over them. The fight was over. All three
went inside.

The shacks and souvenir stands continued; it was like a
village in itself, the smell of cooking strong. I looked for a
café we had passed earlier, a sandwich would do. In front of
one shack, two men sat drinking coffee and watching the
soccer match on TV; they'd had something good to eat judging by the pile of bones in front of them. Roast lamb? Both
had smooth bronze skin, shiny black hair. One of them turned
around and our eyes met. I stare too much. Fatigue, most
likely.

The café was right around the corner but there wasn't
much to eat. "Lunch time is over," he said, not eager to
work. He was watching a soccer match too, and cheering for
a team I didn't know.

"An omelette," he said, "that's all I can do."

"I'm hungry," I said, "give me whatever there is."

He found some bread, olives and cheese, a bottle of beer;
he made an omelette, swearing occasionally at the TV. I ate

nonstop, glad to be away from the church.

I was wiping the plate with the last piece of bread when this gypsy sat in a chair next to me. It was the young guy I had seen earlier; I recognized his eyes which were the most unusual shade of gold.

"I like you," he said, matter of fact.

I said nothing, hoping he'd leave.

"I like your eyes," he said.

"I'm eating," I said. "I'd rather be alone."

"You've finished eating," he said, "and you don't want to be alone."

The waiter did nothing to help, too involved with the soccer match. "Go get them," he kept shouting.

"If you don't leave, I'll scream," I said, aware you don't say things like that here, a sentence in translation. There must be something else you would say to make him leave. In addition, he had grabbed my upper arm with violence, and with another hand he was squeezing my thigh. Tomorrow I'll have blue marks, I bruised easily, but at the same time I was hypnotized by his eyes, the unreality of the situation. When I shouted finally, he ran away, spitting in my direction three times, the small spits reserved for witches and ghosts.

Later, I met the other four. In the car going back, I couldn't tell if they were disappointed by the village or not. The men said nothing to me, their faces blank. Did I intimidate them? They didn't talk much to their wives either, not the way Teresa and Betty did with each other.

Betty broke the silence. She had confessed for the first time in seven years since she stopped going to church for good. She had been angry with God for being unfair to her.

He took her mother and her two uncles and he didn't give her a child, an experience she really wanted. She didn't deserve all this. But today after the confession, she felt better. The priest gave her a penance to do. She wouldn't say what sort of penance.

I was curious about it, but I knew you don't ask outright about the penance or sins you've confessed. It probably had to do with her anger against God, everything she didn't get, felt entitled to. It could paralyze you. What would her penance be, did he tell her to abstain from, or do some more, that was the question.

"What was the message, what did the kids say?" I asked instead.

The kids didn't appear the way they were supposed to. They left a handwritten note which the priest read. The Virgin said she'll stop coming soon but will appear elsewhere, in some other country. A priest wrote this one, I decided. The kids have rebelled! Good for them! It meant they were still OK, they knew how to say no. But the plan was impossible. The village had grown too prosperous, they couldn't dismantle the apparatus—as with any bureaucracy, it would take a long time. And there might be some violent opposition.

They'll have new kids, I thought. That's the easiest thing to do. Nothing will change.

"Did you feel anything?" Teresa asked. She said some people felt a very strong energy field around the church.

"Yes, I did," I said, without going into details. That gypsy man had given me something I had forgotten, a memory of still another time and another man—a gypsy I had met on the bus. Thinking about him, I told Betty a gypsy remedy and my mother's for having children. I had to whisper, it was something men were not supposed to hear.

"Pardon us," Betty whispered next.

"For what?" I asked.

"Things," she said, but I couldn't guess late at night what her guilt would be.

Chapter Eight

The old mansion looked abandoned at ten in the morning. Nobody in the courtyard. Total emptiness in the halls. In the kitchen, the woman who had been making coffee all along was now washing the floors with a wet rag and a bucket of water. Her friend was perched up on the window sill cleaning the windows with old newspapers. Everyone was gone. Maybe the reading was supposed to be yesterday; I had lost my notebook and my program notes too. In Medugorije most likely.

Upstairs in a large conference room, I saw that I hadn't made a mistake—Indira was there and Jane plus our audience—a young couple looking sleepy, a woman from San Francisco and another from Canada, both anthropologists. Indira informed me that the last night's session was cancelled and the afternoon program reserved for native writers was cancelled too because they objected to each other's politics and religion. There was more to it, Indira said, but she didn't understand all their arguments. So everybody left, the organizers included. Betty must have known this, the little hypocrite.

"But our reading wasn't cancelled," Jane explained, "and we are here. I think it's shitty! This is more important than their dumb Derrida dirt!"

"I don't care," Indira said, "They paid, I came. Tomorrow I will go and see the mosques in Mostar."

"That's why they put us in the last program, I'm sure. It's disgusting." Jane was the only one angry, even though she laughed suddenly and couldn't stop. She had taken care to look good, her blond hair was done in several small braids, and she had on a pretty green dress.

I couldn't detect anything except relief. I was going to talk about a play, how it changed from the original idea because of money problems, but I was happy not to dredge it up—it was over, done with. Things were turning out just fine. "It's a beautiful day," I said, "let's go swimming. I'll show you my favorite spot."

"Great," Jane said, "I'll go get my bathing suit."

"You don't need it," I said.

Lisa and Marc wanted to come too, but not right away—they needed to find a cheap room somewhere in town. The hotel was expensive now that the conference was over.

"All of us will have to pay from now on," Jane said. "I didn't think about that problem until now."

"If I could remember how to get to this house," I said, "they might rent you a room." I liked these two, maybe because they were so poor and young. She was a teaching assistant, he painted, he said, and made bookshelves for money.

I don't know how I recognized the house. We got lucky,

that's all. It wasn't different from the other houses around it, even the shutters were the same green shade but I stopped in front of this one and knocked. A man whom I didn't know said yes he had a room for rent and another one upstairs if they didn't mind sharing the bathroom. "But no Yugos, no dinars!" he said to me.

Lisa ran up to see the room, came back to kiss me, Marc said it wasn't real. Jane said the view is out of this world. I left the owner to see it too, but first promised him I'd ask for foreign currency. He said he wanted dollars.

From the window, I saw that the small harbor, 'my' harbor, was right underneath the house, the man who cooked fried sardines must be next door and the man who was now working on his canoe might be his son, but I couldn't remember why or how I knew this house, did I stay here alone or with the blond one? I always took a steep little street near the tourist office to get to the fisherman's place, but today coming from the mansion with three of them, we went in some other direction. And here it was. Maybe it was with the blond one, maybe one single night I had erased. Maybe it was someone else, but who?

The owner didn't seem familiar, there was no reason why he should be if I had met him just once before. He said he'd take marks or francs if they had no dollars. Jane said that she'd move in too, and have herself a short vacation now that the assholes are gone. She wasn't angry anymore, her eyes sparkled; she loved this new room which was better and cheaper than that hotel with all the dykes. The owner looked at Jane and his eyes sparkled too. It looked like he had fallen in love, poor guy. Jane said fifty was too old.

Lisa and Marc stood at the window, their arms around each other. In front of them the sea extended indefinitely, framed on both sides by the white cliffs, and directly underneath, they had a man and a boat too. No wonder they liked the room. It was perfect, plus they had each other. Standing in the doorway I watched them kiss.

That much perfection in the noon light produced edginess, like a reminder of something brutal to come, as violent as the summer itself; I had never thought of it as a peaceful season. In Alabama in July, the trees burned all around us.

"We'd better go now," I said. "Indira's waiting for us."

Chapter Nine

I could hardly wait to get there, but why did I talk so much, why say you'll love it, it's wonderful, why say it's a perfect spot. It was just my little spot, nothing more, they could love it or not. Besides Americans love big beaches and sand, there are tons of better places out there in Barbados or Jamaica. Thank God I didn't say how this is the most beautiful water in the world, imagine if I did. It's good I didn't reveal all those other things you shouldn't blab to perfect strangers about—the memory of love that linked me to it, how my parents met by the seashore and my dad saw her, and how grandma had a famous fish restaurant right here by the port and this sailor appeared one day. It was my sea. I had loved it too long. Magic awaited me here in the deep waters. If I dove deep, Grandma said, I'll find a shell with pearls. Did I ever?

Once I get there I'll stop talking or thinking, I'll jump in, that's what I'll do. It took forever, first a boat ride then a long walk through the pine forest, then another path toward the shore. Barren. Just rocks. And then Indira didn't want to go any further. She settled under the only cypress tree because she hated the sun. She said not to worry, she'd watch us. The rest of us slid on our backs over jagged rocks toward the water where I had promised them beautiful flat stones and fortunately we found one big enough for four. It was a perfectly secluded little spot, yet open toward the sea although Indira couldn't see us nor could we see her. We were nestled in the rock.

I took my clothes off and jumped. Lisa followed, then Marc. The water was still the most amazing shade of indigo but I swear it used to be warmer. It stung now. Jane shrieked hitting the surface, "I'll die," she cried. Marc picked up Lisa, then threw her in the waves. "Be careful," I screamed. "I see a cave," Jane said, "it's an underground cave!" "Don't go in the cave," I shouted back, "look out for the sea urchins!"

It was disappointing, me and the water. The sea was too cold, my legs numb, I was too old for the Adriatic in May. I got out, and then directly in front of me I saw these things, inside the crevices and cracks mixed with dry sea weed—cigarette butts, chewing gum wrappers, rusty cans—tons of garbage from the summer before. The island looked spotless, but nobody could clean this up, thousands of cracks, millions of tourists, billions of butts, not even a tidal wave. The sea would keep it. Too bad I saw it. Maybe they won't.

"It's heavenly," Marc said, looking frozen, his hair standing up.

"I love it," Lisa said, shivering. She was as slim as an eel, with those baby breasts. Together they brought to mind that painting from Picasso's blue period, circus something or other it was called.

Jane sprawled her large body near me and grunted. When she laughed, a lewd smirk appeared on her pretty face; she had spread her legs in abandon. Her flesh had the dimpled softness of Wonder Bread, cottage cheese, soft things, stretch marks like silver paths meandered from her stomach toward her pubic hair which was the most surprising shade of red. Which animal is she? A manatee? I didn't want to look at her crotch, or think about the hidden cigarette butts, but it wasn't my fault—they were there.

Lisa and Marc had their eyes shut. In a towel, all bundled up, they were taking a nap. Twenty years from now, they won't be the same, I just knew it, glad that Jane was distracting me from my sudden gloom. "You're turning red," I said, "go hide in the shade with Indira."

"I don't want to think about the fucking shade, a man is what I want," she said, laughing.

"At least put some of this stuff on," I urged her, but she ignored me.

"A man," she repeated.

I don't remember having a similar thought ever, nothing so specific, or maybe it came out differently. We were attracted by eyes, hands, the way a man moved, a mysterious look. "What kind of man would you like," I asked, curious about her generation.

"Good looking and wild," Jane said, twitching her foot, her face hungry. A female in heat would terrify me, I thought, but these were not my thoughts. Somebody said it. One of the actors most likely, Jim or George, or Bruce.

"Listen," I said, "put your shirt on at least," She made a grimace but let me throw a towel over her, then closed her eyes.

The sea moved, gurgled gently inside the rocks, swoosh, swash it went, entering the crevices, pulling, gurgling, re-treating towards the sea, then back again and again towards the rocks in the same steady rhythm that puts babies to sleep. I was drifting off myself when the smell of the wet stones under me woke me up—no, no, I didn't make love to him in that room for the first time! It was right here! Maybe not exactly on this stone but one like it, near the water. The room came later. Which room was it? Marc and Lisa's or the other one with the views of the rooftops. It doesn't matter. Can't remember everything.

So, we had met here, and we had made love the same afternoon, maybe right away. I don't remember me then— the girl who did this—I only remember the smell of the hot stones, special in the summer. It meant that the island was empty, with no tourists even in July because it was in July we had met—theater season in Ragusa—and he had a lead in a play, I no longer remember which.

Even though it happened here, I don't have any evi-dence to make it real. Nothing but the smell of water and the stone. I would have to remember a detail about my body, let's say discomfort, because it must have been hard on my back with only a towel underneath. He was a well-built man, tall. I couldn't have been on top, nor would they do it stand-ing up, nobody did anything unusual here in the way of sex, nobody even used the word until later. In the seventies? Still, I can't be sure what people did or didn't, I left too young to know for sure, but still I am certain they were not obsessed with it, the way some countries are. I would have heard about it.

Let's say, a man and woman met here but it would be nice to know how it all went from the moment she saw him and he saw her. If only I could isolate one day in July, the coast empty, the sun blazing, the sailboat far away. How I wish I could see us. Maybe he saw me first, or maybe it happened at the same time, some sort of recognition in our eyes. That moment is what I want, I wish I could feel it.

It troubled me that I couldn't separate the moments, days, or years, what happened. Everything merged, vanished into impressions of color and smell, a bit of laughter. I had to disentangle all those summers for accuracy, step by step, when did the invasion start, what was the country like before and then maybe I would see myself too, at least a glimpse. This was urgent, a need to save myself, but I had nobody to help me, a friend who could say, 'I remember you at twenty, you were ....' Then they would remember everything, dresses, birthdays, who was ill when, you didn't have to worry you'll lose or forget any of it, somebody always remembered you there even though it might be different from your own memory of the event and then they argued about it for days, reached a conclusion, then argued again. Mama kept her stories with her at all times, she could pull one out in an emergency, she was saved with "Do you remember when ... ?" It was easy for her; America didn't exist, there was only before.

I have nobody, I thought.

I had nobody now, except myself as participant and observer, and that self was murky, not yielding, wouldn't come up and deliver—to my horror there was no memory of me. None. Nothing real. As if I had not been there, just passed through. A ghost. A film I saw. The reality of something invented and no more. I panicked, like the day Mama had died, real vertigo followed, where am I, where are the walls but then I was reassured by the repetition of symptoms and common sense. No, I had not erased everything, I had re-corded, observed others and if I had done that, it stands to reason, doesn't it, that others would do the same. Absolutely! Stanko remembers me and what I looked like, what I said to him and how we met, but it's also true that he and the others probably recorded casually, like watching clouds or rain, they didn't try to make connections, unify their observations, or isolate me or each other specifically. They didn't work on themselves, lucky people.

Is that what I'm doing? Just like that woman the other night.

I had made fun of her, considered myself immune. Now, her words were no longer superficial like California where she was from. What else can you do except 'work on your-self' if your neighbors move and you move and you change jobs and become someone else, not once but over and over again, running toward some vague idea of your potential self, leaving starting over again across the American continent, from New York to San Francisco. Millions of people, all lost, searching for the happiness promised in the constitution.

I was always grateful for the intellectual component in me, the rational capacity I seem to have acquired in France to think things through, ask relevant questions. It's some-thing. It's better than if I didn't have it. I am able to discern now for example that what that woman said about working on herself might seem to be the same as what I, Ann, am doing but it isn't really. The woman from California would stay in the present and would examine what she likes, what gives her pleasure, what negative forces to avoid, the aim would be happiness which I, Anna, didn't think of. Happiness is hard to imagine. I only wanted my past back. It's different. I experienced a wave of pleasure at my clear analysis. Lying naked on the white stone while everybody slept, I wondered next if democracy might be overrated, did it make anyone happier, all that running, rushing, torment of choice and unlimited possibilities? Peaceful? No. What's the rush if the end is always the same, exactly as if you hadn't budged, same as your neighbor—six feet under the ground, that's what you get. Who said that? My grandpa? It must be him. But he was no help now, buried in the same field he had watered, a pretty place full of clover. He is no help. I don't have a field, my friends move, I don't even know who I had been all along. And intelligence has its limits, can be a dangerous cover-up, to push you further away from truth with abstractions, words like subject position, deconstruct.

That California woman had it easier, she'll continue to speak the same way at least. She probably had just that one voice, maybe a bit different in pitch, whining occasionally, or angry, but still unified with one language into one person. Not my case, unfortunately. In the attempt to sort things out, I was aware presently of several distinct voices in my head fighting for control;

(a) Ann who lectured, explained theater to her class, fair, caring. Good mother. Certainly. Tired of this voice, so tired of her drab costume.

(b) Potentially angry, sentimental, drippy, like who? Didn't care for that one, close to the edge of tears. Embarrassing. Never to be used in public, in New York.

(c) A voice that was calm, like rivers, a voice from the past—grandma's, the one I preferred but it had no function in real life. It was best solitary, a voice to dream with, "Ages ago when I was a girl, when Dubrovnik was called Ragusa …."

(d) The voices I picked up. On the street, anywhere. Voices of strangers, absorbed. I wrote plays with them. They were not my own.

(e) Various theatre personas, gay men in particular, well done but borrowed too. Neither Anna or Ann.

There must be more, I am sure there are. None of them added to unity of any sort, nothing central held them together, without collision or interference. Perfect strangers. Bickering at each other, pushing at my chest. Stop now, my rational voice said, stop it! It's pointless! I did. Crash landing.

I was lying naked on the white stone. My foot burned. It was the month of May. Everywhere in front there was nothing but blue as the water entered the rocks and retreated with a swoosh. Stick to this, I commanded myself.

A splash. Marc and Lisa had jumped in. Jane fell in too. I joined them, letting myself go down toward the deep waters, maybe I'll find that shell with pearls. I couldn't reach the bottom now. Gasping for breath, I came up.

A man I had not seen before was swimming near us. He was attentive, listening, as if excited by our talk. His mouth made sounds, was he singing or talking, I couldn't tell, then

his voice got louder and I heard him repeat in their direction, "I fuck anything from sixteen to sixty, thin or fat, I fuck
'em all."

A New York part of me said, 'madman, child molester,'
the other part dismissed it—no, just his thoughts. He is sure
nobody understands him.

The man was built like a tree trunk with childish blue
eyes and a comical bald head. "Jane, he likes you," I said,
laughing.

"Really? How do you know?"

"I heard him say it."

"I forget you understand them," Jane said grinning, looking at the man directly. "He's too old," she said. "Why don't
you fix me up with the waiter we had the other night?"

"Come here, pussy," the man repeated a new refrain, "I'll
fuck you to death."

There was a menace in his gestures, maybe he understood what Jane had said. Maybe he was retarded, he said the
same words over and over again.

"I-n-d-i-r-a, Indira," Marc and Lisa shouted from the water.
Indira, high up, waved with her scarf.

I got out. My only chance to talk with her. Tomorrow
she'll be gone. I had a specific question in my head, which I
forgot climbing up, or because Indira had so many questions
of her own. She was confused, she said. At the conference,
women spoke about jobs, relationships, and problems with
men, whenever she had lunch or dinner with them. "That
word 'relationship,'" she said, 'is it like 'engaged'?"

I didn't do a good job. Indira's eyes remained as puzzled
as before. "Why are there problems?" she asked. I couldn't

explain the whole country, it was best not to try. I gave her two books to read. And then, for the first time, I didn't understand much either, although recently in New York I think I did.

Lisa and Marc didn't have a problem yet. I saw them kiss in a long shot. It was a prolonged kiss without a break; they were rocking back and forth, glued to each other. For them the water wasn't cold.

The creepy man sat on the rock, his feet in the water. He was clearly jerking off, feeling invisible. They couldn't see him. I couldn't see Jane but maybe he could. "I kept waiting for somebody to tell me, what is 'subject position'?" Indira said, looking bashful.

"I didn't know either," I said, trying not to laugh. "It means point of view, like my point of view of you, or Marc and Lisa."

"Just that? Nothing more? Why don't they say 'point of view'?"

"I don't know," I said. "They got bored."

Indira covered her mouth with one hand, "I thought it was related to the Kama Sutra. You know, subject positions."

"Yes, I thought it would be something sexual too," I said, and both of us laughed. "I thought they'd tell me that some positions are forbidden by the end of the conference."

"Are they forbidden?" Indira asked looking very young.

"Just kidding" I said, feeling American now. "How old are you?" I asked, ashamed of myself.

"Guess," she said.

She had beautiful skin, the loveliest teeth.

"I can't," I said.

"That's good," Indira said mysteriously.

Eventually the kids showed up. Marc carried my things. Jane was sunburned, Lisa starved. "We'd better hurry up," I said, "the last boat leaves at five."

Once again we took the path through the forest. The sea became turbulent, the boat had a hard time docking.

Indira intimidated them in unspecific ways that couldn't be discussed. Either too much perfection, or her five grandchildren, her religion, or what Jane said, "she only drinks water, you know." We had a party after she left, with tons of food, salads, baked fish, olives, figs, all fixed by Marc and Lisa in the owner's kitchen and he even contributed bottles of white wine, his offering to Jane who was leaving next. A woman from Berkeley and another from Canada joined us; Marc and Lisa found them in a grocery store. They were lingering for a day or two, like the rest of us, wishing it were longer. Temporarily we were unified by departures as May 1991 drew to an end.

After the second bottle, Jane read two poems and received huge applause. Her poems didn't resemble her—it was some other shy Jane, all anger subdued. Then she stopped poetry and told about her family, how poor they were. Better families sneered at them. Upstate New York. Father drank. She never had the right clothes. Nobody expressed grief. But damn it, she left all that behind and showed them! Two years ago she came back and read in the town hall with her classmates in the audience, not that her mother cared. Her mother only knows soap operas and junk. Now, it's time to change her lifestyle again, she's gotten into a rut teaching in a small town. "I could see myself in New York or San Francisco for once," she said.

"I'm not sure you want San Francisco," the woman from Berkeley said. "Something deadly about the vibes. I can't explain it. It used to be different once." She remembered that wonderful time in the sixties and the birth of her daughter, born in a commune in the hills and all these people chanting 'Hari Krishna, Hari, Hari.' "My daughter is a very different kind of person, a lawyer, and she is very embarrassed by my stories about her birth. She'd prefer I shut up. Hell, it's my experience too, don't you think? You know there are times I'm not sure it was for real. There was so much dope around, people tripping on this and that and there I was in labor, grunting."

She laughed throwing her head back, and with that movement of black curls, I saw her the way she was then, dancing barefoot, daisies in her hair. Love, love, they chanted, flowers in front of the White House too.

"I knew a very different sixties," I said. It wasn't love I felt.

"I'm jealous I didn't know that time," Lisa said. "Everybody said it was something."

"We might have another sixties soon," Marc said.

"I doubt it," I said. "Nothing ever gets repeated."

"Why not?" he said.

"Because. It won't be the sixties. It'll be the nineties or … the sixties are over. What's over is over," I said, not expecting to be understood.

It's over, I thought, looking at the sea. The sound of a German beer song drifted across the harbor. The water was blue-black now. It wasn't here, I was sure of it. The view of the harbor had tricked me the other day. This house is familiar but I didn't stay here with the blond one. It was another house further up. I had remembered a detail—my blue dress was drying on the terrace and from it you could see the entire town below. The blue summer dress was the key. I might have stayed here with someone else. Why not? Just lust. Why couldn't I be like other people? Because it's out of character, Ann, the teacher, answers. That character was too romantic, with impossible aims. Nothing like sleeping with someone. Too bad.

"It gives you an edge," the Canadian woman said. What was she talking about, what edge?

"How?" asked Marc.

"It's much better not to be part of any culture," she explained. "You see, I was born in Brooklyn but I really love Toronto. Don't you think some people prefer to be displaced?"

"Horse shit." It came out by itself.

"Horse shit," I said again like a mad person. "Nobody prefers it, you invent that later on. All of us want to part of something, all kids do. To be without a country is to be permanently fucked-up because you are condemned to judge because you are on the outside. The doors are shut yet transparent. You know them, but they'll never know you. They can't. You spy, sort of ..." I was talking and talking in this excessive manner, virtually arguing, yet powerless to stop and I heard it—no doubt about it—I had an accent now. The way I said "spy," for example, lingering on the 'y'.

They looked hurt, probably felt betrayed. What have I done? It has been friendly until now. Why in the fuck did I do it? I didn't want to hurt these kids, who had slaved over dinner and had thanked me over and over again for their room. And it wasn't fair—had I had a thick accent, or an exotic costume like Indira, they would've been warned. What's more, I had at my disposal all the ammunition—their language, their expressions, I knew their country better than them. They knew nothing about me. Zero. I had always wanted to explode something, and now I had done it. Couldn't retreat. It wouldn't work.

"Yeah," Marc said, "we forget." He didn't look angry, a good loving son, but Jane was. "You could tell us about it," she said and that did it. How dare she!

"No you can't," I said, a new rage in me. "What would it mean to you? Do you want it in five minutes or ten? You can't share everything for Christ's sake! How often do you ask your black people, tell me fast, what's it really like for you folks?"

Tell us about it, they had asked about the bombing and I was stupid enough to try. Ages ago. The worst can't be told, in retelling you diminish it. Tell you what? My country didn't even exist for them, they couldn't find it on the map. Why do I even bother with the dumb asses, a waste of time.

The mood had changed. They looked gloomy. My fault.

"It's true. You can't explain things easily," the woman from Brooklyn sighed. She had a secret of her own she couldn't discuss. I'm not even gay, I thought. No group of any sort, nothing organized.

"Margo left," the Brooklyn woman said. "We were supposed to see Venice together." Margo met this man in a nearby village and, without knowing a single thing about him, not a single thing, just packed her things and went off with this guy. From the way she described her, I remembered her as the girl with a ponytail. "Is she a friend of yours?" I asked.

"She was. I could wring her neck."

"It's so romantic," Jane said, oblivious to this drama. "Is he a fisherman?"

"I have no idea what he does. He can apparently sing well. But that's not a basis for a relationship, is it? We were supposed to go to Venice together. It was all planned. Now I have to do it all alone."

"Do you live alone too?" Jane turned to me.

"No, I'm married," I said.

"Are you!" they shouted. "How strange!" said Jane. "Why?"

"You don't look married," Lisa said.

"What do married people look like?"

"She means you don't talk about it," the woman from Canada said.

"There was no occasion for it," I said.

"Most people find the occasion, they say WE are going to do this or that, MY HUSBAND thinks …" The Canadian woman had venom in her voice.

"Is he American?" Lisa asked.

"Yes," I said.

"What does he do?"

"He's a psychiatrist," I said, regretting it. A teacher would been better.

"That's why you're so calm," Jane said. "It must be nice living with a shrink, what's it like?"

"We don't talk about his work," I said.

"But you must discuss your problems," Jane said.

"I wouldn't like it," said the woman from Berkeley, "I'd worry he would analyze my faults."

"He doesn't do that. He is a child psychiatrist anyway." Nobody would understand that Marc liked me for comfort, the way people like cats or dogs. He didn't understand me at all, didn't try; I respected his wisdom—why we were together. Why do women talk so much about their partners?

"I have two," I said to the next question, "and they are in college." My kids, I thought suddenly, but not in English.

"It's impossible, you look so young," Lisa exclaimed.

"Not so young," I said.

"You've done everything," Jane said, envy in her voice. Lately, marriage and children have become exotic in the States.

"Come on, Jane, you could get married tomorrow."

"I'm not ready yet," she said.

"Kids are such a big investment," the Berkeley woman said. "I know."

"Investment?" I said.

"Why yes, emotional and otherwise. You have to put your own life on hold."

I haven't done everything, I thought, half aware of the missing part. And it was too late now.

Chapter Ten

Soon everybody left, Jane first, then Lisa and Marc, Marie from Berkeley and the woman from Brooklyn whose name I never learned.

I experienced briefly an emptiness alone, away from others, people you meet briefly, not friends, not close or dear, all those passing strangers who gave shape to a day. I knew all this from my previous travels; it meant switching gears, thinking differently, finding moments, routines to help you along, first a cup of coffee here then a second cup there, a drink at the café around five. At the old mansion, they were getting ready for another conference, a sign said 'SYMPOSIUM ON MARINE LIFE.'

The month of May was ending, the days grew hotter, soon the real tourism will start. Already, everywhere in the upper parts of the town, busloads of Germans, English, Dutch spilled out, all alike somehow in their sensible shoes, cameras dangling, eyes eager. These were bargain tourists, older people tempted by cheaper prices for a week on the Adriatic

coast, everything included, before they die. They moved obe-
diently behind their guide, men and woman similar looking
in their haircuts, grayness, round stomachs, flattened asses.
Something like quiet despair hovered over them, I couldn't
imagine why they did this now, didn't they know it was too
late? Where will they go next year, Greece? They seemed
like children on a field trip in a museum but were more
docile, bullied into submission, without a single prank.

It was time to leave before the real invasion begins with
younger louder visitors in big cars, but I kept postponing it,
extending my stay, lazy somehow.

When I called home, my machine answered with Marc's
clear voice instructing you to leave a message. "Everything is
fine," I said. "Just staying a bit longer."

From the terrace I watched the sea and occasional boats;
slept late. Children's voices woke me up, sweet murmurs of
kids going home for lunch at noon. The owner who had
watered his roses long ago would be seen coming back with a
paper and fresh bread in his basket. I woke up starved, without a single thought; I wasn't lonely, I didn't miss anyone.
Absence of schedules and conversations was soothing, time
had stopped or appeared suspended.

When the streets cooled and shadows stretched, I dressed
slowly, taking my time, and went to sit in the Café Miramar.
This was an old café with a view of the sea and the island,
everything in it had remained the same, large, cool, with old
leather furniture and silent dignified waiters. Here, I ordered
my usual glass of white wine and read in the local papers
that the country was falling apart. A bloody fight with the
football team. Barbarians they said. Some broken bones. Some

square dedicated to the victims of fascism was renamed. The paper said the breakup was inevitable, but I disbelieved it, couldn't imagine it in this landscape with blue waters and the sun. I didn't see any real signs.

I didn't notice the kids either, not right away but soon it was impossible to ignore them. Local boys were following me, in twos and threes, staying slightly behind. I couldn't decide if these were the same boys I had danced with that night or different ones. It was annoying to have to think about them, like flies.

Lifting my eyes off the paper, I saw them again, at close range, right in front of the café. They were different boys, a bit younger. Bored, most likely, maybe school was over. They were chirping and chirping, then they picked a table right next to me as if they couldn't have had all the others. The waiter looked at them disapprovingly; he was not going to serve them. This was a quiet place not frequented by teenagers, local or foreign, probably discouraged by the number of old people and higher prices too.

It was clear—they were after me for some reason. Their whispers were childish, and the looks in my direction were meant to be accidental. I wanted to laugh the way one of them looked up toward the sky then snuck a fast one in my direction. However, a wiry boy with green eyes didn't cover up at all. He stared openly with insolence.

"What exactly do you want?" I said finally.

For a second they were startled, then one of them said, "We didn't know you were ours." Something about the word 'ours' was tender, sweet, yet sad. 'Ours,' I thought, is the same as 'mine.'

"Are you an actress?" the kid with the green eyes said. "No, not an actress."

Obviously they had not rehearsed this conversation ahead of time, there was a brief silence and discomfort with snickers, then a boy with a round face and no trace of a beard said, "You see, we like your image," using an English word for it. That word didn't exist in our tongue, I never said it in English because it was one of those new words, but I had heard my sons use it. So and so was changing his image, growing a beard, a moustache, maybe an earring in one ear, maybe both. My own generation had other words which were always about eyes and soul.

"What is my image?" I said slowly, looking amused, playing with them a bit. They had said 'ours' a moment ago, the proof that the country wasn't falling apart. 'Ours' implied unity, in opposition to. I watched them blush, the way I used to, a painful burning sensation all over the face and neck. So hard to be young.

"Well ..." the boy with the green eyes started ... "You can't explain it. You see it's kinda cool," he said, using once again an English word that was translated as 'ice cold'. Cool didn't exist here now or before, it was not a cool country.

"I like your hat," said the sweet childish one, sort of begging for it with his eyes.

"It's you," the green eyes said, "but it would look good on me too."

Jane had said the same thing about my beige linen suit. The suit and the hat are me and my image but tomorrow I might wear a dress and then what? Who will I be? Maybe I've done everything like that, even had good times, as if in

borrowed clothes, costumes in a play. For none of them fitted some inner part, not in the way I could say it's me. This
is me. What if there is no more me, nothing to attach the
clothes to, some other voice asked and once again I got dizzy.
This was more terrifying than any other fear, it implied disintegration, chaos, civil war, I needed something fast to attach myself to, me, I, us, anything would do.

I took my hat off which the boys interpreted as permission to try it on. They were no longer sitting at their table,
had moved to mine and were fighting over my hat, who'll try it
on first. Green eyes looked good with it on, his eyes shaded, his
mouth full, he struck poses in front of the window glass then
another boy snatched the hat, put it on. This perfectly ordinary summer hat meant different things to them, provoking
them to act, pose as gangsters, lovers, pimps—impossible
without the right props. They were not shy any longer.

My landlord, it was definitely him, had to walk by at this
very moment, carrying his basket, full of fruit. He tipped his
hat to somebody at the café but his eyes took in everything—
me and the boys, one with my hat on, another with my
jacket in front of the window glass. I was sure he didn't like
my image.

Catching up with him, I wanted to justify myself, explain my love for kids, but asked instead about my room,
how much longer is it available. I knew my time was up. He
said politely that the room is reserved for a German couple
who came every year on the same exact day but he could
help me find another if it's only for a day or two. "Isn't your
conference over?" he asked and I detected suspicion in his
voice, or was it mockery. "Who are you?" he asked, and I

said, laughing, "Your guess is as good as mine." Let him think whatever he wants, he had no business asking me.

One more day. It was better like this, all decided by this German couple who'll take over my room for a month. I could get Marc and Lisa's old room but it was better not to. Time to get out, time to leave. No time to get attached. Sooner or later you have to, so what's the point.

I checked about the flight and started packing. Tomorrow at this time I'll be on a plane, I thought, but tomorrow wasn't real yet. The sun was setting, bright red on the horizon, an orange glow in the room. It was warm, breezy, with a faint odor of pines. I couldn't stay in, not the last night. I should say goodbye to Dubrovnik and the coast. Now that I was leaving it, maybe forever, I loved it the way I must have once, but if I didn't push it away it would soon turn into an unbearable sadness around the edges, a longing that had nowhere to go. Anything was better than that, I always knew this was meant to be temporary! "I'll go dancing tonight," I said aloud, "that's what I'll do."

I put on my favorite dress, a white Danskin sleeveless, perfect for the summer, but a bit worn from overuse. It's the only type of dress I liked, no belts, no bra, no ironing, the skirt that swirled when you walked. I regret I didn't get another one at the same time, the same style no longer existed. Should've gotten two, it's rare when you find something that's right.

The old man and his wife looked at me silently; I couldn't tell what it was—concern or disapproval. At the gate he said, very low, "You should go home now, while there is still time. Isn't your husband waiting?"

There you have it. He obviously thought I was turning into a slut. That silly hat. The mood has changed. Their house was full of crucifixes I had not seen before. Even my room had one now.

I said nothing. He closed the door.

Halfway down the hill, from the side street, a crowd of men came running, shouting, 'hurrah! hurrah!,' their eyes glazed. They carried a flag I didn't recognize. A chess team, I decided, judging by the flag which was checkered red and white. The sound of glass breaking somewhere, 'hurrah, hurrah,' then silence. A *fascist flag*, mother whispers, *it's a fascist flag*, she insists but I ignore her.

I was in front of the souvenir shop which sold dolls in native costumes, objects made of wood and clay, about to go inside when I saw her in the glass—the woman in a white dress. She frightened me a bit but that was me, Ann.

The sensation of fear returned, I'll fall apart, for sure. Maybe I already have. Even my memory was full of others but I couldn't see me at all. If I succeeded at all, briefly, yesterday, it was thanks to the memory of dresses I had worn, white, blue, red, pictures of me in them, smiling sweetly, striking a pose. Clearly an actress, in a movie of my own.

My image now didn't tell me much, another disguise looked at me in the window glass—a slim nice-looking woman, of undetermined age. In a white dress going dancing.

In back of her, framed together in the window glass, a chess team galloped in the opposite direction and the crowd cheered from the sidewalks. Their words made no sense, *Srbe na vrbe*, something about Serbs on willow trees. Maybe they won. A party, a celebration. *They want to hang them from the willow trees,* mother's voice translates but I push her away. No, I insist. They are just having a good time.

The boys who had liked my hat were dancing already. The floor was jammed. Mostly young people. You couldn't tell who was who, what nationality they were. Nobody talked. For a second I saw myself with their eyes, as I appeared on the stairs in a white dress, looking a bit sad and dazed. It wasn't real, just a frame in a Hollywood film, but this woman was an interesting image, you wanted to dance with her. Didn't she remind me of what's her name who always played the other woman?

When the slow started, the kid with green eyes got up and looked at me. Watching him move in my direction I knew he was in a movie of his own too—nothing was real ... him, me or the dance floor.

Who is he dancing with, I wondered. What about me?

The moment the record stopped, I ran out fast, and kept running, afraid he might come after me, drag me back, and then what? I could tell I had provoked something in him, and he was too young to view it the way I did. With some perspective. At his age, movies were real. What was he, eighteen, less or more?

Time to go, I thought, falling asleep, time to leave. But in the morning I changed my mind and took the train inland. You can fly from the capital, I reasoned.

Part Two

As the landscape changed I didn't think about the coast any longer. On the train the other girl took over, and I remembered the man with green eyes, and Anna's first return to her hometown after six years. The sound of wheels brought her back.

The night of the arrival, she had done everything as in a film. She had left her suitcase at the station. Nobody knew she was coming. She wore sunglasses. She wanted to surprise them, she has planned it like this for years. And she needed to see it alone, to smell it. This Anna is so feverish, so young, I want to hug her, console her about everything, girl, you shouldn't have left in the first place. It's here that many things should have happened but didn't, or you would be a different person now, I wouldn't even be thinking about this, in the middle of the night, on the train.

I stop, uncertain about everything. Was it really like that? Did I leave a suitcase at the station, or did I go to Yanna's first? I'll never know for sure, will I? Maybe it doesn't matter, yes, it does for some reason, it's just a detail, forget it, you've probably gone to Yanna's soon after the station. It makes sense. She is the only relative, Yanna, my favorite, my crazy aunt. I have interrupted the story, afraid of something. If I let it go, the door will open slowly, it's not locked— now you see her. There is Yanna sitting in a chair, then she shouts and screams and almost faints from so much excitement. She cries and hugs madly and Anna watches her cry, noticing she is still pretty like a gypsy girl but heavier than before. When she finally dried her tears and was persuaded to put on her best dress, together they went to the main street where everyone would be on a summer night.

On the main street, the gypsy band played as before in front of the hotel called Palace, the air smelled of wheat from the fields, and people dressed in their best promenaded up and down as always, looking, kibitzing, when she appeared suddenly that night. I can't see me accurately now but something in my stomach jumps up then dissolves into tears and shouts when she gets discovered by Mira, and the crowd formed and they found him, the boy with the green eyes, not a boy any longer. And then what and what then? Then they drank, shouted, cried the entire night, all of them, the whole restaurant full of friends, and the gypsies sang, 'Love me, kiss me, kill me if you wish,' and they kept breaking glass after glass.

That was the only arrival I didn't fear, later I did for some reason. Fear of what? What was that song, was it called 'Kiss of Fire' or 'Gypsy Soul'? Dad used to like those sad tangos, gypsies too. I had never cried for him, can't even now.

Of course she knew he was dying when she left, but she had been waiting to return for so long, she couldn't postpone it. In fact, it was the idea of return that kept her alive all those years, like a memory of warmth she clung to. She wanted to live, be young like the others, an immense thirst for it, no she couldn't postpone it any longer and six years in America didn't count as living. She didn't know why not, because being fifteen is hard enough without additional problems, she has lost everything there is to lose, including the language and if you lose that, who are you? Maybe she knew all along that there was nothing to be done; she was just trapped in a country she didn't want from the beginning.

There were only two alternatives—to die or to sleepwalk and make do.

She tried making do without much joy. With whom? All those crew cuts and washed-out eyes made her think of dead people, ghosts, frozen lands, everything opposite of life and passion. She wanted to scratch them sometimes just to see if the blood would come, but would scratch herself instead, making small dents on her wrist, just to see if she felt anything or had finally adjusted. On the surface she appeared calm, she had adjusted so nicely, they said, she functioned so well nobody could ever tell or perhaps she had developed a membrane around her soul, without knowing it of course, a shield against the wind, against all absences and losses, and all the familiar sounds and smells. She is so adjusted she leaves him dying and thinks coolly, he is unconscious anyway, I can't postpone it. The last time she sees him, in the hospital, a commercial is on TV: a man hits against the thick transparent plastic and preaches about tooth decay and the protection you get from Colgate which has an invisible shield. Her father's eyes are shut. She closes the door.

A native girl couldn't do this, I think now, it would be unthinkable. It was an American gesture, the stress is on *me, I*, rather than *us*, the stress is on moving on, getting on with your life rather than wallowing in grief, a waste of time anyway, counterproductive.

Still ... what happiness that first day and the second, what mad joy just to be alive, she had forgotten it: Nobody told her anything for two days—how kind they were—she must have looked too happy. They celebrated. Everyone said he was lucky—he had loved her and always said she'd come back. It was destined. He had even written a story about her for the town's paper, an essay called "Native Land" about her and others like her who come back sooner or later because they have to. He knew it. The celebration continued into the next day with visits at Yanna's who made cup after cup of Turkish coffee for friends and old neighbors with singing and crying, and in the evening Yanna told her what she had to—her father died before she came, during her crossing of the Atlantic. He died on her birthday which was a sign of some sort. A reproach? A warning?

I can't see the twenty-year-old girl nor crawl inside her, I can't even understand her now, her happiness during those two days is a memory of feeling, a book I had read. But I see the white dress well, it was her dad's favorite, thin white cotton, sleeveless, cut low in front and in back, a dancer's dress with a skirt that twirled. And this is the dress she put on instead of the usual black you are supposed to wear for a year.

"So what if they gossip," Anna said, "he would like it." She didn't cry at all; her face didn't change. Yanna said people crossed themselves looking at her, is she human, they wondered. They loved and grieved passionately, some even threw themselves into the grave at burials, some died out of pure grief. And here she was in a white dress. What did they do to her? Is this how they are in the West, they questioned Yanna. Doesn't she feel anything?

In fact, his death pushed her in a frenzy of living, wanting to live, not let a moment pass. She had waited all those years, no time to waste, she should have been in love like the other girls. Sixteen, seventeen, eighteen, nineteen, twenty, spent elsewhere, wrong climate, wrong men, away from home where everything should have happened naturally. It's not fair she didn't even get kissed in her hometown somewhere by the river near the willows or a field nearby but in a wrong place, a sinister bar in Chicago where a man took her to a strip joint on a date. The memory of that kiss is stale beer, toothless men grinning, take it all off baby, a beat-up woman shaking her droopy breasts, the smell of death in the air. The man she was with looked like a Nazi. Pretend it didn't happen, just erase it.

She must have appeared strange to them, small town people used to tradition and traditional ways of grief; they had made an allowance for her in the beginning but were more than shocked, Yanna said, when she persuaded him, the man with the green eyes, not to weep for his father either. Life is short, she lectured to him, live now.

His father died suddenly, only five days after her arrival, strange, strange, they said, and everyone expected him to be with his mother as a new head of family to receive the guests at the door, lead them into the sitting room where his father lay on a table, coins on his eyelids, the smell of incense in the air. Instead of running around with a woman who was no longer that sweet, shy girl with a long braid, but the product, his mother said, of God knows what horrible ways of the West. The girl had grown wild, she said, or had forgotten how things are done, that you are supposed to pay a visit, take a spoonful of the funeral dishes, cross yourself, sit a bit. You pay tribute to the dead man. With others. "Her mother was a fine woman," she said, "what happened to her?"

As his father lay on the kitchen table, candles lit, mother all alone with neighbors, he and Anna sat in the park in front of their school and necked. I don't remember what she wore for this occasion, maybe her green dress, the one with thin velvet straps, or maybe her bright red one, but it had to be the end of June, her birthday was over. I can't see his face on that bench now. The later pictures keep interfering. The sharpest one is an old one, of him at seventeen, somewhere near the fountain.

That evening in the park she can tell something is not right, not the way it should be, you can't continue where you left off, the right moment has passed. She is too young to know this, and it would mean admitting defeat, that she had missed the most important part in her life, the time to love and be young like her girlfriends instead of 'dating' sad babies from Illinois who chewed gum, and who didn't even know how to look at girls, let alone the finer things of love. She had kept her own thirst intact, waiting for this return, had never anticipated any difficulty because in her town nobody changed much, you never became someone else. The idea was foreign to them and to her.

The boy (I'll always think of him like that) who at fifteen had given her a desire to kiss someone didn't kiss her before she had left. He didn't rush because they had all the time in the world; they talked; he held her hand once. Now, six years later in the park, he didn't feel the same, he kept kissing her but his kiss was different from her memory of what that kiss would be; she was not fifteen; she had kissed plenty elsewhere even though it didn't count. She almost knows that evening that the desire to kiss him had faded, had even died, his smell was too oily or was it that she had gotten accustomed to the different smells in the States. No, he didn't smell of Colgate or aftershave, but she hugged and kissed him regardless hoping for the desire to come back. It wasn't hard to do, she had kissed many without wanting to on all those drive-in, coke, movie dates in the States where it was forbidden to sit alone on a Saturday night.

"You are alive and he is dead," she lectured him, legs stretched out on a park bench, her feet in his lap. "Did you read Camus' *Stranger*?" she had just asked when two cops appeared and said, "You are arrested. Both of you."

"For what?" she said.

"For having your feet on the bench, didn't you know it was forbidden."

"Where does it say so? Where is your warrant?" she asks an American question.

"You go and explain everything to them," one of them grumbles.

They were led off together, then separated. It looked like Beckett or Ionesco, especially when they led her into a sitting room and a maid appeared with drinks on a silver plate. She wore a black uniform with a white lace apron. On the wall, an enormous picture of the Leader, slim and handsome from his partisan days, looked down on them, smiling like the Mona Lisa. Two men appeared in stiff new suits, curly hair combed off the forehead, in an old-fashioned style like Tyrone Power, and the maid served more drinks, smoked ham, and pickled cucumbers. They said nothing about her feet on the bench. In their clumsy peasant way, they had to arrest her in order to talk to her. They didn't know how else to do it.

She saw through them, bashful like peasant brides, all decked out, not scary at all. They were not going to harm her. They offered food every few minutes then, stammering for form's sake, they wanted to know if she knew the names of any dangerous reactionaries who might be hiding in the States and plotting against the country. That word 'reactionary' was reassuring, it was just like in the first grade.

She knew that all sorts of reactionaries from all over the world, including some ex-Nazis, were hiding in the States but no, she had nothing to do with them, didn't know any she told them, and they were convinced. However, they were not really interested in them, they had to ask because they were cops, what they really wanted to know, without appearing too eager, was everything about life in the States.

She doesn't blame them, who else could they ask? She was the only one who left and the only one who came back. That summer already, there were only American films in town; nobody could compete with Hollywood in cheerfulness, and all the others—French, Italian and a few native war pictures—faded into the background, too grainy, too close, too real. They've had enough of misery, of half-starved Italian kids in black and white, the American world was shiny, brand-new, perfect like a red sports car, like Esther Williams, Elizabeth Taylor, who swam and kissed but their hair remained untouched and after they kissed their lips were as red as ever.

Weren't they asking her, that night, tell us the truth, is it really like *Breakfast at Tiffany's*, is it like *High Society*? They didn't put it like that but they hinted at it, not because those actresses were their type, they just loved the cars they drove.

Among her friends, there were those who wanted the image confirmed, something to dream about, a bit of magic; there were others, less numerous, who didn't want to hear any of it. The second group didn't ask any questions, was silent and brooding, but their pride was familiar to her and it was them she had in mind when she told the peasant cops, "No, it's not what you think. It's not like the movies at all."

She went on to talk about what she knew—the slums of Chicago, poor Negroes, drunk Indians, the power of money, the only God in the States, the one who can buy you anything, make your dreams come true, even a death wish. (Got to make some money, how much does he have, how much is he worth, as good as gold, I'm going out with a Cadillac, a girl said in college, he is loaded.) At this point she was pacing, making a speech, her lungs full of rage; she sounded more Communist than they.

They poured plum brandy and wanted some ordinary information, what can you buy with your monthly check, how much would a good winter coat be, one with a fur collar, how hard would you have to work to get yourself a car, a nice one, the kind so and so drove in, what was that film with gangsters?

Their questions were about concrete things but objects held no interest for her and she couldn't give them a nice, clear answer. They wished she had bragged, made them jealous with junk, and left socialism to them. And she had imagined that they would applaud, say bravo, a good girl, you've resisted the evil, you're one of us. Instead, they were vaguely disappointed in each other.

She didn't tell them many things—that nobody could

recognize their country on a map, that nobody knew about their heroic struggle against the Germans nor about the millions of dead, that they expected you to forget everything you've been, erase it, and be happy, happy in the States. She couldn't tell them that she had never felt poor until Chicago, that special poverty that's not about things only, they wouldn't understand it because there was no shame attached to it at home but in Chicago it invades all of you—the soul gives up. She had seen it but it couldn't be told.

How could she tell them that in the States you could be called a Communist for nothing, in her case for not wearing a girdle (why a girdle, she asked) or a bra, for not putting lipstick on, for not going to church, for having Negro friends—she was less free there than here, a country Americans called a police state. You couldn't hesitate there if they asked you, do you like America? You smiled right away and said yes, yes, very much; Father told her what to do the day they arrived. He said you had to. He said you say, I do, I do. They rehearsed once a week. It was the summer they killed the Rosenbergs.

They wouldn't understand this, people accustomed to endless complaining, spitting out what's on their minds behind closed doors, even about their leaders (fuck him and the party, fuck the works); no, they wouldn't believe her, she thought. There was nothing in the movies about it, they might think she made it up. And she was too ashamed to tell them that it didn't take much to be investigated by the FBI—an accusing letter is enough. She would have loved to say this but couldn't because it would make her mother unhappy, her enemies would rejoice as the rumor spread across the main street that Mara who was known as a fierce anti-communist and a royalist here, was questioned for Communist beliefs in the U.S.

Even though Anna appreciated the absurdity of it all, she couldn't do it to her, poor woman; she had to protect her and her pride, the only thing she had now. She had to lie for her, she couldn't mention that her mother was unhappy, that all those packages and pictures were a camouflage to preserve the myth, and the myth is what she wanted to believe herself, what else was there? She couldn't come back home—her pride wouldn't permit it and there was nothing to go back to—everything was given away before they left triumphantly for the happiness in Chicago. Anna couldn't betray her and tell that she, a woman who was known for her laughter, gossip, stories, now had nobody to talk to, no more stories to tell except retelling the old ones which always started with, "Anna, do you remember when."

She said nothing about Mother, nothing about Dad, but she did want to tell everything about her own life except that too was impossible. Her girlfriends would have pitied her, it was too foreign to them as an idea—that you go out on dates and eventually the second or third time you have to kiss them because that's how things are done. Her girlfriends went with one person at a time, kissed and made love when they were in love; they wouldn't understand the meaning of 'good' versus 'bad' girls either, nor the sad progression from necking to petting in parked cars. The Fifties.

Briefly, I catch sight of me that summer but it's not really Anna I see but those damned dresses again—white, green, blue, green—all worn by others later on, given away.

They must have been envious of all those dresses, and she saw nothing, too caught up in her own dream of return. She shouldn't have come with so many clothes, costumes for love to occur in. She didn't see many things. Forgive her, she was only twenty.

They must have envied her all those clothes but not how she got them. They were at the seashore, all those months she had worked to pay for her school and dresses and this trip now. Humid summers, hot, dirty, the sound of factory whistles, stale beer. Waitress, barmaid, car hop. She worked. They loafed. She was envious of their summers, of their walks, of their loves by the river, in the fields, while the grass sang the way it used to when she was small. Her envy was greater, you could buy a dress but her summers will never come back although she wished for a miracle.

She had exhausted herself on comparisons that year, explaining what was impossible to tell about life in the States. And if you have so many dresses which you can get at bargain basements, like all those dresses she had sent them for example, it's not the same as the one special dress made with several fittings, then delivered on tissue paper. It's different when you wear it. There is no other like it. Desa made it on her machine. Those other things—cars, sofas, chairs—you buy and throw away later, she explained. None made to last, not like her mother's trousseau in linen used to be, her cherrywood furniture.

She had to explain all those difficult words she didn't quite understand—*race, guilt, money, democracy* and so on. There was so much she couldn't tell them and maybe that was the most important part, that portion that couldn't be told, the part that stayed with her. The part that formed her. The loneliness of it, I think now. When did it start? In Chicago? I wasn't lonely before. Where is everyone? The train is silent, didn't they sing on the trains before? When I think of Bosnia I see darkness, I hear songs of lament full of Turkish words. *Sevdah.*

She did all the talking that June. Her girlfriends appeared calm and more womanly. When she left them they were thin girls with braids. Now, that summer, they were back from the university in the capital city; in the evening they promenaded on the main street, swaying their hips, their walk, their eyes told of adventures they had known at school. With their cinched waists, provocative eyes, and bodies of young mares, they looked very different from the girls in the Midwest who on the outside struck you as prim and chaste, burdened with sin, then necked with frenzy in the evening in front of the dorm for half an hour, lights turned off. Her old girlfriends, all future doctors, engineers, architects, would be considered bad in Indiana, look at them, prancing, laughing, proud of their hips, their breasts, no shame, no guilt in them, bad girls for sure, who in return would never see those prim bodiless creatures over there as beautiful—it takes a long time before you can make a switch. Already, she had a split vision, left and right eye, and each could see differently, almost at the same time, pulling away, interpreting. Donna Reed was only beautiful in the States for example, and Audrey Hepburn was a sweet pile of bones.

They said Anna was too skinny which meant she didn't grow up, the way you are supposed to. Her height and weight remained the same as at fifteen and her body too, she never became a real girl, full blown, lush; if anything, that summer with her long straight hair she looked even younger than when she left, childish somehow. It was fine at twelve but not at twenty, they said. Was she unhealthy? Did she starve herself? They examined her. With all those fine clothes at her disposal, she didn't act womanly. This was the time for it, a girl is expected to be like a wildcat at twenty. At home, everything was clear cut and orderly—how and when to be a kid, then a girl, a woman later, it was something known, handed down for centuries. There was nothing to improve on or invent. And each stage ended, not to be confused with another one, each distinct in color, fully lived without major regrets, but that summer they were confused by her childish looks, they for whom childhood was over.

It was so unusual and unheard of, that they couldn't even put their finger on the problem, what went wrong, why she seemed stuck, or had even gone backwards in her development. They shook their heads and kept feeding her, hoping that their cheese their cream their cakes would cure her. She didn't look unhealthy, they said. She swam and ate constantly, but it was as if the juices which filled them out, their hips, their breasts, stopped in her case at fifteen, a refusal, the way some plants die when transplanted, except she only grew crooked, differently than the way it was intended.

Why did they appear happier, more serene, freer too, than any girls in the Midwest? Their womanhood appeared simple, effortless, taken for granted, the rules that governed them were more like seasons—they had no choice in it, they'll do the way it was done before. Yet every one of them was a special color of her own, not to be confused with any other girl and each had a temperament that belonged only to her. They didn't cover up with niceness, they said what was on their minds, they said, fuck him, I hate him, I'll kill him when I see him with another woman, nothing will remain of him if I catch him, I'll tear him apart. They fought with each other too, got angry, didn't speak for days, then always made up with tears and kisses—the whole spectrum of feeling she had forgotten or never learned.

She shouldn't have left them all those dresses, not that many. They must have been jealous all the time without ever guessing she did it to make them happy, or maybe to prove that some good came out of her years in Chicago. It was hard to have a new dress at home, the reason they talked about them so much along with the new fabrics and shoes too. Still, it was indecent to arrive with so many dresses in a town where you only had one new dress a season, maybe two. It was just thoughtlessness, pure negligence, she was only doing what an American girl would do, and they were really cheap dresses which appeared otherwise because Grace, Ava, Liz and Audrey wore the same styles in the movies her friends saw.

She envied them something too but didn't know it that summer, and maybe it's not the right word after all. It was more like regret, wishful thinking, words like *if only, perhaps, impossible,* a longing of sorts for their nights and days in the capital where marvelous things were supposed to occur. At fifteen, all of them whispered about that far away time when they'll go there, and now they've done it. She had done other things, but her years didn't count. They were unreal, as if they had happened to someone else, this other girl who was not quite real either because some parts were missing but nobody knew it. Nobody could even tell. Not the way you notice a person without an arm or leg for example. Her body functioned well.

And while they imagined her in the cars with the landscape of movie sets, she saw them dancing, kissing tall dark men, the kind that grew here, not in the States. It wasn't just the coloring of the Midwestern boys that was wrong, that pale skin and winter blue eyes, it was everything else about them. Nobody had taught them, poor boys, that love is supposed to be passionate and tender; you couldn't even imagine any of them capable of something large, whispering, 'my only one, I'll love you to death,' what the gypsies sang. How childish they seemed, Jim and Tom and Dick, calling for a coke date, their attraction reduced to a reflex. Stiff and military looking during the day, at night they mumbled about being hot and bothered, their sex separate from their faces and their arms. Terrified of it, it was always on their minds, not the passion but this other bodily function which they wanted like a mother's tit, to sleep better. Love American style she perceived as something lonely, something they did at night only, and with shame. How could you love them? Even Ike looked like a baby.

I had not met the blond one yet, had I? No, that was a year later, after Alabama. I didn't love him either, did I? No. I wish somebody would come in. I would stop this madness, be real. Why is the train so empty? The conductor is not to be seen. Just me alone in my movie to the sound of wheels.

To feel real, that's what she wanted, not that she knew it at that time and then there wasn't much chance for it—

she had splintered for good into two parts, Anna and Ann, and they didn't get along. So it was this other girl, foreign sad Ann, who most likely slept with the green eyes that summer, a girl who was both innocent yet jaded. Her girl-friends wouldn't have done it, not without love, not at twenty, but she must have been sadder than anyone, so lonely, so lost, so eager to make believe that time had stopped. She would wake up, they would continue where they left off, on her street, at night, somewhere, by the fountain.

It was a great setting for it—in the fields of wheat. She had imagined her girlfriends making love like that; as chil-dren, playing hide and seek, they stumbled often on couples in the summer months. And now, she was lying in the field of wheat, her white dress on, the air perfectly scented, the sky blue, everything the way it should be but nothing hap-pened. Maybe he felt the same way as she without daring to admit it. They slept like that many times, occasionally try-ing to make love, but each time he grew more angry so that she couldn't stand to be around him, or to look at him any longer.

What do you expect—it was too late, that's all—you kiss one person, you neck with another, you make love to the third in order to forget the first and so on and on until the real desire is no longer in your body; only your head keeps something like a memory of it. The real desire was meant to be for that special man, and you would make love to his body and his eyes; at sixteen I had imagined that's how it would be. Now I am no longer sure of anything ex-cept that Anna, I, would have been a different person, maybe with larger hips.

That first arrival some thirty years ago is clearer than all the other ones because the town was pretty much the same and all her friends were there. The river was clear and so clean you could drink it but they were cutting the trees, tearing down old Turkish houses, and talking about a dam. The very first ten story building went up. She sighed after those little houses with large verandas, each room a different shape. Her mother's friends lived in them, widows with gray hair in black dresses, their wardrobes full of picture albums of old weddings, and the smell of fruit ripening.

That was the only arrival she was not afraid of anything. Later, every time, there was a peculiar terror in her but it had nothing to do with the regime. As the country changed and became more and more open, the fear remained. It was something vague, private, a fear of things going out of control, a fear of *them*, of their irrational ways, of the way they cursed, how they drove. Is it possible she saw them in the same way the whites see blacks when visiting Harlem, or Jamaica?

Still, as that summer ended, I looked normal again, had gained some weight and laughed more easily. I am almost sure I said *them* when talking about the States. But then why didn't you stay? That was the time to do it.

I couldn't leave her alone, I answer, that was the reason. Most likely. I tried persuading her to come back but she didn't want to. I almost have another reason in the back of my head but like certain almost-thoughts it doesn't develop, fades away leaving a nagging impression of frustration, like a person you almost met.

It's dark on the train, chilly. We are in the mountains now, climbing. Through the window, shadows of trees appear and disappear, then a sharp whistle before still another tunnel. I am pleased I have some extra information at my disposal, a biographer must be excited like me—digging, reconstructing slowly what might have happened. Except you'll never know for sure. I wish for all of it, smells and sounds, not just the facts, every possible bit and then maybe I can come up with a theory, catalogue myself, uncover the flaws, assign the blame. The problem is that some years have merged, were never recorded, or were recorded over by more important details which doesn't mean that they were more important. Just more visible, more dramatic, pushier probably, erasing more delicate ones, like the summer with the blond boy. For example, I can't remember why I came back the second time, what for, what was the reason, and if the motivations were not known then, how can you possibly know them now? I am too involved in trying to disentangle my own past to think except in passing that the train is going through the area where the worst fighting with the Germans took place, and not far away in Sarajevo, the First World War started. My parents', my grandparents' time. History books. Stories told. My uncles died somewhere in these mountains; their graves don't exist. The Germans killed them, most likely. Without graves their souls will wander, grandma said, they'll never have peace. I didn't know them. It's easy when you don't. My puzzles are personal for the most part, selfish, even though it's grandma's voice I hear now, sliding over my past, smoothing all the rough edges, her style in telling a story.

The second arrival was six years after the first; that must

have been the summer she was called names in different countries, for different reasons. "Whores!" a man shrieked at us, his mouth a wound, "whore," his cries wanting to kill and with his cry I see myself too. My mouth is just like his. There she is! Me. The sixties already! Do I hate and how! It's simple. I am a Vietnamese, bombs are American, we hate daily, powerless to stop. I could kill easily, but don't know who. But what the hell was I doing in my home town then? That part is unclear.

She had gone to Yanna's as always. Without any dresses or dreams of romance. She has left all that behind. She is tough now, or maybe she has gone underground completely and wouldn't recognize that other girl who missed and loved too much. This one doesn't think about love, past or present or future, she is all action, smash, attack, kill the pigs now.

Yanna remained alone in her two small rooms, what you were not supposed to do in a small town. She had married ages ago to a man who was her big love but it didn't last more than ten months for some mysterious reason. Now, she was even chubbier than the first time, with a beautiful face and luminous eyes and she had many lovers, some quite young.

Just thinking about her, my Yanna, warms me up, how much I love Yanna still, crazy woman, out of her mind. Imagine this—I come to visit her in a village where she went for a cure. Here she sits naked under an oak tree, eating cherries and laughing. "What are you kids staring at," she says to me and my friends, pointing toward her sex, her mouth, her breasts. "It's all the same body, isn't it?" She wasn't embarrassed. We were.

Wrong! A mistake. That happened the summer of my first return, not later. The image of Yanna naked under a tree looks like '67 but it wasn't. I have taken some liberties with history, rearranging images to fit my point of view. I am glad I caught it. I wouldn't have been embarrassed by Yanna naked under a tree in '67. No way. In '62 I was with him, the green eyes, in the same mountain village, trying to make love as the summer ended. And I was embarrassed that he saw Yanna all sprawled on the grass, like a fat cat. I also know that what I call the second time is not really the second but the third because I had met the blond boy the summer of my second return but didn't remember it well because I didn't go back home, preferring the sunlight of Ragusa to my miserable hills. Stop calling it Ragusa, for Christ's sake, nobody calls it that anymore. Dubrovnik! Dubrovnik!

Sarajevo! Sarajevo! the conductor shouts. A long line of people, women and kids for the most part, with bags, dressed for winter. Going camping? I didn't see them again, most likely they went to the second class. When I think of Bosnia, I think of songs about smoldering passions, unrequited love, silent men, women behind veils, darkness. *Sevdah* means love, doesn't it?

When Anna came back home six years later, the river was muddier for some reason and seemed unrecognizable with the dam. It used to meander, creating pools of different sizes, clearings with white sand, and by the willow trees old people sat playing cards in the shade. Everyone was proud of the dam, you could now swim laps, and instead of the stones and sand you now had cement steps. Caught up in the improvements they couldn't see that the old river was much better because the entire town showed up here. Now, only young people came, those who could swim laps.

The mill was gone. They didn't need it any more. The animal market was still there with lambs and pigs for sale but they said that will go too. Peasant carts had not van-ished yet but appeared less visible, as if intimidated by cars. Oxen and horses charged occasionally, going out of control, heading blindly for the car lights and sounds they hated, a futile attempt to stop things that makes you think of the Polish cavalry against the German tanks. But all in all, there were not that many cars around, you could walk in the middle of the road if you wished and you'd see a car or a cart once in awhile, let's say every two hours. They were even in num-ber at this point in time which I recorded. Everyone wanted a car, a new object of envy, and a television set.

All the friends were married. The ones who hadn't left for the capital where everyone wanted to be showed off with their brand new furniture and first babies. Some were preg-nant with the second. They didn't ask any questions; they didn't know what to think about me. They had gone to the university for all the usual practical reasons, and it wouldn't have occurred to them not to work, it would be a waste of four years at school. The American idea for women—career or family—didn't exist, nor did a certain type of helpless female from Hollywood films. She, Anna, I, confused them entirely—neither a woman like them nor like films—they couldn't imagine someone studying vague things for plea-sure, accumulating degrees, wasn't one enough?

And it wasn't as if she had anything to show. On the

contrary. With no car, no proper dress, thin, in blue jeans, she looked even more bizarre than the first time. And if the first time she looked like a fifteen year old girl, now with the hair cropped entirely, hipless, breastless, all bones, she was like an orphan boy, the kind you want to take home and cry over. Poor honey, poor baby, my sweet, it's hard without your mother.

This girl is scary, something in her blank gaze reminds you of disturbed children. To dig her up is not reassuring but I can't very well push her back either. She might refuse. She has a life of her own. I can't crawl into her skin, get to know her better except through some vague hatred that unites us. It's there. It flared up at the conference, ready to explode. My hatred must be a link to things. Which is better, red or dead? If I can hate, I exist, right? Better than dead, for sure.

It makes no sense for her to be back that summer. It was not intended, most likely. She must have come the way some dogs do, years and years later, they suddenly appear at your door step, and here you thought they had been run over. She is changed in every way, but somewhere in her she must remember what remained unshattered of that other girl and could only be found in the air at home. The problem was, her town was fast changing and becoming unrecognizable, the river muddy, the mill gone. There was nothing in the landscape to hold on to, only the smell of willows remained, hovering by the river banks and the sound of words, more tender than anything.

They shook their heads—it must be something in the West that didn't agree with her. Wrong food. Not as fresh. She is not married like the rest and everyone knows you have to. After twenty-five it gets to be harder. Girls fade like daisies, especially unmarried ones. Think about the kids, it's unhealthy to have them late. Not have kids? She must be joking, what is life without them? Of course you will. Hurry up! Everyone, all of them, the pretty ones and not so pretty ones, chubbier and less chubby, had a husband now; in her case it should have been easy—she was pretty when she left, they said she used to look like Grace Kelly, her face that is, the only part of Grace that was any good. It should've been easy for her but look at her now, an orphan boy! Mira, her best friend, was kinder. Her head full of films, she said calmly, "The last time you were more like Audrey Hepburn, now I don't know. Maybe Jean Seberg." Mira loved films and was affected by them more than religion, her mother, or socialism.

Anna wasn't fading or growing old but she wasn't blossoming either, not in those ugly old jeans, the kind of clothes Mira wouldn't be seen in, not on the main street at night when even rough boys and gypsies appeared in their best well-pressed pants and women strolled in new dresses and high heels. Up and down, promenading, who is that person, look at her dress, how nice, did she have it made here or in the capital. They knew she could have better clothes, they saw her dresses the last time and all the other dresses she kept sending, yet knowing she could but didn't confused them even more. They loved dressing up, looking at others, they spoke with passion about silks, brocades, new bags from Italy. After years of hardship they have finally become well-dressed. Anna's clothes, which helped many in the beginning, were not needed any longer.

She offends them when she mentions casually that she found her table and chairs on the sidewalk in New York and that everything else including her curtains came directly from the garbage can. The streets of New York are teeming with junk, she tells them, you just pick it up, like that. Her clothes too, all for nothing, why spend, why add to the junk pile of capitalism, she explains. They don't understand any of it, what does capitalism have to do with clothes, she insults them and their nice furniture bought on credit, after months of deliberation, the right color and the right shade of carpet to go with it. Wake up, wake up, she tells them, your minds will rot soon.

That year she wears no lipstick, nothing decorates her face, not even earrings, she is opposed to marriage too as a bourgeois institution, and she is telling them about the revolution as if she knew it. The children of those who had fought in the real revolution have heard that word for too many years in school and are only too happy nobody mentions it any more except once in a while on May first which often coincides with Easter.

The events in the West—the student uprisings, rebellions, fights with cops and parents—didn't intrude on the rhythm of love, marriage, death, burials, putting up fruits and vegetables for winter. She noticed that her old girlfriends, after years of turbulent love affairs (fully expected and approved by all), had settled into marriages and babies as naturally as summer replaces the spring; even the slim ones had grown a bit thicker around the waist. One or two had even lost a tooth here and there but they didn't seem concerned—it happens when you bear children. They never became fat, not like the blubber in the Midwest, but they developed an air of thicker, fuller, more satisfied woman-hood, a slower walk, a heavier gaze. There was a complicity about them, like a sorority of new mothers and wives, all talking babies' rashes, coughs, what he eats, how he shits and so forth. Nothing but babies and recipes even with Yasmina the eye doctor and Slava who was a professor of math. They didn't go to the river any more, kids did that. And Anna of course.

It wasn't different with their husbands, those mad lovers and former tomcats became thicker too, like well-domesti-cated animals, eating all those stews, taking naps, going early to bed. Just like their wives, the wild girls they used to make love to by the river. And they did all this without doubt or regret.

Anna swam laps with the kids who were babies when she left and liked their company the best, "pass the ball," they said, "do you want some of my apple?" Kids liked the way she did the crawl, she liked it that they didn't judge her or suggest a way for improvement. They and the river calmed something in her.

Nobody was envious of her this time. The country is quiet, sunny while in the West the adolescents raged. She doesn't have a car, nothing pretty they would want, yes, she travelled to many places but like a beggar, hitchhiking and sleeping by the road.

They were even. That time in the sixties, she didn't envy them much. Their so-called revolution for which many fought and died is a sham, real socialism didn't happen (not the one they promised in the first grade), or they wouldn't be gabbing about Italian shoes and bags. Petty bourgeois concerns. And you call this socialism, she preaches. Anna has a sense of mission, first an international fight against the war in Vietnam, then more, Che said. When she gets going on the subject, she could move the stones, Yanna says, proud, excited by some fire in her speeches. She too is opposed to the war in Vietnam, the only one in town who even mentioned that distant war. Still, she wished Anna could put some lipstick on even though she was fighting for the revolution.

That summer poor Yanna worried about her sister's disapproval. The rumor of Yanna's many lovers had spread all the way to Chicago, not that having a lover was considered bad in itself, but you always had one at a time. And here was Yanna with a slew of men, all young, hanging around her door. Yanna remained thirsty for love in a way that was excessive and out of control, the reason Anna liked her and her madness which resembled Tennessee Williams' plays. Her mother knew Yanna would come to a bad end because she was always a stubborn impractical girl who should have known that love is an illusion. Didn't she marry for love in the first place and look what happened. She could've married another man, a steady person, a good provider, she had all those men asking for her hand but what can you do with a girl who jumps out of the window into the bushes when suitors come? Mother always repeated that old story and brought back memory of Anna's own childhood intermingled with Yanna's youth when she was wild, thin, beautiful as the most beautiful gypsy girl, and Anna watched her jump out of the window, then jumped herself too. The smell of lilac bushes is linked with Yanna, her whispers, her talks of love with a man she had seen once, married later.

"Love," Mother lectured, "is to be avoided. Unhealthy upheaval, like high blood pressure, bad for your heart." Back for the first time in many years, she gave the town what they wanted to hear and what she had come to believe. Dressed in a brocade housecoat, out of earlier films, the forties, Joan Crawford style, she held court and showed pictures of her house with rooms full of shiny objects, sofas with plastic covers, mass-produced pictures of saints on the walls. She had adjusted to America through things, but she always craved more, sheets, towels on sale, dishes, a new toaster.

With old friends, the woman with the gold tooth, Desa, the dressmaker, Sara, the baker, she spoke differently now. They used to tell stories taking turns, this happened to me, let me tell you about my mother-in-law, wait till you hear about mine; now, only her mother spoke, either because they've told everybody their news or most likely she had forgotten how to talk with people on a daily basis. She didn't have a single American friend or neighbor who would just drop by for coffee without a big to-do about it, she didn't know them, nor did they know her. She never said in front of the gold tooth or the dressmaker that she missed her old life but spoke about her new one instead, created with the help of pictures, and she believed her new version except occasionally at night when her heart fluttered. She had sent so many packages to so many people, dresses, shoes, name it, and even if she wanted to stop it she couldn't now. She was better than Radio America for spreading the American myth abroad; she forbade Anna to talk about the garbage in New York or anything that could embarrass her.

If Yanna embarrassed her because she was a slut, Anna did it by being unmarried at her age. And since she had not incorporated America in her, nothing of its confusion, freedom to choose and be, nothing but sofas and appliances, she expected her daughter to proceed in the same old way she had known, which was more ancient than what her friends now believed at home. Her reasoning in marriage matters was peasant-practical from the old school—you decide to get married and you do it. Her opinion of men was simple too—men are beasts, they eat more, they snore and sweat, their natures are animal—they need to be tamed. But you need them for procreation and a couple of other reasons. In any case, to remain an old maid was out of the question because people make fun of you.

Even though she had come to put some order in Yanna's life she worried about Anna now; it was marriage, marriage day and night. At the peak of her despair, she even invited a gypsy woman to read her daughter's palm and kept nagging her—do you see a man, when? She even gave her an American silver dollar as if to persuade her to tell the very best fortune money could buy.

The gypsy woman didn't like being bullied. She said, this girl had a split life line as if she had died once. A ghost maybe. The gypsy was scared by this, and kept making spitting sounds against the evil eye. She didn't come up with a husband but said in passing that Anna was very gifted for love, and mother moaned, "Heaven forbid! Let's hope she doesn't take after that slut." At this point she would like to marry her off to anyone, even a Catholic or Muslim, even to a local man, the very last choice on her list, because she would have nobody to tell her life to. To save face, she repeated in front of the gold tooth and the dressmaker, "It's not as if she didn't have many offers, two doctors, three lawyers, an architect, a dentist, and others wanted to marry my Anna."

She went back soon, disturbed by the changes she saw and the new prosperity, which no longer justified her years in Chicago.

The one with the green eyes was married too, which didn't prevent him from looking at Anna as if something of hers had gotten stuck in him. He drank more, ate too much, hung around the old party men who resembled the cops that had questioned them that first time. Obviously he had problems. Still, they had parted nicely, with no bad words. Now they could be friends, she offered. In her mind, that's what he was, a relative of sorts, the reason she trusted him and accepted a ride with him and a party guy. I remember—it was in a large black limousine with a silent chauffeur in front.

She was heading West, all edgy; there is no nostalgia or regret toward her hometown, no desire to stay. That year, the only one, she is American, united with the others, whether out of love or hate she is not sure. The resistance maybe. Her own. Against the melting pot, against things, like a desire to save her soul from the stew, but she didn't know nor could she guess that the fight itself produces a change— the shy sweet girl became something else. Neither this nor that. A twisted plant.

I hate this sentimental voice, don't know where I picked it up—not grandma's, not mother's either—she mimicked well, had an ear for dialogue. It has to be his. Didn't he talk about twisted plants too? He hated constantly, he feared all the time. "A country without soul," he said about America, "a terrible cruel place." "Go to France," he said, "a country with style." A really stubborn man, instead of adjusting, he died instead. He had no choice. I did. Did I?

The first day in France, a man drinking red wine said "You really like this piece of shit, this old whore?" I said yes, yes, many times, for all the obvious reasons, either the beauty of Paris or because nobody forced me to say I do.

Why didn't you stay there, why not? Your fault.

That's an American question, for God's sake! Give her a break! Stop! It was impossible, that's all. How do you lose one country, abandon the second, and adopt a third, how do you do it when you are twenty? And the French didn't feel any warmer. Nothing did.

This is silly and absurd, this questioning, it leads nowhere but how do you stop. You can't just say go, Anna, fade away. Maybe you shouldn't start. And there are no answers, none, more like half-answers, you can't be sure of anything, but of this she is certain—her town didn't produce the girl she has revived, not the girl who hates; it happened in the U.S. I know this to be true because I can see *me* from before, and then there are witnesses in addition. All said a sweet, nice, darling girl. A girl who loved everything. People too.

It's nice to know this, my only certainty. It's something.

I wish I could fall asleep or the morning would come sooner. The conductor said, "lock yourself in, put the chain

on. Things happen." He looked grisly, with sunken eyes. I
locked myself in, then went back to the previous scenes
which had a look of films from Godard—

Heading for the capital with those two. The party guy,
an important local official, wears a leather coat even though
it's not cold. He is lazy looking, overfed, with a drooping
moustache. He smokes. The chauffeur is silent the entire
time. The party guy wants to know, to kill time, what she
does. She tells him about campus unrest, cops, CIA, the
Vietnam war and her role in all the above. She talks like a
ten year old, she must expect him to applaud, and embrace
her for doing such good work. He is neither young or old.
He smiles with a corner of his mouth, his eyes bored, "Oh
forget all that, and let's talk seriously. Did you bring any
pornici from the U.S.? I'll pay well."

It was an English word used in the diminutive—she didn't
recognize it immediately because she had never seen those
films. He explained porn to her using some hand gestures,
he said he saw his first in Germany and got sort of addicted.
He would pay.

This picture, this trip was never erased. In her mind it's
catalogued as *leather coat* and *porn* and her shame that in the
U.S. they called that socialism. She is too stunned to say
anything. They drive on. And for an ending—a jump cut—
the man with green eyes almost raped her in the hotel room
she took for one night. Looking at her with hatred he said,
"You owe me something, don't you? What's the matter? You
wanted it before."

I am not sure if it's me he hated or this other girl from
the West, I am not sure if my betrayal was worse than his or

if they are even, but whenever I came back, I avoided him
the best way I could. There was something mean about him
now, sickly too; I heard that in the old prison they had
orgies.

The last time I came back in the seventies, most of the
old buildings on the main street were gone, nobody went to
the river any more because it was too polluted. They lived
well now, summer homes, trips abroad, cars, everybody had
all the machines, all except Yanna whose life didn't change
except that she grew older. She was medicated more and
more for nervous ailments, she slept in the afternoons. That
period in the seventies is not very clear for Anna or Ann, in
either country, and the eighties were even dimmer which
means that nineties might be a total blindness as I and the
century get older.

She stopped going back and forth, too tired of explaining East and West, and all the comparisons. There was nothing left to explain anyway, she had concluded with gloom, it
will all look the same—the junk will take over. I got married too, had children and this more than anything else
made my mother happy.

I am not sure I stopped coming for this reason or some
other, I am rushing it now, the way some people do when
telling you about their vacations and are full of details about
the first day, then they just skip over things to the end. I'm
sure everything hasn't been said on the subject but my body
gives up—sleep overtakes me just before dawn.

Part Three

I wasn't going to stop until the train came out of the tunnel and I saw the town with the river below. Just for a day, I thought, aware of a certain curiosity but no more. It's a clear morning, fresh. I watch the train leave, disoriented. My town is not recognizable. I don't recognize the train station either, it's not the one I had left from. It's a different location, on the left bank of the river, because you didn't see the town from the other one. The other one was old, dark, smelled of chickens and hay. This one is elevated, airy, painted in bright colors but poorly designed, not good for lonely passengers with suitcases; there must be hundreds of steps before you reach the street below.

I am the only one walking alone. Others are met by relatives; this is still the same. They are walking slowly, step by step, arms around each other, kissing and talking, a grandma who looks like a grandma should, in a black dress, is hugging a girl, crying at the same time, then they'll go home, eat something good, then a nap, then after that coffee and more talk.

I am surprised I don't know any of them. How come?

I am hungry and would like some coffee but I can't think where to go. My town is gone or has gotten rearranged; the hills are there but without forests or meadows. Everything had vanished in every direction I look. Nothing but houses perched on top of each other, big, ugly, in brick. I had always felt trapped by the hills even as a child; now I was crushed, my eyes went toward the river, a muddy torrent. Recognizable though, in spite of everything, helpful in my confusion because it still flowed the same way and divided the town in two halves. It was called 'River of Floating

Children,' because the Turks dumped our kids into it centuries ago. The name must still be the same.

I recognized the bridge too. It was worn out, full of holes,
too narrow, unsafe for cars. You can walk right in the middle
of it, which is nice, you can skip and jump on the way to
school. This bridge was always meant to be temporary, a
replacement for the pretty stone one the Germans destroyed.
That's why it had no name, I guess, the way some important
bridges do. I knew it when it was nice-looking, the color of
rough pine, its birth and my first grade coincide. People
came to sit on it often on summer nights and for a reason—
the bridge had a view of everything, the hills, the river, and
the town too. It was important during the day too—peasants came and went with pigs, lambs, chickens for sale and
on the other side in the clearing, gypsies had their tents in
the spring. They used the bridge constantly, singing, dancing as they went, dressed in bright colors, yellow, orange,
red. I saw all of it. My grammar school is right there, a
perfectly located building because you could see everything
just by turning your head slightly toward the window and at
the same time you heard the teacher's lecture too. As she
talked about revolution, socialism, and better tomorrows, I
imagined this future happiness as a movement, with me in a
gypsy wagon on the road to … To where? "Anna," she snuck
up, "tell us now, what did Comrade Lenin mean when he
said …"

I could always fool her because I always knew better
than others what she wanted and what Lenin meant, a standard answer but well-expressed to make everyone happy,
and I could go back to the gypsies and the tents. They brought

good luck and were lucky—no school, just adventures; they could even walk barefoot anytime they wished. Maybe I was elsewhere from the start, I think now on the bridge, a brand new thought. Who can tell, maybe yes, maybe no. I like the little girl though. This Anna always looks the same, wide-eyed, bright, somewhat dreamy, curious about everything, just like Alec my oldest. Her eyes are clear, just like the river at that time. No hate in her, none. I had a wonderful beginning, didn't I?

My feet are stuck. The bridge is like a sick relative. It's hard to move. Good-bye, I'll never see it again, it'll die soon. They'll just blow it up. Not a bad way to go. Not a bad life either, if you remember it was made out of pine. Who's ever heard of anyone crying for a bridge, you should have your head examined.

I run up to the school, dragging my suitcase on my little gadget with wheels. I wish I could see my old desk, but classes must be on. I can't just barge in like that and disturb them. They would ask questions. And what would I find? They must have central heating instead of the coal stove that smelled and never gave any heat and we just shivered, our feet wet. Of course they would. The kids would be well dressed and healthy looking, not like my own generation, dying with TB, even though there was medicine in the West but not for us, punished by East and West for being independent. There would be nothing on the walls, no pictures of Lenin or any reference to world socialism and Stalin we got rid of in my second grade. No lice, either, crawling somewhere behind my ear, on Mira's neck in front of me. If you're clever you can catch them under your nail then squash them with your thumb on the school desk right over the engraved hearts, right over M loves N. A bit of blood on the thumb, that's all that's left of the lice, then you hunt another one; the physical pleasure of squashing them is bigger than you imagine. My sons would be horrified if they knew.

The school needed sprucing up. The paint was peeling, the steps sagged. No, I won't go in. It's better that way. Some kids are in the yard, the same dusty yard and it's still the same old game of dancing round and round in a circle, then you fall. What is this game called?

It's easy from here. The main street renamed after a partisan hero officially but still called the main street by everyone, the longest street and the best, where every kid would want to live because you can see everything—the street where Yanna lives starts here. And right at the beginning of it there was a photo store, it'll appear any moment now.

It's not there. The tiny crumbling one-story house is still there but the photos are gone. The man behind the counter is selling bread. The smell of fresh bread is nice but I miss that store, the darkness of it, what it might see and do to your face on that particular day. He only took one and that was it. Too bad if you looked the wrong way or smiled with a corner of your mouth, like Mira did once, and Slava bit her lip not thinking that's what she'll get.

He was the one who took all my pictures, but it all stops around fifteen, because nobody knew how to look at me well. Not the way he did. And it's different in black and white. Color is flat, more democratic, I guess, you can't take it seriously. I had relied on him and the store every time I came back to see how the fashion had changed and who are the local beauties that year. The prettiest ones were displayed in the window, you wished for it. The entire town passed by the store, stopped to look and argue about his choice, 'her pretty, look at those beady eyes, you call that hair.' They could argue as much as they wished but the choice was always his. He had his reasons and there was nothing you could do to change his mind. That's how he was. My own picture was there too, briefly, with a long braid from the time I was supposed to look like Grace Kelly and he kept the picture in the window for years. That's what they wrote, what Yanna said.

I bought a piece of poppyseed strudel and asked the baker about the photo store. "Did he move?" I asked.

"Sure he did," he said, waving his arm, "to the same spot over the hill that's reserved for all of us." He meant he died, that's all. "He's lucky he went when he did," he added. He looked surprised, however; at any moment he'll ask me how come I didn't know, where had I been, and quickly, before it's too late, I am out of his store.

Dead, I think on the street, how come? Well, he was old that's all, must have been in his fifties when we left, no wonder he is dead. Maybe he died ages ago, maybe in his store with the pictures of town beauties and babies on fur rugs. Whatever happened to all those negatives, did they throw them in the garbage, imagine if they did, years gone, no record of anything. I hope it's not true, that someone was smart enough to save them so they can see the way things used to be, how people dressed for the weddings for example. And then, he was the only one who photographed the town without cars, hills without houses, peasants on donkeys, you'd think they would want to keep them but deep down I am pessimistic. The need to throw away or forget is strong.

He was a loner and different from others, maybe because he came from the western republic and spoke in a way that was distinguished, at least that's how I heard it. Nobody knew him. They say he appeared soon after the war and set up his shop. He stared too much and nobody knew that he took more than one picture of me, then picked the one that was to be printed. I had forgotten that until now. He always chose the angelic ones with wide eyes but maybe others were entirely different, mean too. I'll never know, and now the negatives are all gone. I'll never know either what was on his mind when he stared at me, love maybe. What he saw would be nice to know. If he were alive I'd ask him.

He always had good things for us to eat, figs, oranges even. "Come back," he whispered, "not this afternoon, come tomorrow, we'll be alone. I have two sets of weddings, nothing but peasants this afternoon. Come tomorrow and I'll do something new, do you want a gypsy picture, I have a perfect costume for you." He never gave me that one, claimed it was over-exposed.

I can't recall the last time I saw him; I had stopped paying attention to him and his store. I had my own camera, later on.

And now what? This wasn't planned. All the other times I had stayed at Yanna's or my mother's friend's, Sara, or Desa, or the one with the gold tooth. Can't do that now. No involvements or tears, you've got to stay on schedule—one day and no more. Some discipline is necessary. If I stayed with them, I know exactly how it would go—one cup of Turkish coffee and one more, then sweets, then fruit preserves, then stories, without a main subject, without an end, circling, merging, and you sink slowly into the cushions, enveloped by the smell of things. Soon you forget you came for a day, and might stay a week.

A nice clean anonymous place is what I need.

The hotel they wrote about is right in front of me, I can't for anything remember what used to be there before. It's a monster in gray marble, fat like some hotels in Texas. Built in the eighties, Yanna wrote about it. How German tourists on their way from the coast would stay here, tempted by the luxury of saunas and shops, and how the economy would boom, except it didn't turn out that way. The Germans never came, choosing to head straight for Germany after the coast, and the Hotel Intercontinental was nicknamed The Bull's Ass, Yanna said.

It looked empty, a bit like that airport in Tanzania where they never got around to getting the planes and the airport remained unopened, then rotted.

The main street looked congested, no room on the sidewalks. The population must have doubled and they seemed much taller. I am so tired and it's sad that I have nowhere to go, a kid in me says, "Isn't this supposed to be home?" Then I get lucky—the old *Hotel Palace* built in the twenties is still there, right in front of the park where I was arrested for having my feet on the bench, not far from my high school which had survived too, gray, serious-looking, built in stone.

I put my glasses on, what if they recognize me? If I stick to a bare minimum, nobody will notice that I speak funny. I must. All those flattened R's and added diphthongs make me sound as if I had a speech defect.

Nothing to worry about. The woman at the reception is too busy to pay attention to my speech. The place is jumping with all sorts of people, festively dressed. On the radio, folk music, the kind peasants loved to dance to, holding hands in a circle.

As I hand over my red passport I am thrilled. I think, "I've passed. Nobody noticed a thing."

Somewhere in the distance a woman squealed, someone shouted then the sound of an accordion woke me up. Next, the sound of a pistol shot. Outside, in front of the town hall, they were celebrating a wedding, a peasant wedding judging by the noise and the flag a man carried in front. That's how they did it as they passed by our house, singing and shouting, with horses and carts and everyone pushed to see them appear in a cloud of dust. I rushed out now.

They were dancing in a circle, a tall man with a handkerchief led the way. A jester offered brandy, his bottle decorated with ribbons, yellow, green, red. I couldn't tell if he was drunk or pretending, it was his role to tell jokes about the bride and what will happen to her that first night when she had to spread her legs and submit. The jokes never said anything about men.

They use to be skinny, just like their horses. They seemed stockier now, bursting out of suits which seemed a size too small. Workers in Germany, judging by their cars which were decorated with roses and ribbons, the same as their horses years ago.

The bride is who you looked at. Is she pretty? Is she young? What is she wearing?

It was impossible to avoid her—she wore white. But this one was very different from those skinny girls my mother felt sorry for. She was heavily made-up and looked like a streetwalker. In the seventies with the new prosperity, they took to makeup with a vengeance and while in America that look had faded, here it hadn't peaked yet. You would think that brides would be different but no. This girl was bursting out of her gown too because she was pregnant and wasn't trying to hide it. It was the wrong gown for her condition because it was very tight all over, then widened, swirling around her ankles for the 'siren' look. Obviously she wouldn't pick this sort of gown now, it must have been perfect when she got fitted, five months ago, and then the wedding was postponed for some reason. The girl didn't seem bothered by all this and danced with a light step, her breasts moving up and down to the rhythm of the accordion.

I went on to imagine the reasons why the wedding was delayed—money, jobs, change of heart—I was inventing a story when a woman nudged me. "Have some," she said, offering a large plate of roast lamb. "Not that piece," she ordered, "that's just two bites." She gave me a big chunk which she said was the sweetest meat, around the bone.

The lamb was better than anything, I had forgotten how good it could be if it's young. They probably killed it last night, had it done on spit this morning. Without asking, she handed me more food, spinach pie, cucumbers, chunks of pork, then she said, "Lord, am I tired. I'll tell you, I'll be so glad this is over. Did you know, I haven't slept for two nights fixing things."

A boy served wine from the barrel. I had a glass or two, wishing I could dance but too full to move. Besides I didn't know how, not this. You couldn't just carry on and do your own thing. Their steps were intricate, precise, they danced hand in hand, clasped firmly, and moved in one direction forming a circle. If I fucked up, the entire chain would get derailed and they would look at me and know.

I continued to sit, leaning against the park fence, chewing on the bone. In front of me they went at it, stamping the ground, thud, thud, heavy strong steps, the ritual that is meant to fertilize the earth and the bride. The bride's mother danced vigorously; one of her braids was undone. A man shouted something I didn't know. Another pistol shot went off. Women squealed and the tempo changed. The music grew faster and their steps too. Men threw their jackets off. The bride looked flushed, her make-up gone. "I can't, I can't any more," the women moaned but they didn't stop.

The accordion player had his sleeves rolled up, his arms bronze and very beautiful. He moved with the accordion, sometimes to the left, other times to the right, effortlessly as if in a tango on a dance floor but you couldn't tell who led the dance, him or the accordion. You just couldn't. It was one of those things, love you might call it, love of music, of whatever danced in his head. And when he suddenly laughed, throwing his head back, his white teeth gleaming, his face carried some mad desire that made you wonder. It was bigger than this town, bigger than anything, something immense, full of wind and fire, but what I saw in his eyes was what I had missed all those years away from home. It wasn't anything precise. No word would describe it, no word I knew.

When did I meet him, was it in the seventies, I think suddenly about the gypsy man on the bus.

It was a warm day with a breeze, a perfect summer day for the region. I looked at the gypsy musician once more and got up, taking the same direction as always, without thinking; you could say it was as involuntary as the return of lost dogs and cats.

Going up the hill toward my old street I couldn't find the fountain that used to serve the entire neighborhood once. All ice in the winter, perfect for sledding and we went, Yanna and I, on a roasting dish stolen from mother who always said, mark my words, nothing good will happen to Yanna.

Old people must be happy the fountain is gone, no more worries, no ice but now they have cars zooming every which way, confusing them. And they can kill you, while before you just fell, maybe broke your leg or arm, nothing major, and how about the kids, where can they sled now with all those cars rushing at you. "Shit," I shout and jump to the side. They drive badly. Do they think they're on horses?

The soldiers' barracks used to be on the corner, but not any more, not that I regret them. Not too much. Through the barbed wire young men stared and said things. We hurried by, blushed, their eyes on our knees. All gone. Isn't it funny that you might hate something but still it's a reference point for something else and even though those barracks were ugly and the soldiers creepy, I would rather have them there on that corner as always. Strange isn't it?

The old dark tavern is gone too, replaced by a little supermarket. It's in this tavern that my father's father drank whenever the mood seized him, where he wasted all his money on gypsies and music, feverish in a state of ecstasy that has no right name in English. Kill me if you wish, that sort of feeling, and sometimes gypsies accompanied him home with violins, singing softly one of those tunes and you knew half-asleep that he was possessed again. Not his fault, they said, what can he do if he is possessed. They said he was consumed by fire, which I imagined as the very best thing that can happen to you. I had forgotten him and his face, only stories remain and that one time when he appeared on a white horse, his chest covered with medals from World War I. He looked amazing, but mother said an old drunk, tormenting a beautiful animal.

The beautiful art deco house built by a Russian architect is still there and the architect's son must be in it. We were together that day in the first grade when the German grenade exploded and many died and he lost both arms and a leg. I was luckier than the rest because I moved away, saved by a fear of some sort; I told the dumb boys not to hit it but they didn't want to listen. Privately, I believed grandma saved me because she loved me so much, more than anyone, and she was a saint, people said, no doubt about it. Her voice told me to move away from the boys that afternoon just before the grenade exploded. I wouldn't dare tell Marc about it. He'd think I was nuts, hearing voices.

The architect's house looks well-kept with flowers and lace curtains. The son got married in spite of everything, Yanna wrote; had three children, a nice peasant wife, clean. Of course, he wouldn't have married a peasant woman if his limbs were intact but they said he had a good life. The boy genius in the next house must be there too, the windows are wide open. What if I saw him, just a minute or so. I can't, I hadn't seen him the other times and now it's too late to start. I had always wanted to but was prevented by one thing or another, yet he was the only one I could talk to about the theory and practice of revolution, and what Lenin really meant. He became an alcoholic, they said, too tired of general mediocrity and everything. There is so much he could tell me about us and the present situation but I am afraid to bother him now, if I had stopped paying attention to him even before we left. And for superficial reasons—he was sickly looking, kind of short. And I had always felt bad about his dog.

Somebody is at the window, him? Don't linger, just pass by.

My street starts here, a slight climb to the right. All the houses on the left side are in the same spot as before, we had played hide and seek in all those basements—Ljuba's, Mira's and Boris'; all private homes built before the war. But on the right side where the cherry trees used to be—the property of an old millionaire who had to give it all up—nothing but three-story houses with ugly cement balconies. The nerve that woman has to shake her dusty rug like that! Peasants, most likely.

I walk by my own house on purpose, I want to find the bridge and the footpath by the creek and then in two minutes I'll be in the countryside. The bridge is not there and the creek, big, foamy, exciting after a storm, has disappeared! The path is gone too. Instead, more houses, a whole new neighborhood on the hill, blocking the sky and there is no point in looking for the meadow, my favorite one, full of clover where I escaped toward the clouds whenever I wanted to.

So, they have tamed the creek which doesn't mean it had died, it must still flow invisibly toward the river and further up I would find it if I just keep walking and then the trees would be there too. Still, it would take a long time, this searching for the open country, and the open country might be too far, maybe over another hill and then you just don't know. It's hard to get used to this imaginary creek. It's hard to get used to this new street where the creek used to be and it's even harder to imagine my street without the creek on the other side, just below the houses, below their gardens which fell into the ravine full of nettles, darkness and humidity. It was our jungle, where everything exciting happened—Tarzan, hide and seek, and poor Boris lost his glass eye once, but we found it. Didn't we crawl up the creek to look through the window and see the butcher all naked with his wife on the kitchen table and it looked like he was killing her? Didn't the butcher leave for Milwaukee? When did they channel the creek? Maybe the seventies, maybe later. My memory of the seventies is not as good as of the other times because everything smelled stronger before.

The street is asphalted now. It used to smell of dust and heat in the summer and when it rained it smelled of rain too. It was dark at night except for the fireflies. It was perfect for hide and seek. "Boris, Boris, where are you? Boris, hurry home or I'll break your bones," I hear Sara call. A brief quiet then, "Anna! Anna! Where are you? You'll get it from me!"—my mother adds another voice, three houses away.

Boris is in the capital now, that I know. He never saw his father the way he wanted to because Sara refused to go to America. Tired of moving, she said. Imagine if my own mother had said that, she could have. How nice it would be if I saw Boris again and talked about everything, the cat we had buried and that kid's dog. He would give me a clue or two about everything, he was good on details. Boris was with me the day the grenade exploded and he lost his eye and he was with me when the house was bombed and our fathers lived abroad and were supposed to be enemies of the State. We had so many secrets, did so many things together and then I betrayed him at fifteen with green eyes who was two years older. Boris suffered, no doubt about it, but it wasn't my fault—a taboo enveloped him—he had become a brother. I can't remember how we lost each other later on or if I saw him again after the first return, probably not. No reason. Just time. No time for everyone.

I had gone past his house with blue shutters. It was here somewhere on the street walking home from that first dance that I had stopped to talk with green eyes and we almost kissed. Funny how I can almost remember his eyes and that funny feeling in my body for the first time, funny isn't it. I am not sure of the exact spot though. It must be lower down where the fountain used to be, not so near my house where we could be seen by mother and Boris, a jealous pest, lurking about, following us.

If I keep walking around here, somebody will recognize me. Haven't I made up my mind not to disturb them? It's only curiosity on my part. I have nothing to say to them, in five minutes I'd be bored and five minutes are no good here, it's more insulting than not visiting at all, better nothing than five minutes and they would tell Yanna and then there is no end to it. Nobody. I'll see no one this time. Mira's mother? No.

Mira's daughter must be big, she was born around the second return in '67 or '68, isn't her name Anna too? Mira was my favorite from the first grade on, even though we never spoke about anything important, just dresses and blouses; she was not interested in anything else. Mira was my favorite but she was not very smart. Not too. Pretty though. With large brown doe's eyes, skin of a slight coppery tone. Her house is right around the corner.

Mira, Mira, a Spanish word. Mira's name opens the doors, the sixties roll into the street and I see a man I was with in that room on the coast! The room I found for the sweet young couple from Wisconsin. That one. It wasn't the blond boy, or green eyes but the one I called Che even though that was not his name. Just one night or two, that's all, no wonder his face is unclear even though Che's is as good as ever.

It's nice to salvage something, to reach a satisfactory conclusion even if it is to discover nothing of major impor-tance. I had forgotten his name and everything else about him, although he must have been from Cuba, Argentina, somewhere warm. "Mira, Mira," he would say, look, look, in Spanish. Look at what? I don't remember what we were looking at.

I am in front of a house which is about the same as the other houses on the street—two windows toward the street, more toward the garden, a basement and a basement apart-ment and another one upstairs. They are all like that except for the hue; this one is a warm sepia shade. This was not the one that was bombed, obviously, that one no longer exists, but it was in the same exact spot and they rebuilt it just like it was except that mother always said the second one wasn't as good because socialist materials were shabby. She would have said that even if they were the best in the world.

I am looking at the house, trying to imagine it the way it used to be but no more. If I go further, my head will spin. Too dangerous. I did it once. Don't push me to explain. You are buried and you can't scream, that's all. I can't decide which of the two was worse, the bombing or America. The first, I used to think. The second, I think now. I recovered from the first—my hair grew back, the wound healed. It happened to others. Boris was there too. At fifteen, it was all gone.

"Are you looking for someone?" a woman asked from the gate. I must have been there for a while. Startled, I said, "My friends used to live on this street."

The woman had a polka dot kerchief tied around her head, must have been dusting, "Please, come, have some coffee," she said, "I was in the mood myself. Excuse the way the place looks."

I entered the old way through the big gate that peasants used to deliver the wood. The lilac bush bloomed in the same spot, but would anyone know about the dead girl who was buried under it right before her wedding, lovesick for another man who later killed himself too? She came to haunt us often in the bushes by the creek, dressed in white, singing, urging us to jump. Jump, jump, follow me, come!

The little cottage is there too, amazing that it could house so many people—a slut with her lovers in one room, an unhappy couple with a dog in the other. They couldn't have a child and their life had no aim, people said. And then the dog drowned.

The young woman started on coffee. She was chunky, with beautiful black hair hidden until now by that scarf. She looked like Lena, the girl who used to bring us milk. Maybe her daughter. She had the same coal black eyes I was jealous of. Lena must be the same age as me.

"Who lives upstairs?" she asked.

"My parents," she said. "If we could get rid of those," she pointed toward the cottage, "my brother would move in. He lost his job in Croatia."

Did we sell the house to her grandparents? Through the window, I saw our immense garden had shrunk. Buildings instead of the trees. Hard to get used to it. Buildings.

"Do you mind if I take a look?" I said getting up.

"Take your time," she said. "The water hasn't boiled yet."

The pump was gone, you couldn't even tell the exact spot, icy water, mother's laundry frozen on the line in winter, mother's face gone too. The pigsty and the pigs were outlawed earlier. Three wooden outhouses were gone and the two ghosts near them, by the ravine and the creek. The water ghosts were friendly, grandma said, you have nothing to fear. Sitting on the wooden toilet seat you saw them through the planks, whistling softly in the trees.

The ravine was gone with the creek. All the trees were cut. A large street extended down below where the ravine was. And on the other side, housing projects created a wall compressing everything, making the garden seem smaller. I couldn't tell if the garden was really that small or if it seemed that way because there was nothing in front of it. Did I invent everything? My kingdom by the creek was now just a piddly yard, some shabby grass. I knew the grass used to be tall because I jumped from the window into it and Yanna jumped too, escaping her suitors.

I had buried the cat with Boris somewhere near the old tree trunk. Some bullies killed it, maybe the butcher's sons. We gave it a proper burial and said someday we'll come here and dig it up. I was sure the spot was right; it was in a direct line with the right corner of the house and the tree trunk was there, if only I could have a shovel. I started scratching the dirt with my hands when the woman appeared. "The coffee is ready," she said. "Did you lose something?"

"Nothing worthwhile. A tin box."

"When was that?" she asked, not curious.

"Ages ago." Maybe I had invented the cat, maybe it was a baby, there were many newborns in the creek. "What happened to the creek? I asked.

"The creek is further up," she said.

"But it was here the last time," I said and realized that the last time was fifteen years ago.

"I like your dress, I love that shade of blue," the woman said and I stopped myself from saying thank you, an American thing to do.

Fifteen years, I kept thinking, how they went.

They must have found me strange the last time even though my hair was longer and I didn't wear ugly old jeans but an elegant jumpsuit that Yanna said looked like a mechanic's uniform. I was all nerves speaking about the theater, my productions, my work. I didn't even look at their babies that time.

I brought America with me, I shouldn't have done it.

They understood nothing about feminism—lazy, self-complacent, they didn't have to fight to become doctors and the state paid for everything—health, maternity leaves and every abortion. They looked at me, not understanding—they've always had women around them, sure they loved them, mothers, sisters, grandmas, their friends, they failed to see how this was something new. They didn't understand my anger at men, their chauvinism, their exploitation, "How could you be so brainwashed," I had screamed, "to work like slaves in the office and at home." They only shrugged, and agreed that yes, men are lazy, childish, weak, they dropped their clothes on the floor, left dirty dishes in the sink, but who would want them in the kitchen cooking, who would want to eat what they cook!

They were hopeless. All the finer points of feminism were wasted on them. Mira, always a coquette, saw no connection between looking good and being a slave—she loved clothes and men's eyes on her. Others felt the same way, without insisting or arguing; they only listened as always to my new anger and fed me strudel and fruit.

They would like me now. I am not pushing anything, no big ideas on revolution or feminism, but stripped of all that who am I?

"Were you born here?" I asked the woman.

"Oh no, further up, you know the village of Teras?"

"Of course I do." That's why she didn't remember the creek, she came to town recently. I couldn't say 'I knew your mother, she used to bring us milk.'

"My father bought the house when he came back from Germany," she said with some pride.

"He worked there?"

"He did. Six years."

"It's a nice street and a nice house too," I said.

"I like it. You know, ages ago, it used to belong to people who left to America. My mama knew them."

"Your mother's friends?"

"Oh no. She only knew them a little bit. She said they were well-to-do. Nice though. She gave my mama all sort of clothes."

"Did she like them, the clothes I mean?"

"Sure she did, she said the daughter was real pretty, as pretty as a movie star with long blond hair and then she changed terribly over there and nobody would recognize her."

"How strange," I said, "that she would change that much."

"It's hard without your own."

"Yes, it would be," I said.

"That's why dad didn't stay in Germany. Nobody to talk to and in America it's much worse."

"Not worse than Germany," I said. "You think she changed because she had nobody to talk to?"

"The girl? You never know. Their ways are different. My uncle says over there nobody eats properly. It's either canned or frozen. They just buy some cans and heat it up. Can you imagine?"

"That's not true," I said, foolishly. I didn't want her to stop.

"I only know what they say. And they say she destroyed this poor man."

"The same girl?"

"Yes, her. He lives over there by the river. He took to drink all on account of her. That's what they say."

"Really?"

"Yes, they say she made him dance tangos the night of his father's funeral and she wore a white dress too. And they made love on the grave."

This was unfair. What a fucking lie. They have no business telling stories like that. I wished I could defend myself. I did nothing to him. If I am to feel guilty about anything it would be about a dog Boris and I sold for movie tickets and cherries without knowing it belonged to the kid genius. Maybe Boris told him. Yes, I always felt guilty about that sweet poodle and the kid genius who looked even lonelier after that.

"Where do you live?" the woman asked.

"In the capital," I said calmly.

"More exciting, isn't it?"

"Yes, it is, but noisy too."

We sipped our coffee slowly, then the woman started peeling potatoes for the soup. I turned my cup over hoping that she might know how to tell fortunes the way my mother's friends did, in this kitchen.

She saw me do it, and laughed, "I am no good at this. I only see a few things. You should wait for my mom, she would talk to you for hours." Still, she examined the cup from all sides, and said, "Many travels and many men. You have one blond, two, several dark men after you."

"Where do you see these men?" I asked, never understanding how they saw blond men in coffee grounds.

"See this," the woman pointed toward various shapes but obviously you had to know how to look in order to see them. I saw nothing. My cup with men and travels went into the sink.

They had running water. Easy. Just turn on the faucet. Electrical stove. Everything neat, clean, brand new. Mother cooked on a wood stove but I built the fire in the morning and the wood sang because the ghosts were trapped inside it then later they came out exploding. Deep snows outside. Flames inside the stove. Fire is full of magic. You stare. Sometimes we got lucky, it snowed and snowed so much and the school closed the entire month, the river froze too and everywhere you look nothing but whiteness and it's still snowing. It might not stop. At any moment Mira and Boris will appear with the sled.

"Did it snow much this winter?"

"Not this year. Here we had mostly rain. The snow is further up, that's where you go for the snow."

"What happened to all that snow," I said.

The sound of a baby whimpering came from the other room. The woman jumped up, and came out with the sleepy baby with big cheeks. "I've been worried to death," she said, "he hasn't eaten anything this morning." She touched his head for fever which he didn't have.

"He looks healthy," I said.

"Mother's baby, my precious, my little male," she crooned.

She kept kissing the baby over and over again, tickling his toes, licking his fingers, she didn't want to leave him alone. "He is so handsome," I said, forgetting you shouldn't compliment them.

"Knock on wood," the woman said, "yes he is hand-some, just like his dad."

She kissed him more while changing him, kisses all over, on his face, stomach, his fat feet. That's where the passion went, I solved an old puzzle about Mira, Nina and Slava—how they changed, grew slow, quiet and contented, you couldn't believe they were wild animals once. All that fire in them. Children got it all—the hugs and kisses, and then the grandchildren continued the cycle of passion that won't get exhausted. Their own was short-lived. It wasn't meant to last. Their time was over.

Mother and the baby were in their own world, teasing, nuzzling, whispering like lovers. There was no separation, not even the tiniest bit, even a perfect stranger could see they adored each other. *Dusho*, she said, "mother's son, mother's soul." The woman called him all sorts of names, some very private, in whispers. I've held back even in that, I thought. Sure I had loved my sons but not like this, not with kisses all over—this would be considered too suspicious in the States, child abuse maybe. What would they think in New York about Mira, whose youngest slept with her and her husband, and Mira only said, "He is lonely without us. He'll outgrow it." Sometimes both kids slept with them, that's why they got a larger bed.

"What about the two of you?" I had asked but Mira didn't pick up on it. Sex wasn't like vitamins to them.

I could never explain why sex as hygiene caught on in the States, nor the obsession with it—how many times a week, how to perk it up, dress it up, better sexier sex, bigger better best orgasms. Obviously it was a profitable obsession, and then money is sexy too as Judy my famous actress friend once said, referring to her well-known agent who was otherwise ugly.

"My mother is late," the woman said. "My brother had a new baby, that's why."

"A girl?" I asked.

"Yes. She is the chubbiest thing you've seen, you just want to eat her up. I prefer fat babies, don't you?"

"Oh yes," I said, not having thought of this before.

It was warm in the kitchen, steamy from the soup. The woman fed the baby bit by bit, a spoon for her, a spoon for him, then she gave him her breast too. From this angle, sitting in my old kitchen, the smell of soup in the air, I thought they were luckier than me—protected by an old circle, they bloom, they live, they die. There were rituals to be observed, the beginning and end of each stage, but I had missed them and now of course it was too late. I could never be part of it. Just an observer. I felt no envy now, just something like regret. How nice it would be to live fully, without thoughts, like this woman. But it was too late for that. My real life was inside my head, a refuge and a prison.

Looking at this woman, it was impossible not to think about Jessica, Joan, and Ellen trying to conceive at forty when they finally got ready for it. And Joan's anger at not being able to, in spite of her efforts. She wanted it all, just like Jessica and Ellen, furious she couldn't get this last item on the agenda when she wanted it. Mary had everything— money, a great job, everything except a relationship. "I need a good relationship," sounded hollow, an item you get with other staples at the grocery store. And all those other friends, people you hear at parties, all improving their bodies and minds, and the constant never-ending questions—am I on the right track, did I choose the right career, the best, the one that's just right for me, the one that satisfies, the very best man, will he help me grow, am I growing, is this town right for me—the doubt never-ending because the answer doesn't exist. It never will. It can't. And besides it wouldn't be profitable.

I couldn't stop comparing, wishing all along it weren't so. But it's not my fault, you are taught to compare, aren't you?

"Do you have any kids?" the woman asked.

"Yes," I said, "two boys," wishing I had a picture now to show her.

"We are going to have a bath," the woman said to her son. They had a bathroom now, everything white, toilet and tub, no need to worry about that ghost by the creek in winter, at night.

"Thank you for the coffee," I said. "I should get going." I touched the boy's foot and kissed it. He giggled, pleased, and his mother kissed him too.

Once again I went past Boris' house and Mira's and that little spoiled prima donna with curls. I recognized a woman or two but wasn't sure if they were mothers or daughters.

It bothered me I couldn't remember the exact spot where we almost kissed coming home from a dance. I am sure I would remember it if the fountain were still there because that was in the background, the sound of water, as he stood near me that night. Even his face is less sharp now, it keeps blurring into a more recent one, the gypsy man I had met on the bus.

It was silly to hope for a peasant cart, all gone ages ago, but I still wished for one, the kind grandpa had, with two white horses.

A woman walking toward me looked strong, with short legs and arms. She had a black dress on, maybe her mother died. There wasn't much to identify her as the milkman's daughter with beautiful black curls, yet it was her, hurrying from baby to baby, a bag of cherries in one hand and potatoes in the other. She still had that large mole on the upper lip but her hair was almost white.

I had not seen Lena in years. The shock of change prevented me from speaking and when I got ready to say something, Lena the milkman's daughter had already gone by, her eyes worried—to call her back seemed pointless, she was not a good friend, just a picture from my past and maybe it's the best not to disturb people. Maybe Lena wasn't her name, mother never called her Lena, maybe Lena was another peasant girl, the one who used to bring us cream. In safety I watched her.

Her walk had the steadiness, the gravity of a weighed-down animal, it was a walk I had noticed before. Grown women had it; not me. That's why the confusion about my age every time. It was that walk that was missing, with even measured steps and a grown woman's dress and swollen ankles, plus that look of permanent worry all of them developed after thirty. Nobody escaped the worry, not even my friends who went to college, but I wasn't sure if it was real worry that marked their faces or a mask, a habit they put on. Still, they were grown up in a way I'll never be, no matter how hard I worried and worked—something will always remain undeveloped in me, maybe my American part?

With Lena in the distance, a bit of black by Boris' house, an old question came back with a vengeance— *Who would I be if?*—a pointless question, the same one every time, you'd think I'd get tired of it. *Who?*

Not like Lena, she didn't go to school.

I went over the list, eliminating some for temperament, others for intelligence or body type, but there wasn't a single one that I could claim as mine, not even Dara, who was intelligent and daring, a tomboy at ten, a doctor in obstetrics later on, even she seemed settled the last time. There you have it. Nobody. Nobody in New York either, not a single person man or woman, who could offer a similar landscape I would recognize in their eyes without having to explain or talk.

Occasionally gay men had it, and even though theirs was of a different kind, we still gravitated toward each other as if lost, in search of a country. Everybody had noticed this, even Marc, who said that if there is one gay man at the party we'll find each other. He didn't offer any explanations as usual. We obviously emit special sounds known only to us, not that I could hear my own.

There was someone. Years ago, a time erased. The girl in my dorm who was passing. Nobody could tell. She'd had everything bleached, girdled, straightened, except her eyes which were on the lookout and terrible. I know this is not Marsha now, who looks more Brazilian, but the other one, the girl she was. We recognized each other. Who spoke first? Something about her eyes was more than terrible. Which means I, Anna, looked deranged too.

A jab in the chest. I doubled over. I'm sick, I'm seeing things. Father died at my age, didn't he? He saw his whole life months before he died, didn't he? I'll die soon. 'Not likely,' grandma says, 'off to school with you!' My pain is passing, will pass any moment now, I'm fine. Still, if the old tavern were here, I would go and have a shot. Something strong. That's why bars exist, for moments like this, when your chest hurts. Thoughts can kill you, and that's the truth.

I am almost at the hotel when the priest appears on the edge of the park, why in the hell did he have to pick this moment for a stroll. I am searching for a button on my dress to hold onto, then spit unnoticeably three times in his direction as protection against the bad luck he can bring with his costume. Other people can do it, certain old women with green eyes, women who flatter you, but he is the worst. Why him? Who knows. I am ashamed of myself for such stupidity and primitivism, didn't they lecture over and over in class against superstition?

The peasants won. Garlic against the witches, garlic everywhere, under the baby's pillow, amulets against the evil eye. I'm embarrassed. Turning suddenly, I see that I have been seen. A man in his forties in a nice summer suit is holding onto his shirt button too. "The Devil take him," he says, laughing, "I'd rather not cross one of them on my path. They always bring me bad luck. Did you know that the day my father died, I dreamt about a priest the night before and then saw him in the morning. I knew immediately things would turn out badly and they did."

The guy is funny. He is still holding onto his button until the priest disappears completely from his line of vision. And I am talking or thinking, "Yeah. That's how it is. I'm telling you. Just cool it, sugar." It's not me. It must be Marsha sneaking in or some other voice I had loved and didn't resist. I even laugh now with Marsha's husky laughter, a bit brazen, Marsha now, not the other person and it all seems normal because it is—it's not just Marsha talking, it's one of my favorite characters—a woman from Savannah, a fascinating person who took over my head and wouldn't let go until the play was finished. Most people don't understand that part, how a play begins, if you told them this person took over your head, they'd look frightened, she is nuts, they would say. It's best not to reveal too much, it's dangerous, Marsha knows all about it. Didn't I dream about a priest last night, just before dawn?

Slightly off the main street, I saw a huge new square, can't remember what was there before. Very modern, with benches and a café. A large fountain in the middle. To the right, the view toward the hills was blocked by the 'Bull's Ass Hotel' in gray marble. To the left, and directly above the fountain, a huge statue of the Leader in bronze dominated everything, his arms extended, lifted in a heroic Partisan stance. But as I came near him, a surprise: his head was gone and they were using the neck opening for a vase. Flowers stuck out of his neck—yellow, green, red—and the body was sprayed with paint. In my own ramblings, I had not paid close attention to what's happening to the country, I had missed too much to catch up and make sense of their internal problems. However, things must have changed drastically if his head is missing. It was unthinkable in '75. Who would dare! The criminal would be found, immediately! They had their ways. Of course he had been dead for a decade but I remember him alive and that one time when, in the second grade, I was chosen to present him with flowers on May First, dressed in a white blouse, navy pleated skirt and my red pioneer scarf.

Everything matched, the roses I gave him were red too. The best pioneer, the best student, an honor only the kid genius shared but he didn't get chosen. "Snake," my mother whispered, "snake, I am raising a snake, imagine who she gave flowers to." We disagreed violently on the meaning of socialism and the revolution. If I, Anna, said yes, it was in the name of reason and clarity, against petty bourgeois thinking, doctors instead of amulets, against the evil eye, against the darkness of all religions as the opium of the people. Against nationalism, for something bigger that would unite us, for better tomorrows, for justice and then we had fought our heroic fight against the Germans and won! Even she couldn't deny that, but still expected me to refuse, invent sickness, instead of giving flowers to the monster who is the very reason why my father never came back.

He didn't look like a monster to me. He was too handsome and then we had similar eyes, the same shade of blue. They say he was one of the handsomest leaders in Europe especially during his partisan days; later, when I gave him flowers he had already accumulated some extra flesh and his face looked a bit pasty, sort of British well-to-do.

My head is fuzzy this afternoon, I am thinking about this or that, including him of all people! But he was the only president I had known, from birth to my departure, and I gave him those flowers after all, and was kissed by him. But who knows, maybe there is another reason.

The movies maybe. Why not? Handsome heroes and gangsters, everything better than in real life. The magic of that screen. After all, part of the money from the stolen poodle went to see *Treasure of the Sierra Madre*, Boris and me in the front row, not guilty about anything, just watching America unfold. It was a great film, and there were tons of others after that, no comparison with the shit I had seen lately. Why aggravate yourself, Marsha says, and watch shit for seven bucks.

On the right side, in front of the brand new cinemas, kids waited now for *Sex, Lies and Videotape* and *Out of Africa*, plus some I had not heard about. Directly in front, a new theater was an improvement over the shabby building with squeaky floors and much hammering in between the acts. I was about to go take a look at the stage when I saw a familiar name on the wall. It was a standard rectangular piece of paper with a black rim, what you saw everywhere on the walls, announcing death and burial. My old dressmaker, the costume designer for the theater, had died last week. It was definitely Her—Desa's old picture was on the wall, and she looked as funny as thirty years ago. I should go and offer condolences to her sister; according to the announcement she lived in the same place as before, just below the Turkish ruins on the hill.

I can't imagine Desa dead—she laughed too much and told too many stories about actors and what they really looked like without that goo, and whose left breast is smaller and what she had to do to even everything out. Some actors stuttered horribly, she said, but they knew how to cover up

with tricks so you could never tell, and they loved differently, uncontrollably, as if there is no tomorrow. 'Uncontrollably' is the word Anna liked.

She made all my clothes and my underclothes and paja-
mas and even stole some material from work to make my
first tutu; it was impossible to buy tulle at that time. It was
my first performance, dressed all in white, on the podium
built for the May celebration, an attempt by the town bour-
geoisie to have something else besides peasant music and
revolutionary tunes. Boris was my handsome prince, with a
patch; we danced the last part of *Swan Lake*. My teacher was
a Russian refugee who taught other things—gymnastics, ballet, and violin. I remember: Desa, mother, Sara and my teachers sat in the front row as I shook my wings and slowly died
on the podium.

Now, going toward the river, I saw the tennis courts
where the gypsy tents used to be. Desa's house was right
there, on the right bank, an old Turkish one with a wooden
gate, and that old fashioned smell of jasmine from her garden.

Inside, every bit of floor would be covered with rugs and
more *cilims* in different shades. You took your shoes off and
left them on the porch, next to other shoes. Can't have
shoes inside. It's not clean. The sewing machine went clippety
clap, sweetly. Her feet did the job. She looked up, did you
find your slippers, go get them or you'll catch cold, she said.
It was hot, June or July, you argue, but put them on. The
fitting over, you swam, she and mother talked in whispers,
you came back, she gave you soup, then you took a nap,
they talked some more, the machine went clippety clap,

putting you to sleep. You woke up, had something to eat
again. Another fitting in two days, she said. You never saw
money exchanged.

I couldn't do it. Through the planks, I see her sister in
black but I simply can't. I have got enough time, but some
discipline is necessary. I can't. There'll be no end to it, it
can't be five minutes, she is old, she would tell how Desa
died and her last words just before she died and the day
before and she would cry constantly. Then, I would have to
talk too. More than I wanted. I don't want to. Next, Yanna
would hear and then ...... Nobody.

I retreated. Careful now. Green eyes lived around here
in his mother's house by the river. Yanna said his mother
had died. For a second, I wished I could go see him and we
would talk honestly about everything, like old friends, forgive each other, but I knew that was a nice Hollywood ending and not the way things end here. He'll always hate me
for some reason. You can't alter that with some words, quickly.
Shouldn't disturb him now. I shouldn't have disturbed him
the first time. What did that woman say, "ruined him and
he took to drink."

Maybe I did.

Not likely. Still ... you never know.

I brought America with me. I shouldn't have come.

Lots of time. I am doing fine. It's all under control. I did
just about everything I wanted to. You can be quite organized when you put your mind to it. Everything is just great.
Why am I feeling bad then? Guilt?

It's Desa, of course. I had always seen her friends before,
every time, every one of them, I should have gone in for an

hour or so. You are supposed to. It's too late now. I can't go back and in addition I know that my decision is rationally correct, but what's rational doesn't help your stomach, your chest, or ease this dread in me. Step by step, uncontrollably, unwillingly, I am once again on the familiar road going over the hill toward the cemetery where they took grandma, the rain falling, October, second grade, three years after the Revolution.

In the cemetery, it's worse than this morning. Did I think it would be easy to find Desa's grave in the midst of so many crosses and red stars thrown together at random? The cemetery had grown in size, had even taken over another hill where the TB sanatorium used to be. I am really lost now, how do you find a new grave, I asked.

The people sitting by their grave only shrugged; "go see the guard," they said. The guard was out for lunch, the sign on his door said. How could he be out for lunch, it's too late for lunch, loafing, most likely. I went from grave to grave hoping to find her, it's better this way, better than visiting with her sister, it was important to tell her what wonderful dresses she made on that old machine. I hoped she would forgive me for forgetting her all those years and her dresses— I went to America in one, a blue dress cut on the bias with invisible pockets and buttons that had to be covered in fabric, one by one. And my navy silk dress copied from a Paris journal, and the light pink one with a bare back for the summer months. I can't see Desa's face at all but see her hands now, the way I must have seen them once, with bandages and a pincushion around her wrist, moving fast, doing a hem.

It was hopeless. I couldn't find her. The cemetery had no clear paths, no symmetry, no order. I stumbled. Potholes. My sandals didn't help. But searching for Desa I met others—my Latin teacher, a woman who was brilliant and limped, a teacher of Greek with beautiful hair, and a literature professor who was known as a flirt. Didn't he have a crush on Mira at one time or did Mira invent it? He suffered so much in provinces away from the capital where life was exciting and all he could do was teach literature and talk about the tragic loves of our poets. He was too young to die, maybe a car hit him, maybe he drowned, maybe he died from love the way he said it would happen.

In the same neighborhood, a few of my mother's friends, recognizable by their old pictures huddled together—the one who told fortunes, and the one who loved men too much, and Sara, Boris' mother who spoke Ladino, the language nobody else knew. A classmate dead ages ago, soon after the revolution, still looking like a kid in a pioneer scarf, thin, hungry looking; most likely TB took her. No sign of Desa, maybe the new graves were further away.

I was lucky with grandma as always. Her place was not far from Sara's, with a tree over her head and a bench off to the side. A nice grave, well kept. When Boris visits Sara he must see her too, how nice they stayed on the same street.

I was exhausted after all those graves and Desa might not forgive me, but grandma would understand everything as always, "Grandma," I said, "look, I really tried. You saw, I did."

Grandma understood everything, my misery now, and all the other miseries before, she was firm, fair, just, it's her face I saw when they talked about God, maybe I had prayed to her all along. "Grandma," I said, "help me. I am lost. No doubt about it." I didn't have to beg for forgiveness or tell her I had never forgotten her—grandma knew.

I wasn't sure if I was talking or dreaming, I couldn't tell if I fell asleep, or for how long. Grandma's face looked at me, young in the picture from her Ragusa days when she ran a restaurant near the port, then a sailor appeared one day, and she doesn't want to tell any more. "Time to leave," she said, "go!"

Over the hill, the sun had set. I got up, kissed the picture, moved away, came back, kissed her some more. Off to school with you, she says, you'll be late, hurry, go.

I wish I could believe in an afterlife, it would be nice, but I can't. Only the ghosts are real. You'd better get out of here and fast. In the absence of sun, everything turned gray. Soon the night will fall. Not the best time to be wandering around the cemetery all alone. You must be out of your mind jumping over graves, something you're never supposed to do. Ghosts can surprise you. If you awaken them too early, before the first stars, they go berserk, they keep you. I couldn't remember that special chant, and my dress had no buttons to hold on to.

The wind carried the sound of people, of laughter, the smell of food. As I came out of a ravine, I saw a funeral party sitting by a bungalow. They were eating roast pig and lamb in big chunks. It looked like the end of mourning, judging by the number of people and the amount of food. They ordered me to stop. "Have a bite," a man motioned to me, drunk, "for his soul."

I did. You can't say no. Nobody does.

"Have some wine too," he said. "Meat without wine is like a woman with one tit." He laughed. Gold shone in his front teeth.

I took a glass.

"We've done everything," he said. "We didn't skimp. He wanted English wool and we got him the best wool from London. The tailor did a nice job, you could die for that suit. Go see."

"Where?" I asked.

"In his home, there."

This was for real. I swear I didn't invent a thing. The bungalow turned out to be the rich peasant's grave with a TV, a bed and his accordion. The new suit was on the bed, with a white handkerchief in the top pocket. A telephone too.

What happened to the gypsies—they were around the graves before, weren't they supposed to be intermediaries between the living and the dead? They were not to be seen. That wasn't good. You had to have gypsies around. They always brought you good luck.

At the grave, the funeral party didn't seem rushed. They kept drinking, some sang. They wanted me to drink some more, might not take no for an answer. Their faces looked peculiar. I ran. I kept thinking, I didn't invent it. I wondered what if the phone were connected.

It was dark when I got back. My sandals were muddy, my dress crumpled. I changed into blue jeans and sneakers, then went out again. I didn't want to sleep yet. I wanted something to happen. The main street was closed off to traffic and a few old people still promenaded in their finery, as

always. However, the excitement, the reason why you hurried every night to the main street was gone, because there
was nobody on the sidewalks to comment and whisper. The
young people were not there.

The square with the headless leader was packed. A rally?
All young, hundreds of them, a sea of blue jeans. The town
had tripled. They were not waiting for anything, a boy said.
That's what they did every night.

"Do you know what's playing at the Café Park?" another
kid asked.

"No idea," I said.

"We're going," the same kid said, "you wanna come?"

"Sure" I said, thinking, this is crazy, who do they think
I am?

A large group moved toward the river, then stopped not
far from Desa's house, in front of the dam. Café Park was
there, an ordinary modern structure of glass and steel.

Inside a large hall, more kids smoked and talked. The
kid who invited me said he didn't care for the band—too
archaic he said. He liked my sneakers a lot, the color and
the brand name, he would get himself a pair the first time
he gets some dough. Another one said, "I saw that movie.
She is a dog."

"She really is," the other agreed, "but the film is not
bad."

"Which film?" I asked.

"*Out of Africa.* Don't you think so?"

"What?"

"That she is a dog."

"She is a very good actress. Beautiful too."

"Her pretty!" they laughed. "A dog."

"She is still a good actress," I said.

"I think he is better. He is so great, get it, that you understand the power of love even though she is a dog."

"She is not a dog," I said. Why was I defending Meryl Streep, what's the point. Maybe she is a dog, all of my American friends would be ugly here, my left eye saw them. Not Marc, though. He looked like Boris, except for that eye. He would be handsome here, maybe more than in the US.

They asked nothing about me. I worried what I would say. Now I wondered why they had invited me along, what age I was for them. They took me for a younger person because I walked the way I walked, or because I was dressed in blue jeans and sneakers. They didn't know how to look carefully, how touching kids are. Soon I stopped thinking about it and drank with them, a feeling of science fiction in my lungs, a travel though time.

"See that one," a kid nudged me, "she was my girlfriend until last month. That prick stole her, see the one with the ugly jaw. She is the one next to him."

"How did he steal her?"

"Fucking ass! Promised her a trip to Rome."

"Did they go?"

"Rome? Never. It was a come-on, you know what I mean. I'm going to break his fucking jaw and let's see what he does next." He looked like he meant it.

At some point, I started walking back to the hotel. In the narrow dark street near the Hotel Park, people promenaded up and down. The main street was no longer it. But this unofficial street was not blocked off to traffic, so the cars and people competed for space since there were no sidewalks. I couldn't understand what force of desire drove them to do it—the promenade was always meant to be quiet, slow, good for your digestion and sleep. Now, in the darkness, both pedestrians and the drivers cursed, fuck your mother, your sister, your stupid head, and yet nobody wanted to give up.

I didn't sleep well. Woke up early, ate fast. One day. It was a success, I had managed to pack quite a bit into a day, and stay on schedule too. Maybe a day or two in the capital then off we go. That's what I am thinking, ready and packed, but as I walk out of the hotel I am really going in the opposite direction, can't help myself as I enter the ugly block C.

I got in as always—the door was not locked. I tiptoed, wanting to surprise her. I'll say, here I am, but only for a short time. Just passing through, I'll say. Just wanted to kiss you, my only one, there's nobody left.

Yanna slept where sleep overtook her, in a kitchen chair in front of the TV, music blaring. She was gray, fat, decaying. The kitchen was in disarray, unwashed dishes piled up, bags of garbage; a fly danced on her upper lip.

I retreated slowly, silently closed the door. It wasn't her—my Yanna was the other one, that wild girl who jumped through the window when the suitors came.

Part Four

I am glad I didn't see her—it's better this way. It's better I didn't see him, the man with green eyes; he would be bloated from too much food and wine, the last time he already looked that way and besides it's not him I had wanted but that other person. I wish I could always remember him like that or maybe remember myself looking at him with fireflies around us at night.

I can't remember him. It happened too long ago. It's more like a memory of love, a story about them. I can't feel what she felt and that's that. I lost it all along with the pain. I can't even imagine the size of that pain now except it must be bigger than my memory of it.

At the window, looking at the new train station, I would like to remember my first departure, the one that would dislocate me forever, but the pain refuses to come up. I can't will it. Every detail is there and every face—Mira, Boris, Yanna, teachers waving, everyone except me. Maybe there is nothing left of it, it's been used up in Chicago, over and over again in slow motion, the last whistle, the very last look at the hills, the friends crying as the train pulls out heading for the West.

Death, I think, would be the way to direct that scene.

I feel absolutely nothing but wish I did. Something small. A whiff of feeling, mild regret would do. The town in the valley just disappears and soon gets replaced by meadows and trees. Just as well, it passes through my mind. I'm free of it, all gone. And what's there to miss? This is some other place. Still, I wish I missed it more, I have gotten accustomed to missing it and what will replace it now? I'll miss missing it, I had missed it for too long. And even though I can congratulate myself for staying on top of things, one day, right on schedule—now, on the train, away from everything, I feel cowardly, I feel bad, I had run away from Yanna in spite of all the good reasons. There is a hunger in my stomach, emptiness in my arms, I didn't kiss her and Yanna was my favorite; I had loved her more than anyone. I should have visited Desa's sister, the way I did before, and the woman with the gold tooth, mother's oldest friend, still alive and what about my old dentist, Sara's brother, the only person in town who went briefly to Israel. At least I didn't run away from Mira and Boris; they had moved ages ago to the capital.

Impolite, improper behavior, I didn't teach you like that, mother says, harsh, an eyebrow raised. Yes, sure, it's easy for you to command. You're dead, feel nothing now. Meanwhile, it's me, Anna, who is uncertain about the most ordinary things—I, she, us, who I am, was, would have been.

Of course I did the right thing. One more day and I would have had to talk about her and about me and life in general and all the tears—no thanks, just as well I skipped it. They don't know how to have a positive outlook on things, it's not in the air they breathe, just misery and misery and the sad past, the only country that celebrates its greatest defeat as a national holiday. Seven centuries ago. Sick, right? I was always afraid of these returns, a fear of something crazy in the blood. Tomorrow, or rather the day after tomorrow, I'll be on the plane and everything will be OK.

We triggered the First World War, I'd better go with Pan Am, I thought.

The train that took the whole night would only take three hours now. Amazing. You can go there on weekends.

You can go to the theater, to a ballet, or to shop. It used to
be a far away city, the biggest one, the one you dreamt
about—Mira and I in the grass by the creek—and of the day
when we would leave our pathetic hills and head for the
university in the capital. There, by the Danube, marvelous
things happened on summer nights, each new generation of
girls who left said so. There, in the shadows of linden trees,
the cafés are full of mysterious strangers and the music never
stops. We never dreamt of going to Paris or Rome, just there.

I almost made it. Just a detail or two was off. I had
travelled there with green eyes and he bought me a ring. A
gold band that would be switched to the right hand, the day
of our marriage. That must have been the summer of my
first return and he must have done it to make it more official, more binding. I was engaged, he said, expecting me to
come back, he said he loved me in spite of our problems. I
am sure we never made love because he loved me too much
or because he really had a problem or maybe I had one—he
had become a relative, a brother—something like a taboo
and an air of regret surrounded him and all the native men
that summer. Who knows why, maybe it had to do with the
softness of the language, what you could say with it, its
sentimental side, or maybe I had gotten used to separations
as a way to be.

Did I write to him after that? Probably not. He did. So
did the other one. I was trying to start all over that year, in
France, then in July I had hitchhiked with the French students and met the blond boy who was from the North and
spoke the language I didn't know. Who knows why I was
with him but it was probably ordinary—he was a beautiful

man in a beautiful landscape and it was hot. No harm was done, it was too short, and besides he got something out of it. Both of us did. No, it wasn't him I wanted but this other thing—to kiss the entire country, to warm up. Nobody would understand that, nobody I know. I was cold, even during the summer months. Of course I didn't know all this, but do you ever know anything completely? Didn't father say, 'you learn and learn and you die dumb'? The more I go over this, the less I seem to know. Will it ever stop?

There is a chunk of time that's missing after that year, too many different people, places all over the U.S. When did I see green eyes next? It must have been in '67, the reference is LLP, yes of course, Limousine, Leather coat and Porn, when he tried to blame me, to make me feel guilty for his whole life.

This was right around the Tet offensive when I stayed briefly with those Argentinians on the coast. Were they Argentinians?

His face from that period keeps merging, fading into another one, that gypsy on the bus, even though that was much later, in the seventies, my last time coming here from Paris, on the Orient Express.

How did I ever end up going with the gypsies and peddlers to Temisoare, was it the name of the town that sounded like the one dad had known or was it that I was told that across the border in Romania they had beautiful embroidered scarfs?

That train station, Ottoman, filthy, full of beggars and peasants in wool hats, was a different station from my old memory of the Wagon-Lits Orient Express we took to Paris, that first time. In the seventies, everything was shabbier, dirtier, as train after train herded workers from Istanbul, Athens, Belgrade toward Munich, Düsseldorf, Hamburg but it was still a perfect spot to see the native costumes, listen to regional dialects, and some ordinary speech of the sort I had always liked anywhere, New York included. You hear everything that way, everyday concerns and dramas, who left whom, who is in love, who died. And the price of things, what is it they want and can't have. Go to ordinary places, sit there quietly and listen, I always tell students. Not that they listen.

So, I must have gone there to listen, invisibly, spy over a cup of coffee but then I can't quite see how I ended up going with those gypsies and peddlers to Romania, to Temisoare, was it the town my grandpa had known, or was I told that across the border nothing had changed and they still had horses and carts. Maybe that was the reason. It sounds right. But nobody told me I was on the wrong bus, it wasn't advertised as the smugglers' bus, although it was known to everyone, most likely. And here I am on a bus full of the demi-monde, toothless old hags and general riff-raff, carrying powdered soup, batteries, and native blue jeans to sell in Romania.

God knows how it all started. This gypsy sat next to me, that's all. Urging me to eat his food, talking nonstop. He had the most beautiful teeth in the world, and swore on his youth in a way that was most original. "May my youth die," he said, "if I do any harm to you. May my youth die, if I'm not telling the truth."

I had never heard an expression like that, it was usually

"may my mother or my father die," but 'youth' was touching.

He didn't know I was much older than he was, and the other smugglers didn't notice it either because they kept shouting, laughing and teasing, "Leave the girl alone, you bum. Stop it."

He ignored them, his arms around me.

In Temisoare, they went to work. I walked and looked amazed. Here, not that far away, time had stopped—everything was the same as before—horses, oxen and girls with pioneer scarves. Streets empty of cars and blue jeans. I would have liked to stay much longer, but three hours later, I was on the smugglers' bus.

On the way back, I carried a few things for them, whatever they had managed to buy or exchange, because they had noticed that the border guards didn't look in my bag the first time. They imagined all sorts of special connections of a political nature but it was only my blue passport—guards couldn't imagine an American girl doing petty smuggling in Romania.

Of course they were right. So were the smugglers. I got their goods across the border. Nobody looked at my stuff, nobody searched under my clothes, in my mouth, the way they searched others. It called for a celebration. The driver turned the radio on and pulled a bottle of brandy out from under his seat. The gypsy sat next to me again and soon we kissed and kissed as the bus rolled on, the driver drank, the road bumpy, and everything seemed out of control yet normal.

I remember, he tasted of salt and marinated beef and

moved like a cat, silently, with precision. I remember his arms were long, wiry, bronze, the most beautiful arms I had even seen. He must have been a petty thief or something like it, his eyes were on the lookout at all times.

It was dark when the bus arrived at the station but the gypsy said it wasn't late. When I tried to leave him, he said no not yet. I was sober now, to pacify him I said I'll call him tomorrow. He had no phone, he said. My mother waited for me, I lied, why not meet tomorrow at noon for lunch, but he could smell my lies, he was a pro and, grabbing my arm, he said, "No, we're going to my place now. Let me just get my things from the trunk." "I can't," I said. "Of course you can," he said, not letting go.

Try to imagine this—a woman fights, screams, nobody comes, it was late, they'll consider it a family argument, a lover's spat. I didn't like being pushed around, he was suddenly a different man, violent, mean-looking, I could imagine him raping me, killing me, dragging me God knows where. "You're hurting me," I must have said. Then he let go and I ran across the tracks, across the street, not looking back, all the way to the hotel where in the quiet I could remember the gypsy as he had been before, sweet and wild, on the bus. Saved by the train which came between us, and his goods in the trunk. Otherwise he could have caught me in two leaps. I was lucky, I often am.

Years ago, when this story was still fresh in my mind, I had told my friend Cathy about it, knowing that Cathy would love a good story with men in it and Cathy said, "Ann my dear, I wouldn't have fought, I would love to wake up in a gypsy tent with such a hunk." 'Hunk,' she said. Hunk was not the right word for him. He was no hunk, he was a panther. It's different. Cathy didn't understand the real situation, it was movies to her, she didn't think about pregnancy, VD, and for what!

Still, *for what* would have been nice to know, I think now, remembering that night and that time in the seventies and with it a memory of that woman—her. Didn't she wear a blue jump suit that year? Yes, with a pair of cowboy boots, her hair shoulder length with bangs, and that was the year she was given a second chance to live all over again, as in that play by Sartre. Most people are not that lucky. This is not really new information, I knew it even then, startled by the unreality of it—I had walked into a dream.

I must have seen Mira and Rada and looking at them the old question must have come up again as always—*who would I be now?* Looking at them didn't help. They had been young and in love and had many pictures to show for it; at thirty-five, with big kids, they were strong looking, matronly, with that look of self-satisfied boredom that comes from socialism, marriage, and the absence of stress. A part of me didn't want to be in their shoes, another portion said, "They have lived fully, you haven't." No idea what *fully* meant except—everything I am not, what they were. Maybe that mix of boredom and worry. I, Anna, Ann, had, through some bad magic, remained a young girl, didn't age like the others or did but differently, keeping a whole set of gestures, movements that they too had once. The proof of everything—the summer I had met the gypsy on the bus, I had stopped at the university to look and compare the theater departments, and the students flirted with me openly although I didn't believe it in the beginning.

It wasn't flattering but disturbing since it offered possibilities for further camouflage. I could step into a young student persona, erase the other years, and with Western calculation have another life, the one I had missed—become someone else. Yes, I did think about it. Not like this, nothing as orderly, but I must have. In theory, it would work, didn't Cathy's grandfather leave his family and open a saloon and marry a very young woman in Alaska? And there was Susan who left her husband, changed her name and everything, and found herself in San Francisco. It could be done but it meant having to work at it, keeping track of lies, and I knew, thank God, that you don't live your second chance this way. Besides, it wasn't the bodies of those young men I wanted and could have had, not even their love but my own, or some feeling I couldn't get to, or name.

Yes, that was the year I wore a jump suit and spoke mostly about feminism. My classmates in the capital lived well, spending freely on clothes and travels; nothing was saved. Yanna was medicated more and more for something they called 'bad nerves,' the man with green eyes drank, grew fat, they said he mistreated his wife. I left the town secretly that year, afraid of him and his revenge, yet the people continued to talk about us as doomed lovers, as their own Romeo and Juliet, except they didn't die. Our sad story—love and separations—became magnified with the years, his own drunken tales grew bigger, more interesting in detail and I couldn't explain that he made everything up. Of course, we did a few things, kissed and necked, which doesn't count because I was mad with grief over my father, but I insisted on what was true—we never made love. Nobody believed me, not even Yanna, his truth was more interesting.

That year I decided this can't go on, this going back and forth, too confusing. Unhealthy for sure. Exhausting. I accomplished in months what had seemed impossible before— I even erased every bit of my accent; those who didn't know took me for someone from Wisconsin. There was not a moment to spare, plays, writing, directing, kids, schools, a very productive time for sure, if you just keep busy, there is no time to dwell on negative components. Peace is what I wanted and peace I got, two days from now, everything will be fine again. All of us need routines, clear structures, we really do.

Something doesn't ring true in all this, don't you think so? It's lucky I'm all alone, just pictures of places to visit, Plitvice, Ohrid, Split. I smell a problem now. I know my official reasons for things, what I tell others, what I said about me, my views on the U.S. and so forth. I am capable of all sorts of nice perfect answers, you'd be amazed. If you asked me, 'how are you,' the answer is 'just great,' right? No moaning or groaning or kvetching, I know what to do and what not, so they don't get offended. It's easy, you learn those things, the way you are supposed to, you say 'Oh sure, I got used to it,' you say 'sure I do,' or 'it was a bit hard but I worked at it." They love the last one a lot. These are my coverup answers, but I can do them so well, so smoothly nobody can ever tell they are not real, I assure you. The other ones I keep locked up for myself at night and I know at all times what's going on and which are which. However, sometimes, unnoticeably, either out of habit or for some other reason I borrow from my coverup answers and start believing them myself. Like Marsha going around the dorm telling stories about her WASP parents, poor thing. She got all screwed up, it was something, I mean really. So I said, Marsha, cut the shit. *And you my friend are lying now* or giving me incomplete evidence because *look here, baby, these are the facts—someone intent on never coming back wouldn't go and get the red passport that year, would they?* I confront lying Ann like a district attorney. Would she? Ladies and gentlemen of the jury, what do you think? And one more detail, it's important—to get this passport wasn't easy. It took a lot of paperwork and time. So, we are talking about intent, aren't we? What did she intend to do with it?

It could have been a purely symbolic gesture, Ann whispers, like a freshman in college in an Intro to Literature class. I, Anna, know this rings false, symbolic gesture, my ass! Go on, let's hear it—why not tell the truth—the capital lived up to its promise that year—the cafés were full, the linden trees bloomed, the music played, and the city was full of mysterious strangers. And didn't I discover that they talked the same way my thoughts ran before falling asleep—circling, gathering, no goal or aim, so that an ordinary question—how are you—is answered with a story about you, your sister in law, your neighbor, the dreams you had last night. Is that what Byzantine means? I have to say I love it, yes I do. Yet you rushed to get on the plane, as if rescued or saved, then wished the following day you had crashed instead of landing in New York.

Go back where you came from, an old voice reminds me. *Sluts, we'll get you.* See the problem? Even now at this moment, when I am trying hard, the best way I know how to disentangle everything, my summers, my voices, and my men, America keeps interfering once again, confusing me with mixed messages, like a memory of a bad stepmother who fed you but twisted your soul. I'd rather not think about it, except I do. Here is a question for the shrinks—How do you cure yourself of a country? All the psychology books aim for the ordinary disturbances, my mother and me, my father and I, me and my brother, why mom preferred him to me and such. There is no cure for racism either, do you adjust so you don't see it, do you fight back, or do you leave? To go where? Whose case is worse, Marsha's or mine? Mine is, according to me. Who hates more, me or her? Who loves more? I'd rather play *what if*, it's more fun, you can let your mind go.

—What if I never left, what would I think about America now, let's see ...

—Wouldn't think about it. I might even dream of visiting Sunset Boulevard, Disneyland, etc.

—If only you had landed in New York, rather than a redneck state, Marc often says, it would have been so much better. Sure, sure, maybe.

—What if the McCarthy years never happened?

—What if the country were colonized by the Portuguese or French?

It would be a different country. Out with that one.

However, there is a possibility, a small one, that I would have opposed it, even at long distance, and why not? Some perfectly nice people hate India and Indians and others hate France for no apparent reason. It simply irks them when you say French, they foam at the mouth, "I hate their arrogance," they say. Why then, couldn't I, in the name of self-expression, hate too? I can't. *Go back where you came from. Nigger whore! We'll get you,* a fraternity boy shouts at me, in me. I can't see him, just a memory of something metallic, ice cold, I feel the same wave coming up, can't stop it. Pure hatred. I want the bastard dead, I do. But I can't give in to that dumb sound, especially since I know I already know my list of hatreds, too boring to repeat. Instead, aiming for the good times, I cleverly switch gear into the opposite—let's think positively what's good in the country, shall we kids.

Nature is wonderful, American rivers and mountains. The trees are superb.

So are the kids, kids from New York to L.A. are always great.

Never had any problems with blacks for some mysterious reason. It doesn't mean they are all angels, they couldn't be.

No difficulties with the American Indians but I had only known two.

My friends are OK, but look who they are—a crew of the alienated and screwed up. But even they leave constantly like Allen and Rose and then they won't be friends any more. Lots of new friends, Allen writes from L.A., fun people. My friends will never be like the friends mama had, the kind you wake up in the middle of the night and say, please come on over, my mother died, it hurts unbearably. What good is all that politeness, have a great time, enjoy yourself, happy New Year. With whom? Words are easy. How many would be with me if I were dying now, if I lost everything? Maybe one, maybe two. Sure, colleagues sent cards afterwards and looked sheepish the first week, then they left the phone number of a new support group, to help me adjust. Mine are mostly telephone friends, machines talking to machines, leaving messages, when you need arms to hold you. Not like mama's friends for sure. Even Marsha is far, busy busy now. Running rushing getting to.

I did it! My hatred moves into a larger perspective. It's comfortable. It's not directed against one person or persons, but the very system of living, its propaganda machinery. I am afraid this system will alter the landscape, even my dreams will not form—Bali will look like Florida, as Hawaii already does. Just guys in Bermuda shorts relaxed and grinning in every country across all the oceans, China, Poland, name it, all melted down into the soup with Pizza Huts, burgers, no more saris, just blue jeans and on top of it all one big smiling face looking like Ike.

Yes, I am sure it will happen. In '67 already I knew the opposition to it was hopeless and it justified my own position—better live in the belly of the beast than on the fringes waiting for it, getting it all over again, a double dose.

Maybe resistance is possible but how? Who would do it and in the name of what? With what better more subtle machine? The image is perfect, there is nothing better.

This is interesting, it calls for deeper analysis, "let's try to understand it," I say to the class. I am a good teacher, I pace, explain, probe; they can never rest. "Let's see now, shall we, what is so seductive about this image," I turn to them, "there has to be something or it wouldn't work." Silence in class, as always. They either look down at their notebooks or straight ahead, bewildered. I have to do it all.

The image is fluid, light, fast moving. Nothing heavy

about it, no smelling of death, or earth. It's never-ending youth. The stress is on action, on doing, and you keep going but nobody knows if you ever get there or not. So, it's a fun image in pastel colors with no shadows, in lovely muted tones that stay in your head because they are so optimistic. Get it? Images of spring, summers eternal. A young couple jogs, a young couple swims in the ocean, they drink coke and keep laughing.

A pretty picture, no?

It also aims for the lowest common denominator—let's not call it freedom, let's call it greed, freedom to be greedy, to win, to have more, always more than your neighbor. It deals in tangibles, what's easy to see, touch, while poor sad socialism never had a chance—too intellectual, it couldn't succeed in practice any more than religion, how many really love their neighbor more than their car? Of course, this will die too, nothing lasts, it will collapse one day, exhausted by its own contradictions, eaten away by its own cancer. Yeah.

I recognized my dad talking now. Definitely him. Imagine that. Mixing his words with mine. Funny how he sneaks up, a man who was against everything, but he had great rhetorical gifts. It was over. This new hate wave seemed smaller than the one on the coast, uninteresting, less raw somehow and it got diluted toward the end, sort of dried up. Nothing left to say. Done. It was disappointing. It is as if my anger had become fictional, more controlled, no longer mine, maybe I had lost that too. A hell of a detour in order not to think about the central issue—who the hell I am now.

It's not as if I ever spoke like that in class. Lies. All invented. I wished it. Even though I am known as a brilliant

teacher, I mostly talk about motivations, gestures and movement, costumes—acting tools. That sort of thing. These are
just silent ramblings, *as if*. They are half real. My characters
would talk like that, Rachel and Rita, if I still wrote plays
but I gave up on that too. In the eighties. What's more, I
wouldn't be permitted to talk like this in class. Students
might complain, the reason why a professor of sociology was
recently reprimanded for his opinions (quite mild in comparison to my own thoughts!) and with all the budget cuts,
everybody got nervous. He was told to cool it. But let's be
fair, even if censorship didn't exist, I still couldn't do it. It
wouldn't be easy. I would feel ridiculous, the way poor Hoffman
did toward the end of his life; he said, poor man, that he felt
silly preaching liberation to twenty year olds who didn't understand him. He felt sad being younger than them, talking
jive. But he had to keep talking. That was his life. And then
he loved the country. It was his. Maybe if I loved it as much
as he did, maybe then I could talk against everything in
class, the way I can tell Marsha, go fuck off, you bitch. While
with America, I am still, after all these years, in the situation
of a guest in a home you feel uncomfortable in, but can't say
anything to change it. Abbey loved it. I don't. I have no
right to speak. I just rant and rave silently on the train, on
subways and buses in New York too. Talking to myself. It's
life saving. And mind you, it doesn't mean it's not interesting. Some of my best conversations in the eighties were in
this style, it can get quite amusing. Maybe I've invented a
new art form. I am lucky. I don't need to write at all. I am
glad. I know with conviction that some of my thoughts are
better than anything, better than any shit they produce on

Broadway. I am fortunate to have so many thoughts.

A brand new thought jumps out of somewhere and attacks me, an ugly rat. What if you had stayed out of hatred, what if you are addicted to it, how about it? Out of the question! Counter-attack with evidence, my students and my sons. I love them and they said so.

Not out of hatred. Still what were those years but a numbness and coverup? It makes you wonder who wrote those plays. It wasn't me. Is this me talking now? How can I tell? I guess English in translation isn't quite real. It's like kissing from two feet away, saying I love you through a plastic shield, the reason I can say, you prick, fuck, motherfucker, go fuck yourself, asshole—just words, nothing behind them. No not my voice, can't even imagine what that voice would be. My plays were full of others I had absorbed—a musical gift, I was told—voices of people in transit, on buses talking, black maids in Savannah, a gay boy in Illinois. And why my language gifts were often praised, most producers objected to, didn't understand, the absence of a strong central character around whom everything is supposed to revolve.

It's over with, I've covered it all. Another half-hour or so. Through the window, suburbs like anywhere, grim. I began looking at those pictures of the natural beauties of our country, Plitvice, Ohrid, Mostar, when a new thought stabbed me, one I didn't expect. The moment you relax, the worst happens, mark my words. This new thought said very low, 'What if you have loved your sons in the same way, in translation, so to speak?'

Exhausted, I didn't fight. I said, yes it must be true. How else? And let me tell you why. *My darling, my sweet, baby, sugar*, are not mine or are half mine or they don't say what I want them to say. They are neither heavy or light, if I use them or not, it's the same thing. My sons said I was a good mother, I hugged and kissed and said *my darlings*, but is that love? Too too perfect, didn't tell any bad parts, didn't want them upset. It had to be Ann but not both of us. Hate is more specific, I suppose you don't need to be fully engaged. Maybe I've loved no one except this way, call it what you wish, maybe translation is not the right word. What word would it be? Was it me they loved or her, this other person?

Now, as we were approaching the capital, I was forced to admit, wishing it weren't true, that my entire life was one big flop, spent resisting, in pain or numb, translating for others and for myself, and here I was a woman on the threshold of old age, it would be different if I were a young girl.

I couldn't decide if my predicament was like a mechanical error—due to mother's decision to leave—or something like a tragic flaw in my person, in this inability to let go of my childhood and adjust. Others did it after all. And what now? Didn't I ask Marc once, "Don't you think in some cases it's better not to open up the lid and re-examine? You poke and poke and what if there is no answer?" I can't remember what he said. I had asked him one morning, he is a shrink, he should know, "I've been dreaming for years I've killed someone, a girl, I think, and I'm the only one who knows." He said nothing. There was nothing he could do.

In the distance, dimly lit, like on stage, I perceived them dancing, swirling silently in different costumes, Anna's and Ann's, and with sadness I couldn't camouflage, I thought it's too bad. I was really pretty. I never quite knew it. And now it's too late. I wished for tears which refused to come.

I was always helped by others, some perfect strangers have rescued me from grief. Instead of being crushed by everything I had concluded about my life, I hear Jerry laugh at the party just before I left on the trip. "You think you got troubles," he said to someone, "now hear this. I've spent years being a good son and good husband and a good father too. I've been nothing but goodness itself. I finally manage to admit to everyone that I'm gay but I've really picked the best possible time for it—I'm fifty, losing my hair, and everywhere everybody is dying of AIDS." Jerry roared, he couldn't stop laughing. Thinking about him cheered me up. That man knew how to handle the absurd.

First city houses appeared. Any moment now. Strangely, after all this, I didn't feel bad, if anything I was lighter, airier. Maybe this was what I had been searching for all along, like a name for my tribe—DISPLACED, DÉRACINÉ, DÉPAYSÉ, DISLOCATED, DP—all absences of, even my own face missing. That's who I was, a displaced person.

Now what?

Now nothing, Anna said, casually, we just continue.

Part Five

Chapter One

The train station looked and smelled as before; something about the stale odor of sweat and urine affected me the way summer nights do, or rather it brought on a peculiar excitement, of being madly alive, of drama before the storm. Then fear invaded me as before. It was reassuring that I had an old fear, unclear, imprecise, and because it was an old feeling repeated, it seemed more gentle, tamed this time. It's here, around this dark, filthy train station full of beggars, gypsies, and peasants in wool hats that I know I have left Europe behind and any minute something could go out of control, and from there to disaster. It's enough to see how they spit, how they drove; nobody waited in the line for a cab. Around me, they pushed, shoved; years ago, coming from Paris, I wanted to turn back; now I thought maybe I should get on the first plane to New York. If not today, tomorrow definitely. I spotted a hotel across across the street.

In the lobby of the Hotel Balkan, the receptionist looked at me with a heavy-lidded gaze. "Alone?" he pronounced in half murmur, like an invitation.

"Yes," I said.

"How long?"

"Just one night."

Another look from his direction then, "Just one ... well ... come tomorrow and let's see if we can arrange something."

"I need a room for tonight." I said.

"Of course you need everything right now," he barked, "all of us do but there's an Italian shoe fair on and a Japanese something or other, don't you know? There's no room anywhere in the city ... unless you want to stick around ... then, who knows, something might turn up."

I guessed what 'stick around' meant. Had I addressed him in English he would have been more polite, no doubt about it, respectful even, but your own you treat like shit.

He was eyeing me, waiting; no respectable woman travels alone, his eyes said, who are you kidding. I despised him. He even looked like somebody I knew, the same boorishness of a peasant in a limosine. The problem was I couldn't think of a single good phrase to express all this, 'go fuck yourself, you pig, you prick,' all those words I learned in the U.S.

Outside, I wondered what to do, maybe find a travel agency and see about a plane, then I remembered the hotel—a strictly native joint—no Italian or Japanese would want it. If it still exists. If I can find it. It wasn't near.

I put my suitcase on the carrier and moved away from the train station heading east. First, you had to go up the hill, a steep old Balkan street full of little shops, to the center of town, then walk across the park. Somewhere there the hotel would be.

It was warm, humid, the streets crowded. I moved slowly. Most light signals didn't work or if they did the cars didn't care. Careful now! Immense gray trams rattled and thundered as if at any moment they would fall apart then explode. My luggage carrier attracted too much attention—obviously they hadn't seen one before. People stared openly, commenting on it, later they would retell the story about this woman and her funny gadget. My cowboy boots had attracted the same attention fifteen years ago.

Here, away from the coasts, tourists were invisible or they melted into the grayness of a city that didn't offer them much. Maybe for a day in passing, maybe two but no more. There were no recognizable statues or churches to photograph, it wasn't known for its food; it looked faintly Mideastern in spite of the fact that it was rebuilt after the war. This gray sprawling city didn't hold any big nostalgia for me either, nothing carefully recorded. For me too it was a place of transit, temporary, linked to hotel rooms with one or two exceptions; I had come here with the green eyes and he gave me a ring on this same Balkan street that summer.

There were no major changes downtown—the same large cafés, same stores, but going east toward the park I couldn't miss the large M of the McDonalds and right next to it a similar type of place painted bright red. A Pizza Hut? How could they order pizza without laughing or making jokes about it—that word used to mean little pussy, little cunt, ever since I could remember, unless they had a different name for it now. I couldn't imagine myself going in and asking for a slice.

Soon I was inside the park where the grandparents sat with kids in front of them. They looked the same as always—solid, sturdy, watchful in hand-knitted sweaters. Here and there mothers sat with shopping bags, all dressed up in suits and high heels. I wondered how Mira would be dressed now and if she would laugh at my sneakers. Thinking about Mira I thought about Yanna and felt both guilt and regret. It was a cowardly thing to do.

Yanna's face was all that remained of my many thoughts on the train. The rest vanished, leaving only a residue of something unpleasant, incomplete; I was once again in a new situation; you've got to adjust.

The hotel was at the edge of the park where I had hoped it would be. A cheap place not known to most people, I can't recall how I found it the first time. In fact, it wasn't a real hotel, but ages ago it was known for its marvelous dance floor, where Mira and others went on Saturday nights. By the time I got to it in the seventies, it was not important any more, except in the provinces.

The café in front was full of young and old, all men. The cafés were always full, any café, from morning to night, giving the impression of a permanent holiday. They take a coffee break and don't bother to go back to work, I had told friends in New York but nobody believed me.

Men looked at me, and then the suitcase. From top to bottom, toward the sneakers, up again, then directly into the eyes, a style that was known as a 'provocative glance.' A way to spot a true virgin because virgins would blush. It was a lazy interest without any rush, with a taste of *locum*, who is that, who is she, their eyes said, a piece of that would surely be fine, not that I am too pressed.

I couldn't imagine how I looked to them, maybe nervous, a bit weird, a grown woman in sneakers pulling her suitcase on a strange little cart.

At the entrance, two middle-aged women worked—one with a bucket and a mop, another polishing the brass handles. The walls were peeling and the narrow red carpet had many old stains but the curving staircase was elegant with bevelled mirrors that went all the way up to the third floor.

In the reception room on the third, everybody was glued to the TV, shouting and cursing, like at a soccer match. I gathered from their talk that the country was bankrupt and that the era of so-called Communism was over. Ended officially yesterday, while I was visiting my old street, thinking this and that. Funny nobody said anything. The kids at that café spoke only about dogs. That's why his head was cut off, I remembered the bronze Tito, maybe it happened months ago.

A man who didn't look any different from the other four around the TV noticed me finally and said, "For how many days?" "A few," I said, afraid he wouldn't give me a room for just one night. I handed him my red passport, knowing I could always use the other one to get out, my escape. "I'm glad you have a room for me," I said. "With all those fairs I was worried."

"There'll always be a room for you," he said. "You're an old guest."

"Thank you," I said. Me an old guest? He had thick black hair and a small moustache that he touched and twirled every so often. I didn't remember him at all. I'd never seen him in my life.

"That's not all," he bragged, "the last time you were here it was with a foreign person."

"Really?"

"I don't miss a thing," he said and winked. A cop? No, just a compulsive liar.

The only foreign person had to be Marc, funny how I had erased his visit. It was short, that's why. Ages ago, after a conference on the coast. Maybe for a day or two, no more. It's coming back now, didn't we argue? No. But he looked unhappy. He said, didn't he, that he'll never know me, never, here, I was some other person. He just couldn't get why I laughed all the time and what was so funny. Poor Marc. I was some other person. It was nice of him to suggest that I stay longer, his conference and reason for coming were over, I was glad he didn't accompany me to my hometown, what would he understand about our concerns. He would look at Yanna and see symptoms but not the way she jumped into the bushes, and Mira would turn out to be just an ordinary little coquette, ditzy like his cousin Lynn. He didn't know Mira when we swam together and everything was wonderful, including the river. He must have known all that, the reasons he said I should stay longer. Marc was an understanding person, it's his profession. There is nothing you could reproach him, nothing irrational, I am sure even his thoughts are good, better than mine. Didn't I meet that gypsy around the same time? Sure. Right after he left.

There were about twenty rooms in all, a kind of hotel where you spent a night and left, maybe after a wedding. The receptionist remembered me because I stayed longer and with Marc. Marc couldn't like this place, everything must have been full the last time too.

It was the best room in the hotel, the guy said, letting me into Number Five which overlooked the park and the church with the gold domes. The gypsy said five was a good number, one that promised a lot. Promised what? Inside, everything was disintegrating slowly, the paint, the pipes, the water was rust colored for a minute or more. The light next to my bed needed a bulb, the sheet was too small for a bed of that size—when I lay down, the sheet bunched in the middle. The bedspread had not been cleaned for a long time; I sniffed it, hoping that whoever used it didn't have lice. The worst of all, I'll wake up tomorrow morning at dawn; the two large windows had only flimsy white curtains.

The manager said they had no light bulbs, and besides the lamp is kaput. "You have an overhead light, just get in the bed, what do you need a lamp for," he said, and went on to tell me that he was worried for a minute about my accent but thank God my passport said where I was born. Indirectly I learned that I had a faint accent from the Western parts and that nationalism was on the rise now that Communism was over.

He waited for me to fill him in, tell him more about my accent and my relatives but it was best not to get involved, or he would notice how much I didn't know. "I've lived abroad," I said.

Downstairs, in the restaurant on the second floor, the old waiter said they still had a few things left over from lunch. I ate what he suggested—stuffed peppers with veal and rice, a tomato salad and two pieces of apple strudel with walnuts. Tired and full, I fell asleep and would have slept till the next morning if the music didn't wake me up around midnight. The entire room shook. The famous dance floor was directly under my bed.

It was pointless to fight. I got dressed and went downstairs to watch.

All the tables were taken and the floor was packed too. I ordered a glass of wine, not regretting they woke me up. It was a perfect spot, you could see everything from this position—both the musicians and the dancers, the works. The dance was unusual, a mix of folk and rock but done with hip movements so that it appeared Mideastern, a modified belly dance. The women had an old type of femininity you don't see any more—soft white arms, round shoulders, tiny waists with undulating hips and an overall impression of languor and abandon that brought to mind Yanna and the word *odalisque*. The men, by contrast, appeared more fierce, like hunters, at least on the dance floor. Plains and wild horses, a gallop in the dust. The gypsy was like that, I remembered.

By now he must be toothless, they age fast, I thought, relieved by this. Just an old decrepit guy. No regrets for my hometown either. That too is over. Maybe a more peaceful time awaited me after all. I felt sleepy, detached, pleasantly empty.

"Don't I know you from somewhere?" a tall man asked, someone I would call a youth in the States. Twenty-five or so, dressed in a suit of an Italian cut.

"I don't think so," I said coolly.

This was a standard approach anywhere but I didn't anticipate the next line. "You're right," he said. "We haven't met. It's just that you remind me of what's her name in *Fatal Attraction*."

Of course I had to laugh but he was quite serious. "You really do, honest," he said.

"It must be my hair," I said as curtly as possible. I didn't look like that witch but there was no way to know for sure how I appeared to them. I must do all sorts of things differently, maybe bite my lips and tons of small facial movements, like tics that American women do when nervous, but the most likely explanation was my presence drinking at the bar. In total freedom reserved for the world of men. A whore? No, whores don't wear sneakers.

"I love your image," he said, just like that other kid. I bit my lip trying not to laugh. Just finish your drink and go back to bed but I was having a good time until this kid appeared and he had no business intruding on my life.

"I love your hair," he said and stuck his fingers in it. He sniffed it. I shook my hair free but wasn't going to budge. I had as much right as him to sit here at the bar. This was unexpected. I didn't think there was a reason to worry about such nonsense, not at my age, this was not on my list of problems, and besides only a couple of weeks ago I was certain that everything in my life had been settled, then sometime soon I'll have—what was it they called it—peaceful maturity. And now, in addition to my own internal matters, I didn't need these kids to complicate my life and follow me around. Did they need a mother, or did I communicate something to them without knowing it? Maybe. In the past, they only liked young women here.

The manager passed by, twirling his moustache. It was very important to keep a good image or he'll start pestering me too. My window gave onto the terrace, he could break in if he wanted to. He won't, just New York paranoia creeping in. Everywhere you go you think murder, muggings, rape.

The last time, they made fun of me.

The young man didn't move. He offered me a cigarette which I accepted politely. Maybe he had decided to act civilized. However, he eyed me in the style of the young Brando, sort of under the lashes. His killer look. Then in one fast move he whispered something and went for my neck, kissing and saying things. He had a sweet fresh smell of young boys about him. Peppermint? Touching somehow. I pushed him away gently and got up.

He followed me. "Stop that!" I said, trying not to make a scene. He only shrugged, not disturbed at all. "I like you," he said, "what's the big deal. Why are you so selfish? I like your hair. Honest."

God knows what he wanted, the actress from *Fatal Attraction*, or me. I slammed the door, thinking for a second, why not be selfish after all.

On the white sheets, I saw cockroaches for the first time, big dark ones. They scattered immediately, as if afraid of the light. I squashed two with my foot, the others escaped.

I left the overhead light on and got into the bed, worried about the cockroaches but not for too long. Sleep overtook me and soon the music downstairs stopped.

Chapter Two

The blinding light woke me up early in the morning; I put a pillow over my head and slept on. Much later, I heard murmurs, women talking, and wasn't sure where I was. Outside, on the terrace, someone was moving about but there was nothing to worry about—the window was stuck. I saw only a woman in a white kerchief watering the plants under my window and, further across the park, the church with gold domes.

At half past ten, I had missed breakfast. Too bad, I was starved. '*Fatal Attraction*,' I thought, combing my hair, then spotted two cockroaches on the floor. They escaped before I could get them.

The manager was in the same place watching some discussion on TV and muttering to himself. "There are cockroaches in my room," I said. "Lots of them."

"Fuck them, fuck everybody," he said. "Are you leaving today?"

"No, not today. I'll tell you when. What about those bugs?"

"There's nothing I can do about them," he said. "It's a Russian breed, aren't they sort of red?"

"I didn't look at them well."

"There's nothing I can do. We sprayed everything last week but they come up from the kitchen. That's where they nest. It's hopeless really, this part of town is infested."

"Why?"

"You think I know? Old houses. They must have been here since the Turks. I'll bet you anything, if the Germans took over, they would know what to do."

He stretched, then yawned; he looked stubbly, had forgotten to shave. "I need a nap," he said. "We got plastered last night. With everything that's going on, it's best not to think, don't you think so?"

"It would be nice," I said. "Am I late for breakfast?"

"Yeah ... but don't worry, just say Mirko said it's OK. While you're there tell them to send me some coffee, tell the waitress to make it with her own hands and put it in a big cup."

The phones rang, all of them at once. "Fucking whore of a phone, fuck the bastard who invented it. Fuck the TV too," Mirko said, then picked one up.

The big ballroom was empty now and hard to recognize in the sunlight. Even the piano and the chandeliers looked different, the dance floor appeared huge. Only one table was occupied, the other guests must have gotten up ages ago. From the kitchen the sound of folk music came on the radio, along with the humming from the cooks. "He had asked her, and she had let him kiss her red, red lips."

The waitress motioned me to sit in the breakfast section

next to a table with a festively-dressed couple. "Mirko said he wants some strong coffee in a big cup," I told her but she only said, "He would, wouldn't he," with a smirk.

At the other table, a man and a woman were talking low, not a married couple, judging by the way they looked at each other, and how he stroked her hand. I wasn't sure of this, was only betting with myself in the absence of any other information. That's all I could tell about them so far, much less than I would know about an American couple whose clothes and gestures would put them into a definite category right away. With a sentence here and there you could guess pretty well their backgrounds, schools, and then it was easy without major surprises, they were clearly defined, you had a map.

These people were trickier, more opaque. The woman was overdressed, with rouged cheeks, in the States you'd think secretary or waitress and you'd be right. This woman could surprise you, she could turn out to be a doctor, an architect, a mathematics teacher, I had often made a mistake in this area, either because their looks didn't help or because I didn't know enough. You were never a grown-up here, that's the problem.

I didn't know how to look or what to look for, nor could I see them as separate from each other; I, me, American style didn't exist or if it did I didn't see it. It merged with others and disappeared like tricky underground rivers and you could never quite catch it or say 'so and so is this or that,' not like in the U.S. where all those friends have clear problems within distinct categories—parents, siblings, money, job, ambition, and it was the quantity or quality that defined them. They were totally open about it. I deserve more, they said. I need a different lifestyle. It you knew certain mathematical components—x + y + z—you knew them pretty well. They made it easy for you and they followed the basic rules of dramatic structure, the three important questions in drama, the main one being, 'what do I want?' That's why the U.S. is so dynamic, I lectured now, with a certain admiration, *what do I want* is spelled out with clarity. Definitely.

Here, nothing but dimness, impossible to see clearly on the outside or inside, and yet everything they did was fascinating, the way this man in front of me picked up a loose hair from the woman's dress, as if in slow motion, the way her shoulders moved toward him and his mouth whispered.

The waitress was a part of the mystery too, not that she would be fascinating to everyone. She brought the ham omelette, bread, and coffee without any signs of professional service. She would be called surly elsewhere but she was no different from other woman in the shops, on the street, neither surly or polite—that's how they are. Without a mask of niceness or any other, her face appeared naked, offered to others without protection. She looked tired, that's what you saw. Smile, smile, I remembered, why don't you smile. Why, why I kept asking, but nobody said why. Smile, don't look so serious, my colleagues said, your trip is going to be great, aren't you excited?

That's it! That kid last night misunderstood my smile. It meant other things to him, maybe an invitation, here I am, come and get me. Maybe. I was too polite, must have smiled even when I said, 'don't bother me,' and of course he took it to mean 'I adore you.' I had learned to smile automatically, maybe too much, maybe at wrong moments, the way some handicapped people learn things, the way the colorblind tell colors. You overdo it.

I thought about her again, the girl who was passing. I recognized her by that too. She overdid everything. I can't somehow think of her as Marsha.

It was a good omelette, cooked with lard. It was the best omelette ever and it came with the room, a bargain at fifteen dollars. With the red passport only. With the blue one it would be much more, maybe double. Sure, there were cockroaches on the floor, and the bathroom smelled of urine, but still it was only fifteen bucks a night. Maybe I got the passport for practical reasons and no more. It's as good a reason as any.

The waitress would have been very beautiful if she didn't have two teeth missing. She wasn't the only one. Everywhere you turned, somebody had a tooth missing. They aged fast, didn't bother with improvements. This girl was tall, slim with high cheekbones, dressed in a pretty navy uniform with matching boots laced up around the ankle, leaving the toes and heel uncovered.

"Not last year, not this year either," the woman at the next table said. She sighed heavily.

"I will remain hungry, so hungry for the sea," she said, pain in her face. There was no way to translate adequately what she really meant—that she hadn't had a vacation by the seashore in two years, what she desired, what she wanted, there was no right word for the unfulfilled need that's unjust, unfair, that was promised in socialism equally to everyone. In America we are free to pursue happiness, here they were promised justice but they got fucked over. I conversed with myself.

"And cherries," she said, "that too, just a handful this summer. I'll stay hungry for cherries too."

I never paid attention to food in New York, I could have cherries in any season, not just in June. Now my mouth reacted, I wanted cherries too. Going back up, I heard mama say, "Anna, my only one, I'll stay hungry for you."

The lobby looked empty. A light breeze came from the terrace. The manager was gone. The maids were having a coffee break in the laundry room; a young blonde with a braid motioned me over. "Mirko says you're one of my own," she said and named a village further up the stream. Where Lena lived, the girl who used to bring us milk. "Sit down, have some," she said, and gave me a cup. The other two were older, with large laps, grandmothers most likely. "Pretty," one said, touching my hair.

"What a figure," the other one added, and touched my waist.

"You'll drive some man wild," laughed the first, exposing a gold tooth on both sides.

"We are better looking than any, aren't we?" said the blonde with the long braid.

"We certainly are," I said, trying to sound just right. I had heard that before, the town's pride in their beauty, their superior intelligence, their humor, and their famous water, not that it existed any longer.

"You must starve yourself," gold tooth said, "to have a waist like that."

"Food is not important to me," I said, aware that nobody

said that ever. A sentence in translation.

"I wish it didn't matter to me," the dark one laughed. "You know, I could eat a whole chicken now."

"Which reminds me," the blonde said, "my son's birthday is coming up and we'd better get us a piglet from the village."

There is nothing as good as a suckling pig, crisp, golden, if only I could have some of that piglet from her village. "How old is your son?" I asked.

"Here is my baby, mother's treasure," she said, opening her wallet. In a photo, a chubby, handsome boy sat princely in a chair, naked, his penis half erect and rather large. The women cackled about his penis and whether he takes after his father when it came back to me—he had carried pictures of his kids too! I had seen him in the seventies right in this hotel, briefly. Amazing I forgot it. It's nice to know we sort of made up.

It must have been after Marc left and after the gypsy that he appeared suddenly in my room. He bragged that he found me thanks to his special connections with the secret police, but it wasn't likely. Yanna told him. Yanna didn't know how to keep a secret because she forgot easily what she was told and only the exciting parts remained in her mind, like this hotel with the dance floor. Still, no matter how he found me, it would explain why I wanted the red passport, only the foreign ones were registered with the police, he said. That would be a pretty good reason. I hated the idea of secret police snooping, bugging; I had a long history with them in the States. Not that I ever did anything major.

It was probably friendly and brief. He had come to the capital for other reasons and had stopped by to show me those pictures. A boy and a girl, big already. I must have shown him the pictures of my sons too, and he must have looked at them for a long time. All in all, he was more civilized, mature, but didn't he boast about his new mistress, wasn't she the reason why he was visiting the capital? Yanna too had said something about his mistresses and how in the old prison they had orgies.

"Is he handsome?" the gold tooth laughed. "I see a man in your eyes."

"He was," I said.

"Your eyes are like fire," she said. "I love your eyes."

"Drive him mad," the other woman roared.

"Go on! Life is short," said the blonde.

Chapter Three

I kept thinking of cherries at the market, I am hungry for the cherries when I saw a young peasant girl selling straw-berries, my favorite fruit. The girl said you don't wash wild strawberries, you'd kill them and what's there to wash, she had picked them this morning. She sold me her last batch and I ate them out of the bag, slowly, letting each strawberry melt on my tongue. Everyone should taste wild strawberries, there's nothing like them. Nothing, I assure you.

The market smelled as before—of fruit, flowers, and people, all intermingled. "Here, come here," men shouted, "Young potatoes, tender beans! Sweet juicy peaches! Try my cream!" Bees were everywhere, attracted by watermelons and pears, but nobody seemed to mind them too much. And as before, gypsies wondered about, women with kids in their arms, reading fortunes. Yes, I was tempted, but let's be seri-ous, what would they tell me I didn't know?

My strawberries were almost gone. was almost by the exit when next to the flower stand I saw a middle-aged man selling *cilims* and old lace. A pair of curtains had the same pattern as mother's old ones we left behind, funny we took nothing with us, all those beautiful pillowcases and table-cloths she had made.

It's unwise, I decided, putting the curtains down. They might not fit and my apartment is too modern for lace. I touched the old *cilim*, thinking maybe. It was quite worn but of a beautiful rose shade you don't find now.

"How much is it?" I asked. He had another customer now, a woman who wanted to buy lace.

"Wait a minute," he said, "till I am done with her." I was in no rush.

The woman left without buying anything, but he didn't seem eager to sell the rug. He was chewing on a toothpick looking at my hands. "You had strawberries," he said.

"They were good," I said. "How much is ..."

"Free for you," he said low, "take whatever you want, then we go somewhere and I love you to death." His breath smelled of garlic and tobacco.

I was sure I had misheard it, no normal person would say this in broad daylight, selling carpets. "How much is the rose *cilim*," I repeated. "I'm in a rush."

"You heard me. Don't be a virgin," he said. "You won't regret it. I've got some wildcat in these pants." It wasn't hard to guess what wildcat meant, even though that was a new expression. He touched himself in a way men did here, as if itching or rearranging their balls.

I pulled away but he grabbed my hand and wouldn't let go. He was slimy, grizzled, he smelled bad.

"Take your filthy paw off me," I screamed very loudly,

knowing instantly this was a bad translation. A clumsy thing to say. But I didn't anticipate his reaction—after all, he had attacked me, what in the hell was he so upset about?

"Whose filthy hand! How dare you call me filthy! Look at my hands!" he shouted menacing me, getting ready to fight. Maybe he was a Muslim, it occurred to me, they had a big thing about that word filthy, I vaguely remembered.

A crowd formed immediately. He was shouting and calling me filthy now.

"What happened?" an older man tried to help.

"Nothing much. I just didn't want him touching me," I said. "He had no right."

"Communism," the old gentleman said, "that's the problem, they assume everything is theirs. Even our souls."

"What's the big deal," another man said, "you won't die of it. So he touched you, so what!"

"She called me filthy, she said my hands are filthy," the *cilim* guy kept shouting.

"I just told him to take his hands off me," I said, "nothing more. I don't know what he is shouting about."

"Muslim, most likely," somebody said, "you know how they are. Tricky. They'll kill you for a word. That's how my brother died in 1943."

Not fair, I thought. Why couldn't he be our own creep.

In back of me, I heard whispers that were loud enough, "If he were younger, she wouldn't complain, would she?"

"Of course not."

"Probably teased him to death and now she complains," a woman's voice chimed in. A bitch, I thought, a goddamned bitch. I didn't tease anyone.

"She talks funny too, did you notice," they said in back of me.

"Must be our fancy lady from the North. They know how to put on airs."

"Most likely. Look at her."

"I personally think she is from our Western parts. They are worse than anybody," somebody said.

"Brother, I agree. How many did they kill! Half of my family went!"

"They are starting again," another woman said. "My sister and kids just packed her suitcases and left Zagreb."

"At least the Germans admitted it. Not them. I hear they say we invented it all. Can you imagine that? Can you! I could kill when I hear it. Half of my family went."

"I hear they call us barbarians, and they did all the butchery."

"Bastards! They hate us for not punishing them. We're dumb! Too soft. We wouldn't even have a record of the camps if it weren't for Israel."

Soon they forgot all about me as if I had been not been the center of this drama but a pretext for them to get together, to start on the real events, now, yesterday, what sounded like the beginning of a civil war. Even the rug merchant was shouting now about something or other. I slipped away.

I had overreacted, that's for certain, I had nobody to blame but myself. Just my lack of experience in an uncivilized country. Imagine, what would happen to me in Istanbul, for example! All their troubles stem from there. Five centuries of darkness. Not a small thing. And democracy is foreign to them, they never had it. Kingdoms, Turks, and peasant socialism, and here they are in the computer era, the twentieth century ending.

I bought a paper and went to read it in the café across the street from the market. The rug merchant disappeared from my head, a minor event that could be erased.

Inside, it was blue with smoke and packed with men drinking yellow stuff in small glasses. They noticed my arrival mutely, bit by bit they examined me luxuriously, every gesture was recorded—my blue dress, bare arms, sandals, bag. I made a good impression, I could tell, but there were a few puzzling questions in their eyes, not a slut, no, but what was she doing here all alone in a restaurant full of men. Most likely they would talk about me later, wishing I could hear how they would describe me, what would they add to make the story take shape. An event of some sort would have to be invented, something I did, or a fascinating man who appeared suddenly at the door, and eventually a drama began. Depending how you looked at it, they were either pathological liars or storytellers, I had always observed that coming here from the States. It was all very entertaining, but you could never trust them. I could never have married one of them.

The paper was a good idea, a nice prop. With a notebook out, I could even pass as a reporter, which would then explain why I was sitting in this café, rather than in some other more respectable place downtown, large, sunny, more middle-class.

The men had gotten used to me. Their eyes were not offensive, but sad; even though they were together, each appeared to be in a dream of his own. I could relax, read the paper, and forget about them. I wished for some coffee but the waiter was not to be seen. The tablecloth was stained with wine, a blue indigo color, and remains of eggs on which flies gathered and buzzed. The papers shouted revenge against this group or that; two football teams exchanged blows, some broken bones. The rest was unclear, all sorts of events had taken place without my knowledge. The last time in the seventies, the papers preached peasant marxism, but no more. The tone had changed. The usual words were gone. Tito was still alive the last time, I can't remember if he had died in the eighties or late seventies. I had won a bottle of champagne when Marc said the country would fall apart, right away. I had said no, it won't. It looked like it was happening now, but I couldn't quite get it, no more than hearing about Michelle's hate-filled divorce in California. "But you were so much in love" I kept saying, forgetting I had not seen them for a long time. "We were," Michelle said, "and now we're not."

The paper said sugar, coffee, oil would double soon but the 1991 harvest from tourism promises to be good, every bed was booked. There were suggestions on how to make it better and more profitable—more bars and clubs, more organized folk-dancing for the tourists, nicer uniforms for the waiters. I couldn't get upset about the invasion of the coast— it seemed far away, and besides it had happened already. It happened in Spain too. There was nothing I could do about anything. It was over. The dollar went up again. Great. I was glad I didn't pay immediately, already the price of my room was down one third from yesterday and tomorrow it might be less. A whole page of pinups with bare asses on page four, and a recipe for a rum cake. A preview of fall fashions from Paris. I couldn't tell if the girls with bare asses were native or foreign, not much of their faces were visible. Foreign, most likely, too slick, real pros, those tall blonds. No mention of civil war anywhere. Problems in Germany, sick kids in Iraq, cripples from Desert Storm.

The last couple of pages were the most interesting—reserved for the dead people. Dead, young and old and middle-aged, men and women, peasants in costumes and those well-dressed, children and babies—stared directly ahead in their old pictures, frozen and yet alive. Underneath the photo there was a paragraph or more written like a love letter, with grief that made no attempt to hide. "You were our only hope, our future, our passion, we died with you my dearest, my only one, my unbearable wound, yours forever, mom and dad." Some had many friends and relatives because the same picture appeared over again and different people said, "goodbye my love, I'll never forget you, you took a part of me into the grave." All of them carried the date and the time of the burial or the announcement of the next step, a gathering at the grave after forty days, and another one in six months, then the major one when a year was over.

Mama snuck in, I could tell by the way my stomach quivered. Alone, in a foreign cemetery without anyone to visit her with flowers and food, to commemorate her once a year at least. The way she said it would be. She always said so. She said, "I'll remain hungry in my grave for you." Here, she would have had a picture in the paper and friends around the grave to warm her up and all the other rituals would be done, the way it's supposed to be, to make the passage easier for the soul while it wanders, looking for that permanent place where peace awaits you. Yes, sure, fine, but Chicago is as far away from New York as it is from here to Paris, you should have died closer to me and I would visit you. It's not practical, imagine it, to take the plane, then check into a hotel in Chicago and run to the cemetery, rush back. You shouldn't have left in the first place! You decided to, not me. So, don't complain!

But why feel bad for her and not him. Two different cemeteries, both anonymous, cold, on flat land where prairies used to be. Her case is worse, she did all the necessary stuff for him, food and prayers, he'll rest in peace. Not her. Mama's soul will wander, just like her brothers' did, all over Bosnia.

I could have done some of it, but I wasn't sure how, had lost it or never learned it in the first place. I had left too young to know how to bury the dead. But there is more to it—I had refused it consciously, the primitive mumbo-jumbo that my teachers lectured against. I had even refused the christenings which the poor woman desperately wanted for her grandsons. It would have been easy, just sprinkle some water and make her happy. I said no. I have every right to bring up my kids the way I want to. And besides it was second-hand—it felt borrowed, no longer real, the same as the Yoruba chants in Brooklyn. Marc agreed on everything. It was his opinion too. He had always cringed at savage rituals of broken glass at the weddings, the absurdity of bar mitzvahs. He left all that behind when he married me, he had escaped, the way he always knew he would.

I am no longer sure I would have refused anything here.

It would have been part of me, I couldn't see it as absurd. *'Who would I be?'* appeared again, the same annoying useless question. Dead faces on the page made me stop. The question is wrong! It implied choice like those personal ads in the *New York Review of Books,* so clearly spelled out, down to precise details: Forty-year-old white lesbian looking for a white collaborative lover. Non-smoker. Into exercise and health. Preferably a soft butch.

I imagined it briefly—I go to see Mira and say, "Look, I've decided I'm gay. That's who I am. And what's more, I am tired of my lifestyle. Time to change it." Mira wouldn't understand a thing. It would be funny.

I would have been ordinary, like the rest of them. It's a peasant country. If you don't think in terms of choice, choice doesn't exist. Who am I, wouldn't exist. I would be like Mira, we came from the same mold.

Thinking of Mira, I almost see myself, this Anna that wasn't, with some extra weight, a walk that's slower and closer to the earth, and I have a very different expression, that silly kid wouldn't fool around with a woman like that, nor would he be interested. I would look too worried, my face would move less. It's funny how different languages affect your face, shaping it differently, wrinkling it here rather than there, just look at the French pout, directly related to the sound U, and everybody says they pout because they are sexy. Just U, I had told my students.

Starting to lecture again. Something annoying about that voice. Who am I lecturing to? Marc? Kids? I had detected it for the first time two months ago and blamed it on what the French so beautifully call *déformation professionelle,* the result of teaching, lecturing, trying to educate, with greater and greater ignorance around you, it's not easy.

You can't assume anything, you have to explain. Instead of Beckett, Camus, Chekhov as reference points, you have to find some other words to reach them. By the time you do, it's two or three steps removed from the original idea. I end up translating, simplifying, reducing until it's no longer what it was intended to be. But if I just went on, nobody would get anything. I tried it once, for a week.

It's a lonely profession, mostly talking to yourself, re-membering what you said, what you couldn't. I should quit, then I'll lose that ugly voice. Will the voice stop? I would like to keep grandma's voice, but it wasn't the best voice to converse with. What I need is something more ordinary, to communicate with others. In what language, though?

Trolleys rattled outside. The men didn't move at all, the waiter just poured more brandy into their glasses and the smoke got thicker. He brought my coffee in a brass Turkish *dzezva*, with a glass of water and a sugar cube on the side. In a friendly gesture, he waved his rag and killed two flies on the table, brushed them onto the floor. I stared at the dead faces in the paper, the towns they came from, the sweet diminutives of their names. I would be Anka, Ankica, de-pending who said it. Boris said Anushka. Every morning he said, Ankica, let's go to the movies, when I'm big you'll marry me won't you, Anko. Ankice, Boris said, where should we go, now that we got rid of that dog. Boris said all sorts of things you couldn't translate into English, English is no good for loving or grieving, not that it doesn't have its strengths in the concrete.

From here, the conference on the coast seemed far away and so did New York and Chicago. I wasn't angry with those scholars any more, they were who they were, that's all. They wanted familiar things too, and who can tell if their desire for breakfast cereals or burgers is any less good than mine for wild strawberries or cherry strudel. You can't argue about the nature of desire, can you, even if you know that it's not good for you, even if it can kill you, like constant red meat. Their desires were different that's all. It was nobody's fault.

Maybe a culture is nothing more than a group bound by familiar sounds and smells, more than any grandiose idea. *Et tout le reste c'est la littérature.* This struck me as highly original, I wondered if somebody had written about it.

Still, all in all, I'm neither here or there, I thought, elaborating on what I knew already. If at least I were Jewish it would help. They are not wandering and homeless really, they have each other. There is no comparison. I am much more homeless, not that anyone would see it. I understood and forgave some of my friends who, after a brief stint with SDS and rebellion in the sixties, flocked to synagogues in the seventies, with kids and bar mitzvahs, making funny excuses and looking sheepish. It made sense. It was nothing more than wanting some familiar sounds and smells to lose themselves in something larger than me, I. Who knows, I might have been tempted myself to go in the same direction if Marc were not such a diehard. He never wavered, he said all religions are dangerous. More blood spilled over stupidity. They spread hate rather than love, he said, and of course he was right. There was something admirable about his position, his belief in the clear blue light of reason, his steady position that never changed. He would be disappointed if he knew that secretly I wished I had a group of some sort to belong to. It couldn't be invented.

I am condemned, I thought calmly, nothing to cling to, no group at all, but didn't notice that this dark smelly café by the market was not different from the one in my hometown, was almost identical to the tavern where my grandfather drank for hours, squandering his fortune, his health and his life on gypsy music and laments that had no name in English. A place like this would have frightened me ages ago, I would have hated the apparent gloom of brandy and glossy eyes. Now, I just kept sitting, enveloped in thick smoke, not waiting for anything good or bad to happen. When I stopped all thought, I was so relaxed that it resembled happiness, a state of abandon, what the men saw. As if inspired, they had started singing an old one, "Tell me, why did you leave me ... Tell me, why did you forget our love ..."

I had drifted off into nothingness, induced by the heat and the steady sound of trams, when a distinguished old man in a tweed jacket appeared at the door. Lifting his hat, he bowed and came to my table.

"If you'll permit me," he said, "I would like to sit with you."

"Of course," I said, pulling a chair for him. He was quite frail, gray, slight of build.

"Pardon me, if you please, for intruding but I was there when you were insulted so rudely and I only wished I could do something. You disappeared so fast and now I had just gotten a paper and was going home when I saw you through the door."

I vaguely remembered the old man at the market. "I was

very surprised when he grabbed me. He just wouldn't let go," I said, sounding a bit prissy even to myself.

"Of course, of course," he whispered. "Terribly unpleasant. There are nothing but peasants here! Just peasants. The whole town is filthy. I don't recognize it any more. They took over!"

He lifted his cane and ordered some coffee and mineral water, then brushed the crumbs from the tablecloth. "Look at this, look at these stains, it's disgusting. But things are changing, have you noticed?"

"Yes," I said, not knowing what he meant.

"The big meeting is on Sunday in the square. I wish I could attend ... if my health permits. Did you hear the King is coming?"

"Really?" I said. "Isn't he dead?"

"Not him of course, but his son and the princess from New York. A monarchy is what we need, I've always mistrusted democracy in practice. Look what it produced in the U.S, did you see that revolting garbage, pardon me for saying it, but I am so ashamed to open a magazine these days, even a newspaper, and pornographic films are playing right in the very center, have you noticed, right across from the old Hotel Moskva. All those vulgar people in front of them, gaping imbeciles! The language they use. I was so offended the other day, my wife had to restrain me."

I had tried to sit through a porn film once in L.A. but it was too boring. Here it might be more interesting; I would learn some new words.

"Mind you," he added, "I am not opposed to nature. In my days when I was a cadet, there were well-kept houses, with beautiful music. The best-known one was in a house that is now a painter's gallery, right by the Arts Institute ... I remember the owner quite well ... Madame Mimi, educated in Paris. Killed by the Germans, poor lady. A true patriot she was."

"You lived in Paris?" I asked.

"Of course," he said, "several times."

"Me too."

"There is nothing like Paris, not even Prague."

We exchanged the names, the streets, Montmartre, Montparnasse, the authors he liked and the wines; some cafés were still there; I didn't tell him Paris has changed too. He had been a lieutenant in the royal army like my father, and of course he travelled to Paris and lived in a way I'll never know, all dressed up in white uniforms and dangling sabres and fancy masked balls—just pictures for me, the time known as the good times or the time before the war.

He spoke like him too although Dad had stopped believing in kingdoms and kings along with everything else in Chicago. How lonely he must have been, alone with the books and languages he knew, with nobody to talk to, in the steel mills in Chicago. He ranted and raved against the peasants too, to me, who had grown up in the country after the revolution. I kept silent, not wanting to offend him, it took me a long time to get it—he didn't mean just the peasants at home but all the other ones, even in Chicago. All these who didn't read books.

"My father was in the army too," I said.

He pulled away a bit. "In a different army, I am sure," he said cautiously, and with a smirk. He didn't want to say a communist one.

"No, the same. He never returned, you know. He died there."

"Really! Poor man. In London?"

"No, in Chicago."

"Oh pardon me, please forgive me. I assumed you were so much younger. Excuse me, I'm quite surprised. Actually, you have a face one doesn't see any more, my mother had it when young, it's the face untouched by the Turk. Didn't you notice how suddenly everyone is much darker on the street?"

"Dark is stronger," I said, thinking dark is what they used to like before, when I was a girl, dark was more beautiful.

"Yes, but they also have ten kids," he whispered, looking around. "We are disappearing." Who is *they*? Muslims?

"My mother came from the central region," he said, mentioning my own town.

"Me too."

"Well ... imagine that, imagine that.." He seemed so happy, I was like a relative he had discovered.

From his breast pocket, he produced a calling card. "Come and visit us, it would be an honor. I'd better go now. My wife will worry, poor woman, I was supposed to be back already with peaches."

He was up. "Waiter!" he shouted firmly, as if ordering the troops. "Waiter, the next time I would have a clean tablecloth for the lady." He paid the bill, bowed largely with the sweeping movement of the right hand that my father used when asking me for a waltz, clicked his heels and was gone, a ghost from some other past. Ghosts, both of them.

His card said, R. Bulat, retired officer of the royal army.

I should see them, with flowers, yellow roses maybe,

that's what they would like. Maybe tomorrow. I knew the furniture would be old, thirties style with a doily or two, the food carefully prepared and very fresh ... maybe stuffed vine leaves with yogurt on the side or zucchini with veal, young roast lamb with new potatoes ... then a cherry strudel or some Black Forest cake. No cake, it would be too heavy at their age. Why not some camomile tea for digestion and then they would say, "It's too late, you can't go out now, you better sleep here," and I would not refuse, but would lie down in their daughter's room full of fruit smells inside, the bed with heavy linen sheets embroidered at the top, part of her trousseau made to last, before the revolution when she was young and beautiful and he, a handsome cadet, saw her at the ball. The wardrobe would have mirrors called '*psiha*' a Greek word, which means the soul; I, Anna, would look into it as always but first I would wake up slowly with the smell of coffee, breakfast pastry outside, a shuffle shuffle of slippers and some hushed murmurs. "Sh, sh, don't wake up the child, let her sleep some more ..."

I didn't know I was crying or why until the loud tram passed by, startling me and I saw that the paper in front of me was wet. Tears kept falling, blurring something I had jotted down, but I couldn't pinpoint what made me sad, I didn't even know I had managed to cry for him after all.

Chapter Four

The paper said it was Friday, the first week in June. Everything on the street suggested a Sunday, the way people
strolled, stopping to look in front of the shops at window
displays, with prolonged gazing; the air communicated a heavy
feeling, muffled, dying for a storm. My birthday would be
coming up soon, but why bother if I had not celebrated the
other ones, was aware of them only in passing. Of course, I
knew factually that I should be bothered, books said so, the
women around me grew agitated although Ms. said that forty
now is like thirty before, and fifty is what forty used to be. I
knew I should be worried the way some talked about love in
detail, and knew it without knowing it. I knew I should be
uneasy but couldn't detect any fear or vanity that was directly linked to me. Maybe because everything else was off,
starting with that birthday in Chicago. I didn't want to think
about that one, or about anything else, I wanted to stop
thinking for good, it would be nice. If prayers could be answered, that's what I would pray for.

The market had ended. Everywhere, people carried peppers, carrots, soup greens; two middle-age woman talked about their apples, one told the other about a heavenly new dessert with fresh cream. Simmer this in one pot, add this to another, handful of raisins, pinch of salt, low temperature, not easy to do, too much time and all that cream is not good for you. On the practical side, I remembered I needed something to cover my windows with.

At the hotel, *Fatal Attraction* was in the lobby, lurking about. He looked at me in his special way which was meant to be professional cool. It was touching and funny, like my sons' attempts to look grown up. "How about it," he said. "I'm waiting."

"Stop it," I said, "just stop. I have sons your age."

"Lucky guys," he said, not blinking. This was excessive and weird. Could he be a gigolo? No, they don't have them here.

"You wanna see *Sexy Lies*, let's go tonight. I hear it's cool."

"No," I said. "Just leave me alone."

"Look at that rooster," the maid with the gold tooth said from the hall. "Leave the woman alone! Scram!"

"What's it to you, you old witch. Jealous, ah?"

"Go, git!" she shouted, "Go fuck off."

"Ugly witch!"

"You call me a witch, you son of a bitch, little prick, fuck you in the asshole!"

"Fuck your peasant soul!" he said.

"And I fuck your mother and father and all your relatives, git!"

She raised the broom. He didn't look disturbed; with great dignity he slid toward the elevator. The gold tooth laughed big, holding her hips, and laughed some more in retelling it to the other two. "I had to defend her," she said. "She is too nice."

"You got to know what to do, that's for sure," the dark one said.

"Sure," said the gold tooth. "When my daughter got to be fifteen or so, I told her what to say—go fuck yourself! Without mincing words. Nothing extra. Just fuck yourself. It took a while but she learned. You had no mother, I bet," she said lowering her voice.

"No," I said, "I don't." I am an orphan, I thought.

"I can spot a poor orphan," the gold tooth said. "Oh Lord, there's nothing like a mother, nothing can replace her, may yours rest in peace." She was crying now, remembering her own, the other two wiped their eyes. I wished I could cry too, but tears wouldn't come.

"Men are pigs," the older one with the dark hair said. "What do they do but squirt and empty their juices in us and what do we get but misery."

"That's the truth!"

"Imagine this! Here I am walking by the park the other night," said the gold tooth, "when this little peacock says to me 'how about it, give me a bit, don't be stingy. We could go into the park.'"

"Did you?" the blonde asked.

"Me? Did birds eat your brain? You think I need another abortion? Seven I've had, plus the kids. I said to my husband, Velko, I am getting ready to retire from all that shit."

They took their uniforms off, got ready to leave. "You wouldn't have anything I could put on my windows," I said, "the light will wake me up at five."

They were confused; nobody had asked for this before. The hotel used to have shutters long ago, but they had rotted since. "How about a large garbage bag," I said, my first curtains in my first apartment on the Lower East Side.

Sure they had those, they said, then watched as I split the garbage bags in half. They were out of tape so we nailed them at the top. It worked perfectly, yet they exchanged disapproving looks. My room did look strange—a dark green tent, and they were women unaccustomed to anything new.

I killed two roaches, then slept for awhile until the sound of moaning woke me up from a dream. It must have been me. My hands shook. I've dreamt I was on my old street. My sons were with me, both dressed in white. We were going away from town when, from the opposite direction, a line of men appeared and passed in front of us. They walked single file, one by one, their hands tied and tied to each other with a rope. There were no guards. The men wore raggedy peasant clothes you don't see any more, but instead of caps they had plastic bags over their heads so their words couldn't be heard. You could see they were screaming. The last one gone, I turned back and saw that their feet didn't touch the ground, they walked in air because they were dead and I had seen a brigade of ghosts. I remembered that my sons were wearing white, the worst color to wear in a dream. Sickness of some sort. At that moment, I was convinced that I was on the eve of something awful, soon everything would splinter and break, all of us, my sons and me. It took a long time, the telephone lines were busy, when I reached Marc, I could hardly speak.

"Everything is fine," Marc said, his voice as calm as always.

"Really?"

"You sound strange, "he said, "are you OK?"

"Yes. I just woke up scared for some reason."

"When are you coming back? You should hurry. There was an article in the *Times* and they say things are really bad."

"Not that bad. I'll be back soon. I've sort of gotten involved with relatives."

"Yes," he said, "you always wanted that."

"What did I want?"

"To be involved," he said.

"How are the kids," I said. "Can I talk with them?"

"They are not kids," he laughed.

"Where are they?"

"They are fine," he said. "Alex is starting his new job in Colorado."

"What job?"

"His summer job, you know about it ... in a park."

"And Andrew?"

"You know he left with his roommate to California."

"To do what?"

"To visit, that's all. He told you about it."

"Yes, I remember, of course. That's why they aren't there."

"No," he laughed. "Are you sleepy?"

"Yes, and you, are you OK?"

"Sure. It's hot already. It looks like there might be a

sanitation strike. The super had a fight with Nate and I had to go and calm them down, they screamed at each other, he called him a kike and Nate called him a spic. It was something. Otherwise I just go on as usual."

"I am thinking of leaving my job."

"Really? What would you do instead?"

"You never know until you quit. Theater maybe."

"It doesn't sound like you. I thought you wanted ... some safety."

"Really?"

"I thought so. You said the theater was the same as TV."

"Marc?"

"Yes?"

"Nothing. I'll go back to bed now. See you soon."

"See you soon," he said. "Please check with the Embassy at least."

"Bye," I said.

He would put the phone down, maybe go fix himself a drink, maybe not. I had no idea what he thought as he was fixing himself a drink, I couldn't see his thoughts, but I saw my apartment, large, sunny, beautiful, facing the Hudson. Bare, uncluttered, except the boys' rooms which were their own problem. No nicknacks. Nothing extra. A nice stylish lobby with plants, safe, a doorman at the entrance, twenty-four hours. Nice polite neighbors, people who say 'hello, how are you' and talk about their dogs. People who keep to themselves, make no noise. I had never been inside any of those apartments, and it's the same the other way around. After twenty years, I know no one.

How come I know no one? Nothing major. Nobody does.

Poor old Mrs. Mintz was dead three days by the kitchen sink. You can't barge in and disturb people, Marc said once.

I couldn't sleep, I grew more agitated. One in California, I kept thinking, the other in Colorado, that's where the kids will go, why not New Mexico, and somehow a new thought entered my head—I'll have nobody, I said aloud. At least my mother had me, even at long distance to tell her stories to. I wasn't perfect but I knew what she was talking about, she wasn't talking to a wall. I'll have nobody, I repeated. Nobody! 'Nobody' echoed inside my head.

Old age which I had never dreaded became real, a gray asylum full of whispering ex-people, one of those nursing homes Marc's mother had gone to, where nobody will know who she had been, what she wanted, and who she was now. My kids will scatter across the immense land, each in his own independent life, too involved in running, realizing, to worry about me. And why should they? Didn't I train them this way, didn't I say don't worry about me, didn't I encourage them to go, have a great time, go travel, ski. The day they left for school, my darlings, nothing on my face showed when really I wanted to howl instead.

I want to howl now but think instead about Cheryl and Cathy. They'll have nobody either. Maybe for Thanksgiving, Christmas, when the entire country does giving and loving once a year, and then everything returns to normal. My friends won't mind though. They're used to it. They have left their parents too. Their bodies have been trained from the very beginning for this final stage when the old are left alone to die together with their own kind, while the young run, fly away. Colorado, Arizona. In this hotel room,

I perceived what was difficult before, what I could never get hold of except in theory—the soul of America. I kept thinking it didn't exist, they don't have one, but they really do. I couldn't see it well before, because it was a different type of soul, formed by all these separations, by people in transit, leaving parents, jobs, friends, starting all over again. The soul was fluid, subject to change, no deep roots, no dark basements, a mobile, pick-up-and-go type of soul. On the thin side. It was airy, light, fun, energetic, and admirable, so self-sufficient, as long as the weather is good. Cool though, maybe like March or the beginning of April. It didn't resemble a bird of any sort, no animal or fish, it was more like a luminous flying machine.

This, where I was, was more like a Turkish bath with steam everywhere, a day in August, dying for a storm. So, Anna, baby, take your pick.

My mood changed. Thinking larger, toward more global problems, always pacified me; my own case, the case of Anna B., displaced person, became insignificant. Just one of many, I thought, going even further away from national differences, to the rain forests and oceans and when I imagined the planet earth circling around the moons and other planets in the system, peace settled over me. I wished I could always be in that state of slow rotation, watch everything from that perspective, the very best there is, when you let go, drift, disappear into sleep.

Chapter Five

Days must have passed. With the new curtains I slept late, then had my breakfast thanks to Mirko. The market came next, then the paper and coffee in the same place. In the afternoons, I found myself on the street called French Street, and was going to head for the baklava store around the corner when I saw a large crowd in front of an old villa which had become a poets' club after the revolution. The reading was well attended, and the loudspeakers carried the poet's words into the sidewalks where people sat in groups. The poet thundered about bloody national struggles going back to medieval times, when they lost the kingdom to the Turks, he said never again, blood and revenge, over and over again, and from the sidewalks I heard murmurs of approval.

I didn't understand much except the part about the Turks. Even though socialism ended officially a couple days ago, everything remained the same; there was no reason for alarm. I had assumed that the transition would be easy and slow, due to basic languor and inertia. Most likely the poet was just carrying on and being dramatic, but the air carried a pent-up feeling, mens' eyes looked strange, their bodies more erect; I watched them open and close their fists.

An older woman said to me, "Honey, it's not good for your legs to stand so much. You don't pay attention when you are young, then it's too late. I keep telling my daughter, not that she listens." The woman sat on her newspaper and I was going to do the same when a young man thrust a paper pamphlet in front of me. "Sign here," he said.

"I can't sign," I said, "without reading it first."

He glared at me, "What kind of woman are you! What's there to read? It's either them or us!" He was tall, bearded and fierce. He mocked me loudly so others would hear, "She needs to read while we die!"

I started to defend myself, but the big words I needed to put him down wouldn't come up except in English and in French. I stammered. Up to now I knew a bit about Kosovo, but everything else I dismissed as unreal.

"Who is them?" I asked.

"The killers," he said. "Don't you know anything!"

"It's hard to believe she doesn't know," somebody said.

"Maybe she is one of them," I heard a voice in the shadow.

The crowd formed, their curiosity about this incident greater than anything they would hear on the loudspeaker. It was best to move away slowly. At any moment now they'll jump on me.

"She even looks like them," somebody said. Who is them, I kept thinking.

"Talks like them too," said another, "did you notice?"

"You know how they tend to be polite and so refined but underneath just a snake!"

"Go fuck yourselves," I shouted suddenly, "and go fuck your mother, your father, fuck your peasant ass too," and then to my amazement they roared. "She is ours," somebody yelled, "you fools, did you hear that! Good for her!" They were grinning, friendly now.

Too too fast. Can't trust their friendliness to last. The same faces as in Alabama, guns in their hands, run, Marsha said, go. I ran now.

On the main square, known as the Square of the Revolution, I ran into the airline office. It was empty and calm.

"There are plenty of tickets," the man said. "They've doubled, you know."

"I have a round trip ticket already," I said.

"That's different. Do you want to go on Pan Am or ours?"

"Pan Am," I said.

"Should we reserve now? For tomorrow?"

"No, not yet. I just wanted to know … What are they doing … what's going on?" Two cops stood outside the office, guns ready.

"Nothing major. A big meeting on the square later on. I just hope we fare better than the Rumanians … This is the end," he said with pessimism, but you couldn't tell if he was happy about the end or not.

A middle-aged man and woman came through the door. "I've just heard on the radio," a woman said, "that I shouldn't go to the coast."

"We are still flying," the airline guy said. "The rest I don't guarantee."

"I was there recently," I said, "it was wonderful. Maybe a bit crowded by now."

"Not any more," the woman said with some satisfaction. "They killed our man this morning. It's in the papers. They say he was hung."

"I've heard from somebody that all the Rumanians at the market will be quarantined. Cholera!" the man whispered. "All infected."

"I've heard the same thing," the woman said. "I don't go to the market any more. We've stopped drinking tap water."

"Stick to the brandy," the airline guy laughed. "It won't kill you."

"I hear that a bit of lemon is good as a preventive measure, and garlic too. I eat it uncooked," she said.

"Let's say I decide to leave tonight," I said, "how early do I have to reserve, I mean would I have problems?"

"Just a couple of hours ahead. Nobody is going to the U.S. It's too expensive and they have clamped down on visas.

"Is that so?" the older guy said. "How come?"

"Too many people. They've got their own problems. I've been there. It's not what you think. I keep telling my son that. How did you get your visa?" she turned to me.

"Relatives," I said. "I have relatives there."

"All the young people want to go," said the airline guy.

"Sure they do but do they ever think about later. Who'll take care of them if they get ill, I ask you?" the woman said.

"Who'll take care of us?" the man chimed in.

"With money it can all get arranged," the airline guy said. "If you have money, they marry you off to an American woman."

"If you want to get married to an American woman," the woman said.

"It's not a real marriage. It's for a visa ... I know somebody who did it."

"I say stick to your own. Mark my words," the woman said.

"Don't tell me this is heaven," the airline guy said. "I'd go tomorrow, anywhere, if they'd want me."

"Not me," the older man said. "I had a chance ages ago but ... my parents' graves are here and ..."

"Which reminds me I'd better shop," the woman said. "We are giving a yearly memorial for my mother-in-law and I'd better go and get sugar and nuts before the price goes up."

"Everything doubles, even milk," the airline guy said.

"Even bread," the man said.

"Fuck my unlucky stars," the airline guy said, "why did I have to be born in this country. We are cursed from the beginning, just blood and war."

"Old people say that the moon is blood red, same as in '41. Blood is coming our way, blood, that's for sure, plucked eyes, throats slashed," the woman whispered, looking like a witch. How else would she know about the red moon, the best is to spit three times when she is not looking. You never know. She had the same yellow eyes as that woman by the creek who was known for potions and went dancing in the moonlight with the ghosts. Boris saw her.

How silly, of course not.

The man and the woman were not going anywhere. They had only stopped to inquire and chat. They said that the Japanese will be buying hotels and the ski stations now that socialism was over. The Germans and Austrians were taking over the coast and the Americans, the woman said, are buying kids, newborns and healthy ones only. She had probably confused everything with Rumania but still it all sounded bad. The paper warned about civil war for the first time, but the arguments and accusations were difficult to decipher since they made references to events I didn't know, and all the past wrongs. I thought we loved each other, I kept thinking. I had.

To calm myself, I walked into the first pastry store and bought a bowl of sweet wheat with nuts and honey, then a slice of apple strudel with cream. Leaving, I saw that the store was owned by a Muslim, his name said so, and remembered you shouldn't eat there because their cream is never fresh. Food poisoning. It didn't stop anyone.

In the park, by the hotel, birds chirped, kids played sweetly in the sand, and grandmothers knitted and watched as always. Looking at them, I was sure everything would be all right, just a false alarm, all this talk about civil war. As a people they tended to exaggerate, dramatize; it's in the very nature of their soul. Total harmony every day would kill them.

The day took its toll. I fell asleep in spite of the music below me, loud drumming from Macedonia, and in my dreams I went back and back but it didn't seem like a dream because I could smell everything and I saw myself, this girl, a child, with a large bow, with a red pioneer scarf, a sea of red flags, fires burning, and they are dancing madly round and round in a circle. She is tiny, she can only reach up to the waists of grown-ups, she can't understand anything they are singing or saying except that this is something, powerful, taller than herself and she might lose herself in it but she is not afraid, not at all, she knows she was born at the same time as the country and the revolution and all those tomorrows they are singing about are about her and all the kids lucky to have survived, to live after the revolution. At some point men appear, led in chains, bearded, scary-looking, and the crowd stops dancing and shouts, "kill them, kill the enemies of the people!" And I wonder who are they talking about, my parents maybe? Isn't that what they are? In the dream I make a choice, "My country is my mother and my father," I squeal, and then jump into a delirious circle. Boris jumps in too. In the background, the sound of the *International* fills the square. We are together, we sing like one person, my happiness is so big I weep.

Waking up suddenly, I am surprised by all this. Nobody ever asked me to make a choice. They were quite decent. Unless I had pushed myself to choose for some reason. We never sang the *International* either, that was added from some other dream.

I ate my breakfast with even greater hunger than before. Two hours later I ate more, wheat with nuts, baklava, or rice pudding at Mustafa's Pastry around the corner. The weather stayed warm, sluggish. I only wished I had brought more clothes, my summer cotton dresses would be perfect, the closetful that never gets used. Instead, I washed my few things in the sink and dried them on the terrace by the potted rose.

The price of the newspaper doubled the next day, and my hotel room was up too. For me everything remained the same because the dollar went up too.

In the bank, where I had to use my blue passport, I was not certain if the resentment I saw in the face of the cashier was imagined, or the reflection of my own guilt. I calculated how much the food would cost in this new situation, when they were trying to switch to this other system. I subtracted the bill against an average maid's salary and couldn't stand it. It was more expensive than New York and I didn't even add up kid's clothes, shoes, notebooks. How do they manage to laugh? They could barely eat. If the maids knew, heaven forbid, that I had all those travellers cheques, they would look at me differently, would they hate me? I had to think up a profession for myself, sooner or later somebody is bound to inquire. There wasn't anything I could do to help, not so many. It was an accident, pure randomness, that I wasn't in their shoes; it wasn't because I had some special worthiness or know-how, but some trick of destiny that took us to the U.S. for God knows what reason. Yet I would have gladly exchanged my life for theirs if you could do it. Thinking this way about the exchange of lives led me inevitably toward science fiction, or our distant future.

The streets continued to be full of young people, handsome in their summer clothes, strolling, flirting with everything in sight. In the cafés nobody looked tense. Obviously a false alarm. Nobody would look that good on the eve of civil war. In front of the shoe stores, women gathered to

look at the new styles in the windows, as always and I listened to them carefully, as if they were reciting poetry.

"I love the red ones," a woman said to her friend.

"The ones with tiny straps?"

"Yes. Oh how I wish I could ..."

"I love the blue ones too."

"They are divine. They'd go well with my dress."

"And your eyes. Are you going?"

"For a week to Greece. I borrowed."

"I'll borrow too. Kids need the sun."

Mira loved dresses but shoes were her passion, sandals
with or without straps, Italian shoes especially, she even
travelled to the capital to find them.

But nobody bought anything now. They just looked at
the stores. I shouldn't have begrudged them their mad spending in the seventies; the short-lived prosperity was over.
Mira must feel really bad, not for herself but for her daughter, a young girl should have nice clothes or she'll stay hungry for them. If only I had come better prepared, with all
those dresses, I could give them away.

I walked aimlessly, stopping occasionally to eat; a few
times I had the impression I knew a face on the street but
wasn't sure. I followed one woman, convinced that when I
catch up it will be Mira, but it wasn't her. Mira would be
much older-looking now. Once in profile I saw Yanna too,
maybe she came for a day. I panicked, then was deliriously
happy just imagining what would happen next, but the dark
woman turned into another person.

With the garbage curtains I slept well and dreamt constantly without remembering much. One night I was awak-

ened from a dream about a flood by prolonged cries of someone getting strangled. They were the hoarse cries of a woman
who kept screaming, "You are killing me, kill me, stab me
now!"

I got up but saw nobody in the hall. The cries came
from the room directly across from mine. Just when I was
wondering what to do, a cry confirmed they were just making love. How foolish of me, how dumb.

I didn't sleep the rest of the night, disturbed by their
madness and the general humidity but I was also curious
about them; I couldn't imagine them.

The couple walked by just as we were having our second
cup of coffee, I knew it was them by the way the maids
perked up. Dressed, they appeared civilized and under control—he, tall, handsome, she, slim and feminine to a fault,
both young, twenty or so. The girl had a walk with special
movements around the waist that you couldn't translate into
English. A verb for trees in the wind, branches breaking
from too much movement.

The maids laughed, had more coffee and began:

"Let them," the gold tooth waved her hand in permission, "if not now, when."

"It's the right age for it," the other said.

"He looks like a mean brute who would rip you to death,"
said the blonde.

"My husband was like that ... oh my God ..." the gold
tooth said.

"Did you see how she walks," the gold tooth said, "probably hurting."

"It'll pass," the dark one said.

"It won't. She'll get it tonight ..."

The gold tooth who had defended me against *Fatal Attraction* now said, "You shouldn't sleep alone either. It's a waste of that body of yours.

"But ... I have somebody," I said.

"If you had somebody you wouldn't be here," the other said harshly.

"She is waiting for a new apartment," the blonde maid came to my aid, having invented a new version of my life. "People just won't leave, isn't it true, cousin?"

"Yes ..." I said, "it's hard to kick them out, even though it's mine ..."

"I thought you were getting a divorce," said the dark woman.

"Did he keep the apartment?" said the gold tooth.

"Yes he did," I said, crossing over.

"Still ... you have a good profession, lots of free time."

"It must be nice to be a journalist," the blonde one said. "I always wished it but ..."

"You travel a lot don't you ... ?"

"Yes, you do," I said ... "especially when you work for television."

"Put in a word or two for us, will you, cousin," the blonde one said, "tell the bastards about our wages, so help me God I wouldn't survive if it wasn't for help from the village."

"I will," I said, convinced at that moment I will write a major piece about them very soon; there was nothing in the papers about waitresses and maids, just pinups and guys bitching at each other.

How easy it was! Better than anything I could come up

with. After all, why couldn't I be a divorced journalist waiting for an apartment? Why not? And I had relatives now, the blonde maid calling me cousin.

Chapter Six

On the trolley for the first time, I didn't know what to do. People stamped their tickets into the machine, but some didn't bother. "I don't have a ticket," I said to the driver as low as possible, afraid everyone will turn and look at me. "Can I buy one from you?"

"I'm out of them," he grunted.

"Fuck the ticket, just sit down, will you," said another man. "How far you going?"

"The market."

"What's the big deal, only two stops," said another.

In the heat, the market carried the pungent odor of people and fruit. I bought cherries this time, ate them immediately, then remembered Rumanians and the cholera. I couldn't identify Rumanians but gypsies were everywhere this time, packs of kids with brilliant eyes and hair of different colors—black, blond, red. The guy selling *cilims* in the used objects section wasn't there, but in the same spot a woman sold spoons, silver, pots, and pans. I bought a little lamp from her but didn't see anyone selling light bulbs. A man said, forget it, all gone. Don't bother with the roach spray either because it's imported from Croatia. He suggested his own remedies using baking soda, but he also said they were smart insects and do no harm, why kill them. Better than the rest of us sinners, we are the nastiest animal on earth, he said, sounding like somebody I knew.

In the café across the street, the waiter acknowledged me and in a gesture of friendliness lifted the tablecloth and shook the crumbs on the floor. "The same?" he said, remembering I liked my coffee medium bitter. The men remained the same—dark, gloomy, drinking the same yellow brandy in small glasses, their eyes glazed. I hoped the old lieutenant would drop by for a chat but he didn't; ill, most likely.

The paper continued to talk about national problems, bankruptcy and transition. No mention of civil war. A whole page of pinups in string bikinis. More fashions. Hunger in the Soviet Union. Problems in the Ukraine. Racism in the U.S. Three pages of dead faces were still the most interesting, and I read each biography in detail. Some looked familiar. Several women looked like me. A dead actress made me think I should go see a play, at least one, before I go. In between the theater section and university lectures I saw a small article about AIDS. A hundred cases, they said, all imported. There was no mention of prevention, because it wouldn't work. Pharmacies were out of most things, the papers said, including heart medicine. I wondered if condoms had to be imported.

Lightbulbs couldn't be found even in the largest hardware stores. A saleslady said maybe next week, but another

one said it wasn't likely. The shortage had to do with the
problems with Slovenia. "If they don't start sending us the
bulbs we won't send them our meat, then let's see who wins,"
she said.

It was hard to believe. The blond boy was from there,
what would he say if I met him? You never know. We might
talk about acting, his new roles, or he might rant and rave
about nationalism and self-determination. It might be embarrassing.

All this left me with a lamp but no bulbs. You could get
pissed. Without any premeditation I walked into the
McDonald's restroom because it was the cleanest place to
piss in and stole a lightbulb. It was easy. I giggled and thought
about Boris and the dog we stole. We didn't intend to do it.
The dog was there, following us. I should go see him, and
see Mira too. Another time. Not yet. It would be talk, talk,
explain tell about her. Nothing can be explained, telling
only makes it worse.

Walking away from McDonald's, I saw thousands of
people in front of the Monument to the Revolution. They
were shouting all sorts of things, with tons of new words.
Many different parties, each with a slogan and a leader, different democrats, different radicals, but I didn't expect to
see the bearded men behind the black flag, weren't they
known as the killers when I was a kid, didn't thousands die
for the red one?

Very confusing. Every possible flag was there except the
old one. The killers and the enemies had changed, who
were the good guys? Too bad mama didn't live to see it all,
but you never know, she might miss the old days. Without

your enemies, how do you know you are you?

Don't get involved! Keep your mouth shut! It can be danger-ous! At any moment somebody could point a finger and they'd find a reason to accuse me. What would be my guilt? Same as always, probably. Bad thoughts. Wrong position. Besides, what did I really know about their hatreds? No more than they knew about mine. They must have a reason to be angry, why else would they be up in arms but I knew also that the other flag was part of my childhood, and I couldn't wipe it out even if I wanted to. I couldn't tell if my longing was for one or the other, I couldn't separate them, and then you can be nostalgic for things you didn't even like. Now that socialism was ending, did they expect you to snap and adjust overnight, let's forget everything, long live the new model. What hypocrites! They probably cheered until yesterday for the other side!

I heard myself make a speech. Will I be the last socialist? Nobody will dare admit it any more. I'll have to whisper about it behind closed doors, the way mama whispered about monarchy.

A young man spoke on the podium, waving his arms, shouting against all sorts of people. The new anthem was familiar, they used to sing it in emigré circles in Chicago. The mob responded. And to what? Everything he said was muddled, without a single original word. The third rate think-ing you see in commercials, victory parades, support for our boys. That kind of thinking. And while he screamed, red in the face, against the past dictatorship, he was no different from those he wanted overthrown.

At least we had a theory, I thought, satisfied that there was a reason for my beliefs after all. Go give me a better theory than 'each according to his need,' and all the people I had admired believed in it too. There was Sartre, Yves Montand, both dead it's true.

"The princess is coming, the princess is coming," the whisper travelled through the mob.

"Our little princess, our very own," squealed a little old woman with senile eyes, then began to weep.

The crowd shoved and pushed to see better. She had guards around her, handsome peasant boys, who made sure she was not touched.

The princess smiled and spoke about her genuine need for roots but she only knew a few words. A man translated, her aspirations, her needs, and her love for the people. Nobody minded that she spoke only English, they loved everything she said, her simplicity and her demeanor. She was an elegantly dressed woman of the sort you see on Fifth Avenue or Madison, with poodles. Now, she had a kingdom and followers, but it seemed funny, like one of those old films—a white queen in an African tribe.

"Our savior," the little old lady said.

"How innocent she is," a woman wept, hands clasped.

"Primitives and fools," a man muttered next to me, "we deserve everything we get." It looked like he was talking to me. His voice was familiar.

"Absolutely, I agree with you one hundred percent," I wanted to say, grateful for his intelligent point of view. There was somebody to talk with. "Why couldn't we have a democracy, why not include everyone in it, Socialists too, why this need to kill everything, not everything was bad," I thought I said. No, just my thoughts.

A limo appeared and whisked the princess away, then another speaker got up. When I looked for my interesting stranger, he was gone, leaving a mild regret. We had almost talked.

Sometime during the new speech, I was aware that a short grandmotherly woman was watching me, like a cop, had even moved closer for another look. She wore a navy blue suit of that simple cut that had remained unchanged all over Europe for the last fifty years, with a matching bag, a chignon and navy blue pumps. It was exactly what a middle-class, middle-aged woman should look like, what all peasants aspired to; my mother had dressed that way. The woman's face seemed familiar but I didn't know from where. I watched her leave the man she was with, slowly she came towards me. I didn't move. Her hand was on my shoulder. "Anna," she said with that painful stress on 'n,' "it's you, isn't it?"

'A-n-n-n-a,' it echoed on the street. Was that me? My old name, visible on the street, now struck me as thicker, wilder, more tragic than Ann, who was simple, reserved, and slender. Those two would not like each other, oh no. Good thing my body took no sides. Alone, to myself, I was maybe some other person. "Go, run, escape," somebody said. Too late. Trapped. No. I could speak French, or I could say sorry, a mistake, I'm someone else, I'm not who you think, but a part of me wanted to be found out, recognized as this person, while the other portion begged to be spared. A couple of seconds determined it—it was too late to run away. I could have done it, I had my sneakers on. Just like in Alabama. Maybe for similar reasons. "Yes," I said, giving in, "yes, it's me." This woman was not going to harm me, take me prisoner, she hugged, she kissed, she cried. "I knew it, I just knew it was you," she repeated, wiping her tears daintily, at the corners before they had a chance to spill over.

I knew her now because she wiped her tears with a silk handkerchief that was too small. She was a daughter of my mother's best friend, a feisty woman full of stories about her suitors and ghosts who came to visit at night. She had one gold tooth that gave her a bawdy look when she laughed and when her eyes and the tooth glimmered. In her sentimental state, she changed entirely, became ladylike, maybe because of those embroidered silk handkerchiefs she used to wipe her eye with, so very delicately, the way you just don't see any more. And Zina, the daughter, was doing the same.

"Mishko," she shouted toward a man. "Why are you standing her like a pole, come here, look it's Anna, look, she hasn't changed at all."

"My husband," she said, introducing a tall man in his fifties in a suit and tie. "We've met already," he said, "maybe twenty years ago, at my mother-in-law's."

"Sure," I said, remembering only his profession, doctor—considered a very good match, the very best, what mothers aspired to, including my own.

"Mishko, I knew it was her, I just knew it, but I kept thinking, Zina, woman, your brain is gone, what would Anna do here in our misery."

"I didn't know you lived here," I said, not knowing what to say.

"Now we do. We moved four years ago because of the

kids. Student dorms are horrible. How is your family?"

"Fine, everybody is fine," I said, hoping she won't ask for details.

"Zina, this will go on forever," he said, looking at the rally. "It gets worse."

"We were just having a little stroll," Zina said, "and now let's go have lunch. You can't even think about saying no. We wouldn't permit it."

Don't even think about it! If you didn't run away, the best is to give in. No doubt about it, this will be long, not one of those brisk half-hour, see-you-later lunches. It was a Sunday afternoon; away from the main square streets seemed deserted. Lunchtime had settled over the city. We walked slowly, Zina's arm under mine.

Their building had a massive old door and a turn of the century style; they said it was a private residence before the revolution. Zina huffed and puffed and complained about the lack of an elevator.

"It's only three floors," I said.

"Your shoes are comfortable," Zina said; "I wish I could wear them."

"Why can't you?"

"Be serious. They would make fun of me. An old lady in tennis shoes, they would say." She couldn't be more than a couple of years older than me.

The living room was modern—nicely furnished, sofas, bound books and a wall unit with cups and festive plates. "We had a much bigger place at home, right off the main street, next to that big hotel, and Mom came over every day … oh well …" Zina said wistfully.

"It's not bad now," he said, "we had converted the veranda into a bedroom. They have their own bedroom now."

"The kids?" I said.

"Yes," she said, "before all of us slept in this room. It was a bit crowded."

"Now she studies in the kitchen, he in the bedroom and we are here," she said, pointing toward couches in shades of brown and gold.

Mishko came out of the kitchen with coffee, sweet preserves, water and brandy on a plate. "Here, to your health!" he said raising his glass.

"To your homecoming!" she said.

"To us," I said.

They had taken their shoes off, how peaceful, how sweet they looked in their matching slippers, what was that smell coming from the kitchen, nutmeg? "How long are you staying?" he asked.

"Just passing through," I invented on the spot. "There was a conference on the coast so ..."

"When was this?"

"A couple days ago."

"I wondered. Nobody is going there now. Did you see the papers? Most tourists have cancelled. What a waste, oh my God ..." Zina moaned. "Millions gone."

"Listen," I said, "don't tell Yanna if you see her. There is no way I can go ... I'm leaving right away."

I expected them to be shocked. Blood is blood, they would say. People travel days to visit the graves, and here she is without any excuse. Guilty. I was. For all sorts of things.

"I understand," Zina said. "It would be tricky. The trains are on strike."

"Since when?"

"Two ... three days ago."

"We are disintegrating," he said, "have you noticed?"

"I have," I said. "Tell me, what is happening, I am lost really. I understand the 'end of socialism,' but I didn't know we hated each other so much."

"Do we have to start on this?" Zina yelled. "That's all we talk about. You could go crazy."

"But I don't know," I said.

"I don't want to bore you with details." he said, "you were a kid when you left. You wouldn't understand much. But look at it this way—we've lost ourselves. Completely. Like a sick person. Worse than a physical illness. Massive schizophrenia. We don't know any longer who we are."

"Did we ever?"

"I don't know. I used to think we did but I'm no longer sure. I used to think our problem was that we never grew up. We never had time for it, or the right conditions. It was either the Communist slogans, or Western ones. Both deadly. Did you know that Africans from the remote areas when they come to Europe get TB immediately. Not immunized."

"Please, Mishko, don't start now on disease before lunch."

"I am trying to simplify our condition for someone from the outside, to reduce it to the basics."

"I don't care what you say," Zina said, lowering her voice as if somebody might be listening, the way her mother did always when talking about *them*, the Bolshevik vipers—"but our best times happened while *he* was alive. We lived well, we travelled, everything was quiet, no strikes, nobody heard of drugs, kids were polite. And now we might have a civil war, Heaven forbid!"

"Sure," he said. The corruption was covered up. Before only a few stole, now everybody does. Democracy ..."

"We are not ripe for it," Zina said.

"Maybe not, but democracy implies some disorder."

"I don't like the disorder," Zina said. "I can't imagine anyone liking it." What's a lightbulb, I thought about my own corruption, and besides I wasn't going to make a profit, just read a paper at night. "Where do you buy your lightbulbs?" I heard myself ask.

"We stockpiled months ago," he said, "do you need one, what's the problem?"

"They are out of them in the hotel," I said.

"Why don't you come here," Zina said. "Why be alone. You can have this couch. Promise you will ..."

"I'm not staying, Zina, or I would ... thanks anyway ..."

"I wonder what's keeping them," Zina said, worried. "I can't complain, they are such good students, every exam on time. Maya is in a new field, ecology of rivers, and would like to go to California for a year but her boyfriend said no."

She stopped as if reminded of something more urgent. "Mishko," she said, "we're out of wine. Go get us a few bottles at the drugstore?"

When he closed the door, she picked up where she left off, "So, California for a year, that's what she wants. However, her boyfriend won't hear about it!"

"Tough!" I said, a bit too harshly.

"It's her boyfriend," Zina said with wide-open eyes. It

meant, this is serious, this is her husband, her life, her future. And ... your husband ... he lets you ... alone?" she added.

"I don't ask him," I said, again with unnecessary harshness. I couldn't stand that question, 'lets you ...'

"You couldn't do it here," Zina said, "although the young are different, have you noticed, now you even see men with strollers, funny, ah? You know I retired early ... last year. He was able to get a new job but I couldn't and it was strenuous. I spent three years on that train every weekend rushing here to cook."

"Zina! Are you serious? They would have managed. Three grown people."

"Sure, but they would have eaten junk, probably just opened cans and heated them up. It's unhealthy ... So, I retired and we came here but mom took it hard. He really doesn't mind, your husband? You ... don't get bored all alone?

"No," I said. "I need to roam, I think. It's in my nature."

"Roam!" she laughed. "That's what you say now. If you had stayed here you wouldn't ... it's because your mother decided to leave ... that's why you are the way you are and why you look so young in those sneakers." She sounded jealous, or maybe not jealous but sad.

"I don't look young, Zina, go take a closer look! My hair is quite gray, see."

"It doesn't show. It blends in with the blond. And you move like a young girl."

"I danced ages ago," I said, thinking about something Zina had just said. Did she imply that everything she is right now is her mother's doing? That my mother is responsible entirely for my own dilemma, my doubts, and the way I walked? There was so much conviction in Zina's voice that I, Anna, would now be round, settled, and without my sneakers, in a wool suit and pumps, that even though I distinctly remembered I had come to the same conclusion a few days ago, now I opposed this woman in the same way I had opposed everything always, my America and their socialism. Out of pure stubbornness. My socialism was not like hers.

"Maybe not," I said, and a bit of my childhood came back, a portion so distant it appeared invented. "I ran away with the gypsies at five. They were horrified when they found me in the wagon, can you imagine, with all those stories about them stealing kids and all. They were very nice but I was disappointed when they took me back."

"I can't believe it!" Zina said. "You of all people! You looked so quiet, so perfect, even my mother said so."

"Quiet," I said. "Is that what I was?"

"Absolutely, quiet and dreamy, serious, a good student."

Like a spy, I thought, I wasn't quiet. I had bad thoughts. I stole a dog with Boris and we sold it for movies and cherries. And I led them against the butchers' boys. And here is this stolen lightbulb. No, it's no. My dreams were bigger but they weren't girls' dreams. I wouldn't have been like her. No matter what they studied or did, it all ended up with cooking and kids. Just mothers and mothers and an occasional slut.

Here, I registered my own contradiction—what I intellectually disapproved of, bodily I had wished. They didn't mix.

"We ran into one of your friends the other day, the one who looked like that Mexican actress, dark with a small waist."

"Mira!"

"Her. She still looks adorable. Her hair is short now, still well dressed, you know how she was. They live not far from here, although I heard they might be divorcing."

"Why?"

"Who knows. It's always some other person. I've heard he is ... well ... peculiar."

She shuffled into the kitchen to check on something. Chicken soup? It had to be. I could smell parsley, carrots, everything cooking slowly, steaming the window panes.

"I'm so happy you are here, you can't imagine," Zina said. "My mama still mentions you in her prayers, you know she often goes to your grandma's grave. You helped us so much, did you know that? I wore nothing but the dresses you sent, I was the best dressed girl in school. I was much thinner then, you remember how skinny I was."

"Yes," I said, "you were."

"Your dresses fitted me perfectly, and later mom altered them a bit. I was even married in that dress, a beautiful white one with a high collar, tight bodice and a ballerina skirt. I wish I had kept that one but we sold it at some point."

I didn't know her well. She was just a serious girl a couple of years older than me, not the kind who roamed around the creek with boys. Her mother was more interesting, or maybe her stories were, how young, how pretty she was, how much she loved to dance, how tons of handsome men courted her and there was nothing left of it all.

"You must have some pictures?" I said, and Zina laughed, pleased, "You're still the same after all. Every time you came over, every single time you were in our house, you asked for the album. I could never figure out what you saw in it."

"Who knows," I said, not able to explain what I looked for. A clue of sorts. To everything.

From the wall unit, Zina produced two albums, leather bound and perfect, every picture in its place chronologically, nothing like my own two shoe boxes in New York, everything pell-mell, the people and the years.

Zina sat next to me, eager to tell, and began from the beginning. These albums were a story of her life, of the bright girl from my hometown who studied and then married well. The same photographer took the earlier pictures, in black and white; in the background, the same painted waterfall gave an illusion of depth. Did he kiss her foot too? Probably not. He gave me oranges, figs, an orange for a kiss. Then time passes and here is Zina in the capital, the street empty of cars. She is with Mishko, looking very shy, soon after her graduation. She'll get married in a month.

"God, you married so young," I said.

"No, not that young, Mama married at seventeen. Everybody married soon after college. Here! Do you remember?"

My graduation dress. I had worn that dress just once. It must have looked spectacular here, even though it was made out of some artificial material, nylon or polyester, too hot for the summers in Chicago. The memory of loneliness inside that dress is bigger than that word, even now my throat tightens, I might stop breathing.

"We had a picture of you in it," Zina says, "at your mother's house, before the prom, but somebody stole it. You were so glamorous at that time, a real movie star. You're lucky, you've lived," she adds with some regret of her own.

"You looked much better than me in that dress," I said and meant it. It was nice that the same dress could stretch and serve for a happy wedding picture.

Zina's life continued in the pictures chronologically— nothing had to be invented—her first job, which was her only job, and the husband was the only real boyfriend too. The first kid, after he graduated from medical school. On the island of Brac, she looked rounder. Another child, and a furniture set, still looking brand-new. This life was predictable and boring, but who can tell if change itself is an improvement except you get addicted to it like crack. I was starting to lecture again to someone, my sons, Marc, the whole world, wishing it weren't so.

"Are those your real teeth?" Zina's voice brought me back to earth.

"Why yes," I said, startled.

"I lost quite a few with kids ... and you forget until it's too late. You always had beautiful teeth."

"Dad had good teeth," I said, a liar and a hypocrite. I took care of mine.

"Tell me," she said, "how do you manage to look so young? Is it America or what?"

"It's an illusion. I don't think I look young in New York. My guess is you don't know how to look at me."

Something was bothering her. Most likely, now that she was retired, with grown kids, she had no real function, neither a young woman nor a grandmother. No hobbies either, who's got the time. And she wouldn't understand her moods, the sadness that would eventually manifest itself in headaches, bad nerves. We were not that different. I, Ann, who

could advise, see, analyze others in detail, people and plays,
am quite opaque to myself too, muddy, in great need of
light. We are primitives, the whole country is.

"Do you still paint?" I asked. "Your pictures were all over
the school."

"Oh, you remember!" she said. "I stopped all that after
high school. Who has the time?"

"You have all the time now," I said. "Hell, go and paint."

"What for?" Zina said, her eyes strangely Oriental. "It's
too late now."

"For yourself!" I said, sounding like a cheerleader. At
this instant, a full century separated us in practice, but there
were other centuries we shared, some Ottoman misery in
the soul.

"I'm sorry," Zina said, "I forgot to ask you ..." No doubt,
she was going to ask about mother when the kids appeared
at the door and I didn't have to circumvent the question
because Zina had other things on her mind. "Please don't
tell them it's all wonderful. They are stealing our kids," she
whispered. Who is they?

"Guess where I found them?" Mishko said, beaming.

"At the drugstore," Zina said. "Are you hungry?"

They looked like him, both dark and very tall, but the
girl had Zina's blue eyes and round cheekbones. They shook
hands and sat down to eat. Zina looked at me nodding, see,
do you understand why I had to come all that way on weekends to cook, see—my little angels, my darlings, my life,
that's what you called your children.

She must have had it all prepared early in the morning,
how else. The chicken soup came first, the very best, fra-

grant, full of carrots and greens and a bit of meat, livers and
so on, and the chicken was from a village because Zina was
suspicious of the ones in the store. The sauteed breasts in
lemon sauce came next, with potatoes au gratin and mixed
salad which had her own dressing with dill, plus acciden-
tally she had prepared *Blanche Neige*, the kids' and my favorite dessert, with floating egg whites in a thick sweet sauce.
Nobody said anything serious. We ate nonstop.

"It's not an accident," the daughter said laughing. "We
have something new every day, a cake, a rice pudding, a pie.
She is the reason I can't lose weight. Would I be ..."

"Don't look at Anna," Zina said. "You don't live in
America. Here, men don't like bones."

"They are not that thin in America," I said.

"They certainly look that way," Zina said.

"Just movies," I said.

It was such a good lunch after which you lie down for an
hour or so, stomach full, mind empty, but damn it, even
here America kept interfering. Question and answer period!

"You see," the boy started, like an elder in the village
tradition, "first she wants to go for a year to California.
What if everybody left?"

"I only want to go for a year," the girl said, "who is
talking about immigration?"

"That's what you say now," Zina said, "what if you meet ..."

"I'm curious," the boy said, "they are obsessed only with
money, aren't they? I mean it comes up in all the films. It's
true, isn't it?"

"Yes," I said. "You're right." How much do you make,
how much is he worth, a million dollars, thanks a million,

looks like a million, time is money, bankable, get a star. "Yes, it can't be denied," I explained. "I would say money is to them what food is to us."

"Well said," said the husband. "Well observed."

"But food is different ... there is a memory of hunger here while money is abstract."

"I agree with you," I said. "Money is not a childhood wish."

"Rollo May," the husband said, "that's who!"

"What is the wish?" the girl said.

"I don't know," I said, "what was in the beginning. Love maybe."

"We talk about money too," Zina said, "and how!"

"Mama, it's different," he said, "sure we do ... how much is bread and meat today and so on. The idea of making money and wanting more all the time even when you have enough is foreign to us. It would have to become symbolic first."

"What do you study?" I said.

"Economics," the boy laughed, "don't I sound like it?"

"No, you don't."

"Mama told us you are in the theater."

"Sort of."

"Everybody thought you'd go into medicine. You were such a good student," Zina said. "Theater is so ... unpredictable." Zina meant risqué, almost like being with the circus.

"Personally," the girl said as if to herself, "I think they are obsessed with sex."

"Who is obsessed?" Zina said.

"Americans, in films."

"They are quite obsessed here," I said, "let me tell you."

"Do you remember," Zina said, "when we didn't have a word for it?"

"What was used instead?" I asked. "Nature?"

"Well," she laughed, "ah, Mishko, we didn't use any words."

"Sex was a textbook word ..."

"Wait, mom," the girl turned to Anna, "why do they talk about it so much, why don't they just do it, I mean why make a whole film about sex."

"I don't know," I said, "maybe sex is to them what nationalism is here. It used to be forbidden. America is a puritan country ... it's hard to explain, we don't have it here, do we, sex as evil and temptation. Look, money and sex you can get if you try, while love is harder, maybe sex is a substitute too, a second choice to the original wish ... but I am no expert ... just rambling."

"I've heard," the girl said, "they make love on the phone and they never see a person. A friend of mine says, that's what they do in New York ..."

"I've heard," the boy said, "that they send sex messages on computers and that it's even worse. You never even hear a person."

"We are exhausting her," the father said.

"Let's say I went for a year," the girl said stubbornly.

"Could she have a job before she got there?" the mother asked.

"I doubt it. It would take a while, people look for jobs all the time, lose them, get new ones, especially now."

"All the time," Zina gasped.

"Not all the time. Often."

"Apartments too?" Zina asked.

"Yes."

"Why?"

"For different reasons, money, jobs, change. They love to change over there. They really do."

"It takes a lot of energy, all that," Zina said. "I wouldn't like it."

"It's not for everyone," I said.

"But if I get a scholarship ..." the girl started.

"Who is it for?" the boy said.

"Young people, strong. It's better for plumbers than poets, that's for sure. I'm serious."

"See what I mean," Zina said. "I thought so. Do you remember a classmate of mine, Ivan? He flunked out of school, a real troublemaker, well, he now has a fancy restaurant in L.A. Came back last year with a big car. It's a strange country," Zina added.

Ivan? The butcher's son? I agreed inwardly that this type of person had a better chance in the U.S. than Boris who had studied philosophy, but Zina was making Ivan too attractive with his car and no degree, and was defeating her very purpose in what was meant to be bad publicity. Instead of repulsion, the U.S.A. shone, madly fascinating, if someone like Ivan could do so well.

"It's best to see for yourself," I said, "why couldn't she go for a year?" My attempt at subversion.

"What if everybody left," the boy said. They didn't want her to go.

"What if she fell in love," Zina said. She wasn't going.

"She'll go for a year, and she'll come back," I said.

"Could you live here?" Zina switched the subject, sneakily. "We always thought you'd come back some day. Everyone did. Kids, Anna left a real-life drama behind her, this poor man, my classmate, was madly in love, poor David and he never got over it, took to drinking, wasted his life. They say his mother died from pure grief."

"Please," I said. "How could I ever do so much?"

"Mama, you ask a question, then you drop it, she didn't even have a chance to answer it," the daughter said, turning toward Anna. "She does it all the time."

"What was the question?" Zina said.

"Could she live here. What would you miss about America?"

"I don't know, I haven't thought about it," I said. "Here people look at you too much, in New York you can be invisible ... What would I miss ... maybe an illusion of freedom, not political but the other one."

Soon I found myself talking as if the CIA had paid me, about a mythical America, the open roads that extend forever across the immense land and if you fail in Chicago you pick up elsewhere, St. Louis, Phoenix, L.A. and you just keep going, stopping occasionally to refuel. Infinite possibilities, you can invent yourself, and become someone else, the country is so big, no end to it. It was a song to America from one of my plays. A tribute to the dream. The dream was good. The best dream ever.

From this angle, with them, well fed, warm, I loved this country I had created on paper and the mythical search from New York to L.A. had its own heroic scale while the old and new selves circled around the travelling person as angels without disturbing.

Coming to the end, I felt disturbed, schizophrenic, didn't I condemn all that just recently. Yes. Didn't I strive for unity? On the other hand, why can't a human being contain more then one governing idea, why not two or three? Didn't Marc say that the real proof of superior intelligence is the capacity to hold two opposite views and not fall apart?

"So much, work, all that, moving searching," Zina said. "Do you know anyone who lives normally?"

"Mama means the same job, same apartment, same husband," the girl translated.

"I suppose I do," I said, "but I can't tell you about the whole country. It's hard to talk about America. It's a continent, it's like many different countries and groups. I can't describe it simply. You would have to go see it for yourself."

"The way I see it," father said, "if we didn't have America, we would have some other country. America just happened first. My fear is that young people can't see well because they are only attracted to the surface of things. Communism harmed us, especially our middle class, but it never destroyed the family. Capitalism will. Now we have whole families without men, all gone to Germany, when they come back they bring the worst with them. Topless bars and striptease. Drugs. I see America only as the largest symptom and no more.

I saw it in my own way—if everyone, kids, husband, and wife were running off, each in the name of self-realization— this lunch I had loved wouldn't exist or it would be a different lunch, or it might happen once in six months but then it wouldn't be the same. Like making love once in six months.

A big to-do, so to speak. I shifted my position again—was aware of it—a moment ago, I had felt bad for Zina, who had nothing to look forward to now that the kids are grown up, a woman who could have done things. Wrong again. Zina's life was not wasted—this was a happy family, all in all, bright kids, nice husband, why would she be better off if daily she appeared with her briefcase around seven, like Judy, and then spoke about her job and her company nonstop? Who is getting exploited, I ask you? They slept in one room and most likely didn't fight about each other's space. The kids won't have major gripes against the parents, accuse them of indifference. The parents gave everything and children will give everything back in turn, that's how it was. But it will all change, very soon, any moment now—women like Zina will be gone—no more grandmas left, just women searching for 'new maturity' in their special units, searching for the better retirement spots. In towns designed for them away from teenagers and noise. And then young couples will have their own segregated quarters too.

Happiness, I concluded my silent lecture, was not about the unlimited opportunities and roads that go on forever. Maybe it's about something limiting, attainable, as small as this apartment, this lunch, the nap we took next, Zina and I on her couch.

Outside, on the street, the air carried the strong scent of linden trees, mixed with cooking smells here and there; somewhere in the distance I heard church bells. At that moment in the orange light just before the darkness, the city appeared like a beautiful man, a gypsy with shiny eyes. A short-lived magic hour, then very fast everything would vanish as the sun disappeared blood-red somewhere over the river.

I had done nothing but eat and sleep the whole day, yet now my body was wide awake; light in my sneakers, I wanted to go dancing. At the same time, my head whirled with images flying in all directions, Zina, her album, her food, my dresses, the puzzle, the mystery of everything. Zina, my mother's friend's daughter, is what mama had wished for me, except the poor woman never got that satisfaction. That's what 'middle class' meant, that type of order. Good kids, good food, everyone together. There was nothing about them I objected to, on the contrary, but now, on the street, alone once again, I knew that was not me, never could be. From the outside, I had all the trappings—schools, job and my beautiful apartment that mother had approved of, but Zina was inside it all, she believed it, while at best I could pass, if I tried hard. A part of me always escaped, didn't want to be caught by order.

Strange, Zina didn't push harder about my mother. Maybe Yanna didn't tell her. Maybe she told no one. I was no longer sure I had written to her about it, I was not well around that time.

Not bad, my answers about America. Nothing to be ashamed of. It was one thing to hate privately for personal reasons and your own satisfaction but I had always been a fair person and a fair teacher, had refused to simplify anything for anyone, either this country or the U.S. It's a part of me I approved of, the constant part of my person, the one that's most like Marc, some intellectual stubbornness in both of us, not to give in to stupidity. No, America can't be described in a word or two. Not a nation. A continent. After all those years, still a mirage. It's good I didn't tell the worst about it, I could have. Was I trying to protect it for the outsiders, the same way some women do whey they say 'Oh, my husband has his good side.' Or was I protecting my sons, Marc and me?

The street I walked on was deserted. The orange glow had faded, soon the night would fall. The church bells continued, a dark sound, thick. Did they ring this way before Belgrade was bombed? My mind kept jumping from this to that, from Zina to *blanche neige*, to her mother and mine and nothing was simple, not even that word mother. When I hear *mother, mom*, in English, I see a particular person, nobody I had known, maybe an ad on TV, who the hell knows— but *mom*, American mom, is a woman in Bermuda shorts fixing sandwiches, calmly and efficiently placing Band-Aids on, soon she will drive a whole bunch of kids to a baseball game. It's not as if she didn't feel bad occasionally, sure she did, and often she wasn't sure she was doing enough, and then she read books on child care. I had never known a woman like this yet I suspect this mom really exists, the way the French *maman* does somewhere in Paris or Lyon. I always see a woman who is charmingly flirtatious, who laughs and kisses kids with a delicate perfume on. *L'Air du Temps?* Next, she steps into a car that her husband or her lover drives. None of these mothers change, their pictures remain constant year after year and the native one is always the same too—a woman who cooks constantly and whose face is sad beyond words. She is the opposite of the other two— heavy, like bread, like earth, like graves, she often wears black because somebody is always dying and she is always feeding sons who'll go off to war and then she'll have to bury them too.

But there is only one mother, you can't shop for her, pick and choose, reject, think about if maybe she is just right for you. Just one, I thought on the street as the light faded completely. No other would ever be as good, and this one loved too much, excessively, you could never shake her off. The biggest love ever. No other country would ever be as good. It's not the fault of the U.S. Of course not. It simply paled in comparison. This type of love isn't good for the economy, it creates attachments to people, places, graves, no wonder they have a different type of mother over there, a cooler sort who traveled in wagons, away from friends, was lost over and over again, suffered and loved alone. And the search for happiness is good for the economy too, imagine if everybody were contented with a minimum, let's say two summer dresses, just imagine, no, capitalism couldn't exist without the lack of something, wanting to get it, the search for substitutes, all those needs dying to get fulfilled and yet never knowing. Never knowing propelled everything, and you never knew if the real thing or the substitute propelled you, the new need created while you were running to fulfill the first, a mutation of the need. I couldn't figure out if the nervousness came first and then the economy, or if the economy created everything, or if perhaps they were so intertwined you couldn't separate them.

Boy! You could get dizzy just thinking about it all! It's stressful even at long distance, fuck it, girl, you're at it again, shit! And here only a couple days ago, I had decided to leave America to Americans and just seize the day. Now, after having had such a good time, I was off into it again, just thoughts that have nothing to strike, pure poison. I had been sucked into it by Zina's kids, the question and answer time, translating, explaining, my usual job. Same as always. Damn! But now, stumbling in the darkness, I almost laughed—it was all useless—the reality of my thoughts is only an intellectual game, like playing chess. I take your king, you have my queen, I could take any imaginary position, have a major fight, even kill, but ultimately none of it matters—it's in my head only! Like the famous French resistance, all that talking the intellectuals did in the cafés during the Second World War.

There was nobody in the lobby. Silence. The manager was gone. He has not been there for awhile, was he replaced? No other sounds anywhere, nobody watched TV. Maybe I was all alone in the hotel at night. My room, which until this moment was fine except for the cockroaches, now seemed strange with those green bags on the windows. I didn't miss anything until this visit to Zina; now, my body remembered her couch, her food. You get used to things. I'd have to adjust again the next morning.

The lamp and the lightbulb didn't work, maybe there was something wrong with the socket or the cord. There was no music downstairs on Sunday nights and I welcomed the cries from the room across the hall; either the same couple or some other went on killing each other and I felt less alone. I wished I had told Zina about her, why not? Maybe next time. I can talk about her now, I won't fall apart or anything. I can even say aloud, she is dead, my mother is dead. It's over.

Chapter Seven

The next day, the weather grew hotter still, even in the morning. Back at the market I hoped to find some wild strawberries again but was told I couldn't count on it. The season was almost over, the woman said, then sold me some peaches.

At the café everyone acknowledged me with a nod, the waiter and the guests—I had finally passed the test—a serious looking woman who comes daily and reads a paper. The waiter even changed the table cloth, replaced it with a nice clean one without holes; then, putting back the salt shaker and the toothpicks, he asked in a low voice, "Madame must be a journalist."

"Yes," I said, "I am. How did you guess?"

"I am good at that sort of thing. My profession demands it. Horrible, isn't it," he said gesturing toward the paper. "What do you think?"

"Not good," I said, remembering Mishko, "We are falling apart."

"My opinion exactly," he said almost in a whisper, "but it's best not to say anything publicly right now. I can tell you, you're a smart woman but I just keep my mouth shut. You just don't know who is who anymore. At least before, it was easy—you only had to worry about *them*."

I agreed. It's hard without *them*. Everyone will come to regret *them*, you'll see. If he only knew how little I understood what was in the papers. It was incomprehensible, after fifteen years. Not only did Communism end virtually yesterday, and all these new parties were shouting, calling each other names, the country seemed bankrupt and now each republic wanted a divorce for reasons known only to them. I didn't know who was behind it, which foreign power, I couldn't decide if everything was triggered by an economic problem or some new need to find themselves, just like Michelle in California who divorced for a similar reason. "He took over my head, he wouldn't let me grow," she said.

The pinups were gone, not that I liked that page full of tits and ass but still I had gotten used to them. I missed them in these conditions, no matter how lewd, they were real. Their disappearance from the paper I interpreted as an ominous sign that things were getting worse. Only the dead remained the same, three pages of them staring straight ahead in their black and white pictures. An unusually large number of retired military men, some ex-heroes and famous Partisan fighters, were dying daily, most likely under stress and who could blame them. Everything they had fought for was dying. The dollar went up again. An article called "Seduced and Abandoned" said the U.S. sent millions for Tito's villas, as long as they needed us. They dumped us now, the article said.

If there was anybody who could clarify the whole mess, it would be Boris. Zina said he was teaching at the university and had gotten involved with the newly formed Democratic party. I kept thinking about him but didn't call him nor did I call Mira although I wanted to. I was afraid each time I came near the phone, maybe that I would have to explain America to them again. Maybe I would get all entangled in dinners and lunches and would have to adjust to my room all over again. Alone, it was easy. I roamed all over the city, entered the stores, listened secretly to conversations, hidden by a newspaper. I remained fascinated without knowing why, and the people that I observed would have laughed—most likely to each other they were ordinary.

It was in this mood that resembled falling in love, walking aimlessly, I found myself in a section I didn't know. It was about the right time to have my evening drink, in a café called *Zvezda*, a pleasant place shaded by linden trees on both sides. The waiter was nice too, except some men started pestering me in the usual way—stare, stare up and down. Soon I'll turn red, then will have to lower my eyes and the blushing will spread. I said damn, looking at them in the same way, slowly, shit, I said, lingering over their thighs, their chest, and they shifted their eyes, laughing. I solved that one.

The waiter said, bringing my wine, "They took care of it, their treat," and pointed to the three men who bowed. I was no longer angry with them, just funny young guys in a good mood. One of them came over right away, and with exaggerated gestures he said, "I'm their ambassador. My instructions are to bring her royal highness to our table. If she is willing."

"Sure," I said, going over. "Here I am. You must have some urgent questions for me."

"Absolutely," said one. "Would you like to see a play?"

"What play?"

"Next door."

"Is it good?"

"Depends," the ambassador said, "I'm the only one worth seeing."

"Don't I need a ticket?"

"No, not you," he said.

"No, not you," the other two sang.

"All of us are in the play." He is the priest because he is so fat, look at his gut, and this ugly man is a cop. "Me," the ambassador said, "I am special. Girls love me."

We were having a good time when a woman ran towards us, furious, "I've had it," she screamed, "I've been looking for you all over the place, didn't you hear the five minute bell?"

Stage managers are the same wherever you go, no playfulness in any of them, poor things. "Calm yourself, woman," the fat guy said, "you'll get a heart attack. I'm not on stage until eight."

"That's not the point."

"Calm yourself, meet our royal highness … name."

"Anna."

"… who is most likely an actress herself."

"No, she is not."

"Come with us," the fat actor said, "it's a dress rehearsal." Through the stage door I entered the theater in the round, just as an old song came on, 'We are Tito's young soldiers, with us marches our whole land.' Somebody snickered, then the lights came on.

On the stage a woman was mopping the floors and humming to herself. She was dressed in an old gray skirt and sweater, her hair covered with a scarf. The American Ambassador appeared next, looking like a pimp in pointed white shoes and a suit of the latest Italian cut. "How's life, granny," he said. She stopped mopping briefly and said, "Great. Fuck it! I figure it can't get worse. That's why I am so optimistic." And *Our Joy* started without intermission.

The five actors did many parts, some funny, others not, and the play had no central character because it was about the entire country, the invisible part you might call soul. I couldn't tell if this soul was good or bad, it kept shifting this way and that, refused to be pinned down, but as the play ended I recognized it the way you know someone, or a certain tune. Written by Vesna, born in '68, directed by her too. She had to be the dark-haired girl arguing with the stage manager about the lights.

I'll go tell her I really liked it except this wouldn't be understood in New York, I'll say it's good even though this would be called avant-garde, she'd get a hole in the wall. No budget to speak of. Too many pieces, no central character to root for, no motivation—everything I lectured against yet kept writing in the same style as hers. Was it genetic? What was it? This had to be the reason why I couldn't do a simple story, why a family drama, inevitably, against my will, grew and grew to include the entire building, sometimes a whole street. But what I had perceived as a failing on my part, no longer was, maybe my plays would be a popular entertainment here, not far out at all, maybe it's a common style in the Balkans. As ordinary as kitchen sink play.

It was all very interesting to think about, the culture, the art, the artist, and the angle of view; I said nothing to Vesna. She looked busy. Backstage smelled of dust, paint and old costumes, and I had a familiar sadness. This too is over. My theater years. It was good I kept thinking with something unlived in my gut, all those plays that were not born. Desa is dead too. She took me backstage for the first time.

"Let's go and rejoice," the ambassador said, ready to continue the play. "We have time for one more drink." He introduced me to new people but I didn't see the other two. "What happened to … ?" I started.

"The ugly and the fat ran off to do another play."

"How could they?"

"Their part ended at nine and the other play starts at nine-thirty, no problem. I do the same tomorrow. Where in the hell are you from?"

"New York."

"Get off," another guy said, "what are you trying to do, sound important."

"Sure she is, dumb-ass, can't you hear how she talks. Are you deaf?"

"I thought she might be from our less barbarian parts. Are you really from New York?"

"Yes."

"Poor you!" the new guy said. "Bibi," he turned to the ambassador, "don't you think we live in heaven, do you think we would need anything extra to make it perfect?"

"No," the ambassador said, "not a thing."

"Light bulbs," I said.

"Of course," Bibi said, "it slipped my mind. But what's a light bulb? Do we really need it?"

"Of course not," said the other. "We don't need apartments either. You should see my place, my grandmother's chicken coop was better."

"It's cozy," Bibi said. "He just complains."

"Who, me complain? All those New York actors should have it so good."

"At least you are working," I said, "doing two plays a night."

"What do you think we should be doing instead?"

"My actor friends mostly talk about getting parts. While they work in restaurants, bars, anything they can get."

"I don't believe it," Bibi said. "You are trying to make us feel good."

"Listen," I said, "I really liked the play. Tell her, will you?"

"I'm not going to say a word," the guy said. "If she hears one more compliment we suffer."

"Tell me then," I said, "what else should I see? I'm leaving in a day or two."

"Don't go back," Bibi said. "Stay here. It's only going to get more exciting."

"How about *The Spider*," the other guy said.

"That's shit," Bibi said.

"You don't know what shit is. *The Spider* is not bad. How about *Spring Awakening*."

"That's German."

"So it is, and it's done in a Balkan style, but still a very nice production, go see that. I just remembered, no tickets, it's been sold out for the next six months."

"You're such a fool," Bibi said, "Of course there are no tickets. But Anna goes there and says, Bibi sent me, the door opens and she gets the best spot in the house."

Once again the stage manager appeared and hustled them back in. Bibi said, "A word of advice, don't tell anyone you're from New York. It's better. Everybody is poor. We are rapidly falling apart, that's the truth?"

"What will happen?" Anna asked.

"Nothing. We just continue," he said, switching to the last line of *Our Joy*.

I continued alone, on foot. Another warm night, humid. Still early. My body carried edginess, a need to prolong the play, another drink, more talk, a party would be nice. Instead, I had to figure out how to get to my room where nothing much awaited me. A sloppy gloom would envelop me, the kind of gloom Americans don't have, an all-over type of gloom.

On a side street, deciding which direction to take, I heard music from a window that was lit. Coltrane. Imagine meeting him here. What a surprise. And with it, a memory of years gone by, summers hotter than here, more humid, clubs closing on the South side, the pain and dope all around us. Take something, take anything, just get by, the man says, junk flows in his veins, only the pain in mine. We meet in between. Your eyes shine, he says, putting the trumpet away, what are you on, you shoot up, it rubs off, he nods, look at your arms. My arms seem black, the ambulance never comes,

soon he'll die. What would this man in the window understand about mornings in Chicago and the loneliness that
was much bigger than mine?

I stayed on, leaning against the poplar, nobody on the
street. A fast number came on, the pain all gone, summer in
it too, cars, cabs, lights change red to green, keep going, step
on the brakes, asshole, learn how to drive, go, avenues straight,
large, the city stands up, no shade, not much, hurry up, it's
hot, thank God for the wind, cooler inside, my curtains are
the color of indigo, my sons are laughing, candles, balloons,
kids, here it comes, it's falling, a real storm, my grown-up
years whiz by me in different colors, some OK, others not,
but all alive thanks to this sound.

Thank you brother, I want to say, thank you. You make
me feel so good, the drummer on Division Street mumbles,
his eyes liquid, his pupils like glass. I love, just love that
piece, I say. You're so fine, he grins, and baby, this one is for
the two of you. We are together, Marsha and I, going south
on the Greyhound bus. In a month, in July, the men with
the guns will stop us.

The man in the window was obsessed. After a brief silence he started all over again. I saw him smoke in profile. I
was sure the first piece was called Alabama, I had used it in
a play for the sound I called loss. Strange how this music
had travelled, found me here at night, the way I had stumbled
on this music ages ago and knew right away that's what I
needed, I recognized it in the same way I had recognized
Marsha and who knows maybe she was the reason why I sat
under this tree now.

The second time around, there were no scarred arms, or

bars closing at dawn. Coltrane's music took over the street, in it we merged, the man in the window, me, and the man who'll die. The air became full of miracles and resurrection all of a sudden, nothing was lost, I kept thinking, death doesn't really exist. Something of America took root after all, call it jazz, call it soul, call it Coltrane. This will always be a part of me, I couldn't wipe it out even if I wanted to, yeah, some of it was good. I gave in, wishing more than anything I could thank him for all this, write him a letter, give him a hug except he had died ages ago. I wished he were not dead and so young, I could tell him all sorts of things, how he had reconciled me, given me parts of my life trapped by a miracle inside that sound. I went on and on, gushy, sentimental, not different from my parents and relatives, all people prone to weeping, the entire suffering nation capable of extremes, some of them deadly, others loving, an excess in the soul, not liked in the West, viewed with suspicion, known only by the few.

Chapter Eight

Coltrane still on my mind, humming all along, be-bop, almost nostalgic for New York, eager to see my kids and Marc, I rushed into the airline office thinking I should go now, in this mood of reconciliation that resembled happy good times.

The guy looked surprised, "I thought you left," he said. He urged me to leave now, right away, things are getting worse every hour, he said. Pan Am wasn't flying any more, bankrupt, he said, but I could go on YAT, still flying to New York. "OK," I said, "tonight," and he stamped my ticket.

I ran to pack. Maybe I'll have time to get a gift or two, then have one final stroll. This is it, my temples throbbed, tomorrow I'll wake up in New York. Now that I was leaving and reconciled with everything, the pain took me by surprise on the street, in one single blow it knocked me down. Coltrane left me too. I was hit from every side, all those people pulling at my arms, don't go, not now, stop, while I said, please let me, I have to. She has fainted, somebody said, I saw her fall, I pulled her back in time, she almost got run over.

I was inside a pharmacy. A woman in a white coat said a man had carried me inside and I was very lucky that he pushed me away from the train. Otherwise, I had nothing, just my blood pressure had dropped. These days it happens all the time, because of everything, including the air pressure which is unusually bad. It had to do with the winds or air currents in this part of the world, the pharmacy was full of people whose case was similar to mine. Some were crying, some talked about the prediction that the Third World War is around the corner. I cried too, from relief. I didn't have to go. I tried, but something or someone stopped me. It was a sign of some sort. It wasn't my fault. I was saved at the last moment for a reason.

"I am not ready to leave yet," I told the guy at the airline office. He said, "You are losing your mind. What's this 'not ready.' Your ticket will expire." He had a right to his opinions but as far as I was concerned, this explained everything—not ready implied that some day I might be. And then you just don't know what's in your stars, what the next day will bring. He looked at me in a peculiar way.

In the days that followed, the air pressure grew worse, but I slept well in spite of the music downstairs, which continued uninterrupted until dawn. Awakened, I joined them a few times in a dance, too sleepy to worry if I did it right. They galloped and sang like it was their last night, and nobody stopped them because there was no one. Mirko the manager appeared briefly, but didn't stay long and there wasn't much for him to do since most of the rooms were unoccupied. He looked unkempt, didn't shave any more. The maids looked worried, they said they might lose their jobs soon, now that the hotel would be sold to a foreigner who in-tended to demolish it, rebuild from scratch, then turn it into a casino. They didn't think themselves fancy enough to qualify as maids in a casino. All this, including the sale, was just rumor but still they were starting to wonder if they were going to gain anything from the fall of socialism that they too had cheered once. In their minds they were going to get everything that the West had—pools, cars, shops—and still keep all the rest intact but somebody had deceived them.

Late at night, I heard the couple make love, uncertain if it was them or another one. Their moans and cries filled my room, at times I was sure they were really dying. Yet, half awakened between two dreams, I found them reassuring, comforting in the emptiness of the hotel, it's only them, I thought, turning to the other side. I had gotten used to them in the same way I got used to the chronic flasher across the street, who after twenty years on 83rd Street, was just a friendly presence watching, a lonely man dying to be looked at. Nobody would mug you in front of your door, not with him staring out there at night.

The cockroaches remained the same, every morning on the floor, but I left them alone. They didn't get into my bed or my clothes, a nice gesture on their part. I watched them move from one side of the room to another, armies of roaches in different colors and sizes. I wondered about their habits, their nests; some rust-colored, others pale brown; dad never killed them either in Chicago. He always said, how would you feel, I ask you, if someone stepped on you.

Occasionally, it looked like they were watching me.

After breakfast, I was back at the market, then back on

the street, listening, and women included me in their conversations. Turning to me casually, they said, "Did you see
that man," or "What do you think of these pears?" A girl
coming from provinces even asked me how to get to a certain store, another one in a café told me her whole life, or
only those parts she referred to as 'her story.' They had a way
of telling that kept me spellbound, a certain clumsiness perhaps, and while they described their various torments and
asked for advice, I had the impression they were not looking
for a solution. Everything, their story and them, remained
unfinished and mysterious; after they left I couldn't define
them easily with a few words.

Nobody was going anywhere any more. Within days all
the conversations about vacations stopped. Nobody talked
in front of the shoe stores or went inside. At the market they
were buying big bags of potatoes as if the autumn had already come. Refugees appeared, their belongings tied up in
bed sheets. More of them daily. In back of them, I see skinny
horses, mud, rain falling, grandma's, mothers's time, a Balkan
memory passed on to me. Drunks remained the same in the
café near the market where I read the paper every day and
couldn't deny any more that the civil war had almost begun.
Not here, but somewhere not too far, they were already dying.

Stories about death and horrors appeared remote and
hard to believe—men had their throats slashed, hearts plucked
out, ears cut. Not '41. Now. It sounded like a repeat of old
stories mother had told me when we came to the U.S. but I
refused to believe her. My school books had us marching
together, united, and the enemies were the same for all.

(Down with Fascists.) Now I was told that in Croatia they were really on the German side, with some exceptions, while here, in this peasant capital, they fought and died in both wars. This past was apparently a well-kept family secret, a pact of silence in the name of unity, out of forgiveness and love. They hated their own forgiveness now, like abused children, they wanted their past know. While on the other side, nobody wanted to have those old deaths dug up. It's invented, they claimed in Zagreb, and besides it's nothing, maybe twenty thousand or so.

"Murderers!" people foamed at the market. "My whole family went."

"And mine."

"Their souls will come to haunt us."

"Did you hear that *Srbe na Vrbe* is all over Croatia?" It really meant hang them on the willow trees.

Wait a minute, I wanted to say, all this is past history, over with, why now, what provoked it? The end of socialism? Why can't you forget and move on? On the street I heard rage against Croatia, and feelings of pure betrayal against Slovenia, whose separation was premeditated, carefully planned German style. I didn't know anyone from there except this actor, and briefly at that. In my memory, his home resembled Austria more than anything, and his people were on the stingy side, but I couldn't hate him for such silly reasons. Even though we communicated in French, I always though of him as one of us.

In Croatia, where all those horrors took place, I knew nobody. My old photographer didn't count. So what if he kissed my foot a couple of times, so what ... Nevertheless, I couldn't help thinking in the midst of all this did he kiss my foot out of forgiveness for his past acts, did I remind him perhaps of a girl whose eyes he had plucked out? It's silly, of course not. Did he kiss my shoulders too? Maybe once or twice. I know he didn't rape me. On the other side, I am no longer sure who killed my uncles. I had three. I always said the Germans, before. It's a nicer way to think, Mother said, she didn't want to poison me, that's why she waited until we came to the States. She said the Germans killed one, but our fascists killed the other two. I would have many relatives if they were alive, wouldn't I? I'd still rather believe the Germans did it all. Without them, everything would have been fine.

I thought of Dubrovnik again. I couldn't imagine not seeing it again, I couldn't imagine them hating me, and for what? Religion? Is that enough? I go carefully over everything—my room with the view, the landlord with roses, the boys who loved my hat, what else is there? Maybe I have missed something, lost in the beauty of the place, blinded by the sun.

Here in the gray Balkan capital, the air was full of rage and betrayal. Men shouted, fought with each other, women lugged things, swept floors, with kids or without, or pregnant, women always doubly fucked in war and in peace.

I, on the other hand, must have looked calm, even serene, most likely I did. That's why they said all sorts of sweet names to me. An old lady called me an angel, and asked me to read the price of ham because she couldn't see. I did, she shook her head, it wasn't cheap. I went in and bought her a pound and a bone she wanted for her soup. She cried so much, poor old thing, she said *dusho moja, pile moje*, my little bird, and this got me crying again even though I wasn't unhappy. Who could say what I was, serene or lost, but their case was worse than mine.

My fear of this country and them—the vague terror of eruptions taking place—vanished overnight, melted away, leaving only a memory of it, maybe at five I was afraid of the dark, something small. Even the tales of Croatia didn't scare me too much, I just hoped they stick to knives and don't switch to anything modern. What's there to be afraid of?

To be fair, I suspect I've been trained and well. I'm used to it, so to speak, I've lived in Chicago, New York, the violence is in my bones. I'm a pro. That's why I say, this is nothing, oh, come on, to all those worried people. This is just a family feud, I say. Of course I am a pro—look what I have seen—violent death daily on TV, more in the papers, summers are the worst, mob killers, serial killers, sex killers, family killers, kids killing kids, crack, sometimes just names, dead in the electric chair, and much more. With a couple of thousand dead in one city every year, who needs a civil war. Blood flows, no matter what you call it.

And subways! Jesus, all those begging, crippled, asleep. Some days it looks like India. Really. And my own apartment, rigged for safety with special keys and a doorman interviewing each person, my apartment is not safe really. On the street, better look carefully, who's that behind you, keep your keys ready, walk fast, no pocketbook, sneakers are good, run fast, scream very loud, pretend you are insane if they mug you. That works, go out of control completely. This is nothing, I concluded, you exaggerate, you always do.

I had a crowd around me, mostly kids. I was a hit for a day. They preferred me to the man yelling about Croatia. However, those sweet kids mostly wanted to know about the latest dance steps in New York, and I couldn't tell them much.

On the street one day, I went further—maybe I had reversed everything, including my fears, and the safety I fled to, each time I got on the plane, was an illusion too, invented by me. America only looked safe because that was its image, blond, hard-working, and under control, the same reason Americans love Germany so much. However, deep down, under all this, the chaos is amazing, except you don't see it well because it's each crazy person erupting alone. That's why it's not called civil war but crime, maladjustment, bad parents, sex abuse, and so forth. This lonely violence terrified me more. It could happen day or night and you have to be on the lookout at all times. Here, so far, everything appeared well defined, I reasoned, and then the number is still smaller than August in New York.

Relax, I said, get a grip on yourself, see it in perspective.

I only spoke once on the street, didn't feel like it any more. I cried more often, alone or in groups—everywhere you turned someone was weeping about this or that, their lost lives, dead parents, the country. Their tears seemed so much bigger than mine, my own grew smaller, then stopped. All in all, everything was fine. I loved the absence of long-term goals, days without stress, nights to roam. The only intrusion on my joy was an occasional thought that sooner or later I'd have to leave because there'd be no money left. Even this never developed fully, just a minor irritation in passing.

I thought about calling the embassy, but forgot it every time, what could they really do for me anyway when I had other problems to solve. I was running out of things to wear. With the hot weather I was washing constantly, drying my dresses on the terrace along with another guest, an old lady from Pittsburgh who had come back to live here now that she had no one. She had a pension through, from many years in a factory. She gave me her iron and Rose (that was her name) said I could use her hot plate or anything she had. After years of living alone she was a genius at ordinary things and within minutes she accomplished what others didn't know how to do—my lamp worked after all. I love Rose.

On the street they were dismantling the statues, changing the names of streets. They even had a committee for this. The other republics had done this already, they said in the papers. It looked like two separate wars were going on— one deadly but still unofficial in the Western parts and this other one, with words. Small groups gathered on the street talking, shouting as if before some major event, didn't my textbooks say that just before the German invasion, thousands had surged into the streets of this city yelling, "We won't take it!" and "Death is better than slavery!" Weren't we the only nation in Europe to resist from day one, didn't we fight with guns taken from the enemy, and starve often, while in the East and West various leaders discussed whose sphere of influence we'd fall under once the war was over? Wasn't Stalin to get us, didn't the U.S. want Greece?

I didn't invent this. It's really in my textbooks, those big moments I wished I had known. At the core of moments like those when people suddenly surge into the streets, flying with no fear, there is something amazing, unknown to me, passion beyond words. Ecstasy maybe. I had only known the second best, the country at its beginning, with songs and flags and the dead still rotting in the countryside. The time of peace was short. Not even fifty years. And now without a real enemy to attack, they were going for each other, in some special madness that was foreign to me. Let them leave, I said, what's the big deal, let everyone secede, then I had to remind myself, I wasn't divorcing or having a nasty custody fight. Even a seemingly civilized woman like Tracey had burnt all of her husband's manuscripts, destroyed his suits after she learned that he, after years of sacrifice to put him through a medical school, that he had the nerve, the bastard, the prick, to fool around now with a younger woman. Didn't she run away to Mexico with their kid? What would the French do if Brittany left them? Would the U.S. mobilize the troops if California declared its independence? These were just silly questions, because I couldn't hate easily here, nor understand why everybody wanted to leave, weren't we an amazing family, different and the same, an old dream.

Of course I knew what I had wished for, of course I did. However, it all looked hopeless, finished, gone, and in the days that followed I gave up on everything, my old memory of the country and even any hope for its unity, the way we were. It was over. It left me. The map of the country shrunk too somewhere in me. When I closed my eyes, I only saw the new one, looking sort of crippled. The dream remained like any dream, like grandma's voice, something I had wished for, with other wishes in my life, the perfect kiss, or perfect love, or perfect socialism, but it was over without any effort on my part. No way to explain. No time to think about it, that's why. It took over. It happened daily, new every time, the mad uncertainty of it. The fluctuating moods. As good as art. At this point in time, my country and I stood identical, waiting, either at the beginning or the end of something, I wasn't sure. To Marsha I wrote, I am in love.

One day, America left me too, just floated away, an echo of a dream and with it all my troubles with Anna and Ann, all those stupid questions about those two. In the same day, women called me my child, my pet, while kids said auntie to me. A sweet word. All this meant that I was neither young or old, depending on my mood or theirs, how the sun fell on me, from what angle.

Rose and I ate often. She cooked on her illegal plate openly now, although the maids always knew about it. Rose could do anything, read fortunes, cut hair, even sew. With all her possessions, including her sewing machine, she was waiting for things to quiet down, then she'd decide where to live. On her scales one day, I saw that I had gained weight. My face and breasts appeared fuller, giving me a look Yanna had once.

The maids talked about kids and food on the terrace and worried constantly. The gold tooth had grandchildren in the West, one daughter had the bad luck to be pregnant now. This was not the time for it. Rose said her father was from there but her parents never fought, on the contrary. Secretly I was glad that my case was simple for once. Nobody could say to me, go back where you came from. No way. I told them I had lived in the U.S. until recently, and contrary to my worries, they took this calmly, matter of fact.

I guess I didn't fit their idea of a well-to-do American woman. They had decided that my destiny was the same as Rose's, a lonely woman who returned to her own flock where in addition she could live well on a pension. I told them about mother too, how she worked nights cleaning offices in Chicago and it was her job that paid for dad's hospitals and my schools. This was her secret that nobody knew at home.

My mother's life didn't amount to much, I said—she lost brothers and most of her family in the war, after the war it was hard, later she lost her husband and her country too. "I think about her," I said, "even when I sleep." The women cried and said, "yes, yes, we know." The blonde one ran off to get the brandy, the gold tooth lifted her glass. "May she rest in peace," she said, "may the earth be soft to her. She has raised a fine daughter."

I liked those words more than anything, they would never know how much. Maybe that's all that was needed, this ritual with brandy, to make her happy, may she rest in peace. A skimpy event for sure, but these are hard times, what can you do. Still, a pretty day, blue gold. And with a flock of swallows that appeared in the sky, suddenly like in a fairy tale, I imagined I saw my mother's soul not resting in peace, but rising up from the concrete slab, in one movement bursting like Superman flying home, free at last, unbound by earthly miseries to be where she wanted. She could stay in her old neighborhood, with grandma, and then I would join them too.

The joy I knew was real. I even heard mama's laughter, the way she must have laughed once, gossiping in our old kitchen, and she even had that special smell that was just hers.

The maids were laughing around me, seated in a circle, sharply outlined in the noon light. They crossed themselves, took another shot, then went back to their brooms. Swallows circled and chirped for a while, then disappeared. I picked the dry clothes from the terrace, then started an article about the maids for the local paper. I heard her laugh, I kept thinking.

It stayed hot. On the street, the mood changed again. Something new. An eerie silence enveloped everything, replacing the old shouts and speeches. Nobody wept even though there were more dead in the papers. The faces of women inside the stores appeared virile, as if made of stone. Here women fought the Germans, and the Italians were afraid of them. Grandma's grandma killed two Turks, I remembered.

Time stood still or seemed suspended.

Then for one whole day there was no mention of fighting in the papers.

Chapter Nine

On a perfect blue day, windswept after a storm, I found myself in front of the National Theater just in time to get a ticket. In five minutes, I could see *Spring Awakening*.

"No tickets," the surly woman said at the box office.

"What are you doing here if there are no tickets?"

"I am paid to sit here," she said, looking like a grave.

"Guess what," I said, remembering that guy, "Bibi sent me."

"Why didn't you say so in the first place," the woman said, "wait here. I'll tell them. What's your name?"

I had to laugh, she treated me like a kid.

"What's so funny, eh?" she asked.

"I don't know," I said, not knowing.

"She doesn't know," the woman shook her head, "no wonder we are lost if nobody knows. She doesn't know, imagine that."

I couldn't stop laughing, provoked by her gloom. Cheer up, woman, I wanted to say, they've stopped fighting, things look good. "I heard a truce was declared," I said. She didn't react to my good news.

A girl let me in by the stage door; then, just as the play started, somebody told me to sit in the front row. I had seen *Spring Awakening* before, a long time ago, written by Wedekind but why did I think it was a play about fascism? This version seemed to be all about love and springtime and it was like some marvelous music you can't describe.

During the intermission, I went outside. It was breezy, fresh, a spring night. The magic of the play lingered on the faces, in the laughter, the chirping of young people who appeared dressed as if for a wedding, a celebration. The ground was all white with petals that a wind had dislodged. Maybe the fighting had stopped for good, I thought, and they know.

In this moment of lightness and spring I too was somehow included, glad that for this occasion I was wearing my clean white dress, white sandals, and a silk shawl with embroidered roses, bought at the market from a Romanian woman. Everything at that instant seemed the way it should be, the air, the petals; there is nothing like a good play. All I wanted was to see the second act, to give myself to it, when I saw a woman in a pink dress coming toward me. Run away? Where to? My happiness was young, I wanted it protected. This woman in a pink dress was familiar but I didn't know from where. Definitely American. She had that positive peppy look, ready to confront the world; she even looked like that announcer on Channel Two who always grimaced then smiled whenever she spoke about whales in captivity. "Hi," she said, "you don't remember me, do you?"

"No," I said, "honestly I don't."

"The conference in Dubrovnik, just recently. I was there for two days visiting a friend and she said I should talk to you. Don't you remember me? We spoke briefly at that party."

"About sexual politics? I seem to remember ..."

"That wasn't me," she said, "we spoke about food. You speak the language, I'm told."

Her name was Joan, she was from Palo Alto, on a Fulbright in anthropology, and she was doing a cross-cultural study on 'Patterns of Migrations' that would eventually become an important book because it would also include a similar study of Poland and Hungary. She had to get it done because her tenure was coming up. She was worried, she grimaced like Jane Fonda. "You see, I'm told things look bad, and some say I should pack and leave immediately. Maybe I should but how many times do you get a Fulbright, and I've paid for my apartment here in advance, my house in California is rented, and it sort of irks me to leave before my work is done. What do you think?"

American eyes are different, I noticed, they are right here, the glance doesn't extend far. The mouth moves more. The eyes stay still, teeth shine. "What do you think?" Joan asked again.

"About what?"

"The situation. Is it really dangerous? A woman at the embassy told me that the CIA had predicted a full scale civil war six months ago. She says Bosnia is next."

"Really? I thought the fighting had stopped."

"Apparently it was in the *Times*. She says they're right on the mark."

"Well," I said, "the CIA should know, shouldn't they."

Thinking no, the CIA wouldn't be involved in this, what would they gain, but still you never know, you just don't, look what they did in Chile.

"You don't seem worried," Joan said.

"They don't look worried either," I said waving towards all those young people.

"No, they don't," she said. "I'm glad to talk to you. There are only a few us from the States here and it can get a bit lonely. You really think I shouldn't worry?"

"No," I said casually, "what's there to worry about? What can happen to you that couldn't happen in New York? You're American. If all hell breaks loose, just head for the embassy."

"Aren't you American?"

"I am and I am not," I said.

"They told me your parents came from here. Actually, you look more like us than them. You're so fair."

"I'm a false blonde." I said.

"You dye it? It looks natural."

"No, my heart is black," I said, teasing her, what Yanna used to say to describe herself. Joan took it seriously, "Are you depressed? It's hard to be a single woman in this town."

The second half started but the magic had vanished. With her around, I couldn't get into it again. It was all her fault, she had trapped me, why didn't I say no. And at the end of the play, she was there again, waiting, eager to talk.

"Did you like it?" she asked.

"Yes," I said coolly.

"Not my kind of play," she said, "too impressionistic. But I got most of it because it's so visual. It must be nice to speak the language, you must speak quite a few."

"Don't you speak at all? How do you ...."

"It's like this, one, I don't really need to, everyone speaks English in the Anthro department, and they want to practice. Two, I'm going back in a couple of months, and I won't need it again. I can order a meal and things." She stopped suddenly, her eyes went away from me, "Mmm, who is that?" she said and giggled.

We were still in the main lobby waiting for the crowd to thin out. "You're looking the wrong way," she whispered, "not that one, in the corner, in a tee shirt, you can't miss him. He's gorgeous."

I saw him finally, a man in his thirties, tall, dark, but not that different from all sorts of people on the street. He stood leaning against the wall, oblivious to everything; his tee shirt stuck to his body, his forehead glistened from sweat.

"So sexy," Joan said, "doesn't he look like a young De Niro with a touch of James Dean?"

"No, not James Dean," I said, "More Montgomery Clift."

"I don't mean his looks, something else about him."

"It's his tee shirt," I said. He looked a bit like Marc around the time we met in front of the Chilean embassy, protesting the CIA coup.

"An actor," I said, "he is the guy who played ..."

"Of course, that's him," Joan said. "What would you say he is ethnically, a Muslim, a gypsy, or a Serb?"

"I don't know. They look the same to me."

"They are something, aren't they," Joan said. "The men here are so ... every second one looks like a movie star ..."

"Only when they are young," I said. "They age fast. They are excessive, that's why."

"… but with AIDS and all, I'd better watch out," Joan was pursuing her own concerns. "I was told they are mucho macho and all that, and condoms are out of the question. Is it true?"

"I thought you would know better," I said. "Aren't you in anthropology?"

"I don't do that kind of anthro, mostly statistical, analytical stuff, tables. Books don't tell you about condoms, do they? How do you say it?"

"Condom?"

"Yeah, what's the word?"

"I don't know," I said. "There are tons of words I don't know. Just say the English word, but it would surprise me if they had them. They are out of everything, including heart pills."

"Who said that?"

"The papers. It all depends if they are imported or not. Right now they can't afford even …"

"He is so sexy. To tell you the truth, I'm so horny, it's been a while since I fucked anyone," she said with the honesty that passes for intimacy among some women. That word fuck offended me, or maybe the sound of it did. A harsh sound. I didn't mind when the maids said it.

"Well, I'm probably not his type," Joan continued, lifting her shoulders, twitching her foot, playing with her hair.

"I don't think there is one type any more," I said. "Now they even like older women."

"But they don't like redheads, do they?"

"Who knows. In the past, they didn't like blondes either, and now they do," I said, knowing that Joan was not their type, even though she would be an attractive woman in the States, tall, slim, with clear gray eyes. Everything about her was too orderly, too well-plucked, too white to be their type. Her haircut had the same neatness as Princess Di. But when she said 'fuck' a moment ago, a lewd gleam appeared in her eyes, lust twisting her mouth, and because it contrasted so sharply with her Puritan body, this gleam appeared bigger, more vulgar, or even pornographic, while a peasant coupling in the bushes wouldn't be.

The actor stretched now, yawned, a half-smile around his lips. Another man was talking to him, occasionally touching his arm. The other one was good-looking too.

"He is probably gay," Joan said, a resigned look on her face, "I'm so tired of gay men everywhere you go." Now, as she was saying goodbye to him, adjusting to the end of this potential affair, her face had the wistfulness of a young girl. Sad to watch. No friends or relatives.

The actor in the tee shirt was heading for the door, a bag over his shoulder. If not now, when, I though, running up to him. "You have a fan," I said.

"Good. Is it you?"

"Her. She only speaks English though."

"I speak some bad English," he said in English, that half smile on his face.

"You're doing great," Joan said, grinning widely. He was attractive, not that I would have noticed him on the street. It was the contrast between his eyes and mouth that made him appealing, the way he bit his lower lip slowly, while his eyes danced full speed.

"This is Joan," I said, "and I am Anna."

"Marco," he said.

"That's my grandfather's name, no, my granduncle's."

"Mine too," he said.

"Actually, you even look like my aunt Yanna," I said. "When she was young."

"Yanna what?"

"Yanna B."

"It's because we are cousins," he said. "Bibi told me about you."

"Joan, this is my cousin," I said. "I didn't know I had one."

"You don't look like cousins," Joan said.

"Yes, we do," he said, "around the eyes. I hoped you would show up. I didn't know where to look for you."

He knew everything about me, he said. To show me how we were related, he drew a family tree on the floor; he was surprised I didn't know it already. I didn't believe him in the beginning, but it had to be true, he knew too many details, and they were the same ones I had heard, even the story about crazy Marco who went to dig for gold in Alaska, then came home to die.

"Where are you from?" Joan asked.

"Montenegro. Very very beautiful," he said. I had never been there. It seemed too far. At the café next door, he introduced me as his cousin from America and ordered drinks to celebrate my return. He couldn't get over it that he found me only because I mentioned my mother's last name to Bibi and Bibi realized we had to be related—our clan was not big. I didn't remember giving him my mother's name. Enough of the family tree, I wanted to say. Be a good host. Joan

looked bored and lost, poor thing. Leave us alone, she
mouthed toward me and I did. Went to congratulate the
director and we ended up talking about theater in New York.
He was dying to go, New York was his dream, he said.

They were where I left them, next to each other. Joan
was telling him about her beautiful house near Palo Alto,
and she has everything, the view and the stream. "Like a
Western?" he said.

"No," I said. "Red trees, different than here," I remembered the smell of eucalyptus, and the slight tremor under
my feet.

"You'd do very well in Hollywood," she said.

"No," I said for some reason.

"Who says they'd want me," Marco said.

"Why wouldn't they? You'd have to try and see," Joan
said. "You can't get anywhere unless you try." (Accomplish,
against unbearable odds, challenge, challenging, if you have
guts, a winner, we got a winner—it rang in my ears.) I watched
my thoughts change. Damn, damn her, I liked myself less.

"Well," Marco said lazily, "what would I do there, would
they want me for, gangster or Mexican parts?" His eyes
laughed, looking at me. He looked like an outlaw.

"You have to start somewhere," Joan said primly, "nothing gets done in a day, you know."

"Should I pack?" he winked at me, letting me know
something.

"You'd certainly live better," Joan said.

"That's an honest thing to say," Marco said, "Most Americans I meet want to sell me democracy. I could live better,
true, but it might be too much. I might get bored." His words

had a mockery that Joan didn't hear, because two drinks had got to her head; relaxed and flushed, she told him his hands were very expressive. She knew how to read palms, too.

Will they or won't they, that was the question now. The drama had started. My role was not to interfere.

I left them again to go to the bathroom. Next, I ran into Bibi, then he introduced me to other people who told morbid stories about chopped heads, yet everyone laughed.

Back in my seat, I didn't know if I favored him or her, or was impartial. Once again I was in the good mood that had been briefly interrupted by Joan. In this café, with actors and wine, the spirit of the play returned, and I met Marco's friends, including a beautiful girl who had played the witch. Thanks to Joan, no doubt about it, I had discovered a cousin I didn't know I had, and now, in the same spirit, I wished to give her something too. What's the big deal, I wanted to say to him, she is a guest, be a good host, don't be stingy. Besides, what would it cost him?

It looked like yes, Joan would get him, condoms or no condoms. Even his question confirmed a switch. "Are you going to live with us?" he asked, and Joan flushed. "It's hard to say," she said. "What would I do? The language is hard. I would never speak it well and certainly there are fewer opportunities."

"What if you fell in love?" he said, very low.

"Well, in that case ... who knows," she giggled.

It was time for me to get up again, but he reached for my arm and pushed me back into my seat. "I'm sure you could," he said.

"Could what?"

"Stay here."

"You think?"

"Of course," he said, but not in English. "It's like this, you might have their ways but you have our ass." He was enjoying himself, his eyes laughed.

"You're such a peasant," I said. He muttered something like a curse.

"You don't look like cousins," Joan said.

"We are. No doubt about it. He just told me my ass is not American."

"He can't see your ass," she said.

"It doesn't mean just my ass. It's all of me."

"Right," he said. "Everything."

"This is one hell of a weird country," Joan said, irritated. "I wish he'd talk straight. How could you live here?"

"I don't know," I said. "Maybe I could."

"You mean you wouldn't miss the States?"

"I don't know," I said. "Maybe not."

"How come?"

"It's complicated," I said.

"Don't you have a U.S. passport?"

"I do, so what," I said.

"What is it then," she said. "You don't like us, how come?" She had retreated, her eyes hurt.

"Damn you, Joan, stop pushing me. There's so much I do like."

"Let me explain, it's like this," he came to my aid, and went on to tell a story all of us knew. A gypsy kid is lost. He cries and cries, looks for his mother. People try to help him. They'll take him home. No, he sobs, I only want her. What is she like, they ask him. She is the most beautiful woman you have ever seen, he says, the best, her skin is soft, she smells better than anyone. Then this dirty woman appears and he runs toward her. "That's love for you," Marco concluded. "That's what she wanted to say, right?"

My ambassador. I was embarrassed for him. How could he be so drippy in front a perfect stranger. Even that word 'love' is dangerous, better to use it sparingly. "I love the way you told that," Joan said, leaning on him, pure lechery. "I'm off to bed," I said, tired of everything, him, her and me. I'll never have peace.

"I'll drive you," Marco said, then asked where we lived. I lived nearby, I assumed he would drop me off first. In the car, he invented a story of dug-up streets, cables, and blockages, the reason he had to drive fifteen minutes to deliver our guest safely. He ran to open the car door for her, and with grand gestures he wished her a good night. Joan gave him her phone number and said they should meet for lunch sometime. She didn't suggest we should meet. She only said goodbye rather curtly, blaming me, and for what?

He drove in total silence, in a bad mood, jaw set. When he stopped in front of my hotel, he turned towards me abruptly. "I knew your little tricks," he shouted, "bathroom, bathroom, Bibi, Bibi, director, more bathroom. It didn't work, did it?" His eyes flashed with hatred and vengeance, what mother called our Ottoman cruelty.

He laughed next and his laughter infected me too. Then he was vicious looking all over again. "You think I'm a fool, do you? Is that what you think?"

"There is nothing wrong with her," I said.

"I didn't say there was, did I? But why pimp for me? You think I need somebody."

"I was not pimping. She looked lonely. She liked you."

"What do you think I am, a beast? If I need a whore, I'll go get a whore."

"She is not a whore."

"I didn't say she was. You pushed her on me. I didn't want to be with her. I wasted my evening. I thought you were my cousin, don't you want to talk to me? Whose side are you on, anyway? You thought I'd fall for her house, is that it?"

He acted insane now, probably had too much to drink. All of us did.

"Good night," I said, "I'm going in."

"Why? The most important question is, what do we do now that we got rid of her?" He laughed and laughed and got me laughing too.

"There's a place near the market that's open the whole night, real gypsy music, I bet you don't hear that often, let's go."

"Not tonight, I'm tired," I said. It was late, nothing on the street moved.

"Fine, go leave," he said and looked at me. I reached for the door handle but he was faster. He kissed me.

"Stop it," I said, "what do you think you are doing?"

"Kissing you," he laughed, kissing me. He was so familiar, the reason I didn't fight hard, a relative I couldn't push away. When his hands reached for my breast, I said, "stop, stop," again.

"Fine," he said, "see, I stopped." He stretched in my lap, ready to fall asleep. Stroking his hair, I thought of incest for some reason. He had a smell of young boys about him.

"I could eat you up," he said, his hand on my thigh.

"We're cousins, don't you remember," I said, moving his hand.

"Only on my father's side," he grinned.

"Tell me ..." I began.

"Anything for you."

"What's going on? I can't tell. I thought the war had stopped."

"Stop? How could it stop if it didn't start yet?" he said, kissing me. "They should leave us alone, that's all ..."

"Who is they?"

"Not you. You shouldn't leave me alone ever. You love to kiss, don't you, but you talk funny."

"Do I really? What do I sound like?"

"It's different ... slower, old-fashioned. It's like a play we did once. You remind me of that actress, same eyes. I'm going to drink your eyes."

"Which actress?"

"You wouldn't know her. She did many films but there's one scene I really like, a brilliant performance. She gets shot at the end."

"Germans?"

"No, ours. She says, let me see, something like this, 'you scum, you bastards, and you call this a revolution.' You say it, go on, 'you scum ...'"

I did, imagining the German guns.

"Great," he said, "You could do tragic parts."

"I wish I didn't remind you of a dead person."

"She isn't dead. Vera does comedy parts now." Again we laughed, and again we kissed. "Please come and see me to-

morrow, will you," he said. "It's a new Yankee play and I
need your help. The director, you met the maestro, keeps
saying it's fine but I don't think so. There's a cloud over my
performance. I'm no good ..."

"What's the play called?"

"*Fog,*" he said, and I laughed. This was funny. "Imagine
pimping for me," he said, almost gently now.

"I wasn't pimping for you. I was pimping for her."

"Enough of her!"

"You said it first," I said, kissing his hair.

"You like me, don't you, just a little bit?"

"I suppose so."

"Don't say, I suppose so, say, Marco, I really like you."

"Oh Marco, I really like you," I said, snickering.

"I love your eyes," he said, kissing my eyelids. "Let's go
in, don't you want to? I know you do."

"I can't," I said. "All this is too fast for me. And all
those people will think I'm some sort of slut."

"Let's go to my place then, let's go get your suitcase. My
place is better than this dump."

"Are you mad?" I said, and got out of the car. What was
he trying to do, get me to move again? It was cold, everything was deserted, gray. Not dawn yet. From somewhere I
remembered, this time is dangerous, the ghosts run back to
their graves just before the cock crows.

"Why are you scared?" he said, looking scary. "Who do you
think I am? A beast? A Balkan barbarian, is that what you
Americans think? I'm not going to eat you up ... well ... I
might ... come here. Why do you shiver?"

"I don't know."

"I promise I won't attack you except with your permission," he said and roared. "Come here."

"I'm leaving soon," I said. "I have to."

"You love the guy?"

"I'm not sure I love anyone," I said.

"Wrong, wrong line for you. That's what's her name's line. You should say something like this: 'Oh it's hard, I love everything too much, too many people, but you Marco, I'll love even more.'"

"You make me laugh, Marco," I said, laughing.

"Let's go. You'll love my place. It's good for arguing because you can't escape. There's nowhere to go. It's about this big." He demonstrated in the sidewalk in three leaps. "I have a view of the river, come, let's go. I want to make love to you, and you want to, say you do."

"Is that thunder?" I said. "What's that in the park?"

"Lovers most likely. A ghost or two."

"I'm cold."

"Your fault. With me around, why should you be cold?" He was so much bigger than me, all of me fitted under one arm.

"How about this," I said. "I'll come tomorrow to your play and then we'll see. When is the play?"

My words were drowned in a thundering sound, then everything around us shook. Out of somewhere tanks appeared, thick, large, moving fast. The soldiers looked terribly young. They sang something I didn't know. Adolescents I had not seen before emerged from the park rubbing their eyes, their clothes in disarray. Some shook their fists, some

cheered, but everybody moved closer together. "Fuck it," I
thought I heard Marco say, "It has started." It has. No fool-
ing around any more. They, we, were going to fight with
them. No way to stop it now. It was too late to run away.
Will he go? In a glance, I saw him dead, blown up. All those
kid soldiers seemed dead already. That's how it goes. Nothing new. I might die too. Big deal, sooner or later you have
to. I couldn't tell what he thought, his face was the same as
moments before, angry, childish, sweet, defiant, all at once
and that something else—wild, excited by all this, in which
I recognized my own. It was exciting. No doubt about it. The
way torrents, volcanoes, hurricanes are, the way he laughed,
baring his teeth. I wasn't tired any more. The real drama had
started and nobody could predict the middle or the end. The
first impulse to run away was short. The fear drifted away, or
it appeared tamed, then I lost it. It all seemed inevitable,
destined, this man, this war, this dawn, I heard myself think.
Soon the sun will rise as always. In the same mood of accep-
tance that resembled life known, seen from before, we kissed
some more, then wandered into the park and made love
beneath a poplar, next to a bench. The rumble of the convoy
continued, became like white noise. When it stopped, the
kids went on a rampage, shouting, howling, dancing, beating
drums; half asleep on the grass I couldn't tell if they were
celebrating or grieving but it all seemed normal, familiar,
some old ritual in which I was included.